COSMO TOPPER, BANKER

Fortyish, respectably suburban, to the eye contented enough, but dead to romance, adventure, and hope. Normally, Topper had little on his mind but his banking, his wife's depressing and possibly imaginary ailments, and whether or not he wanted leg of lamb for dinner—usually not, but he got it anyhow.

That was Topper's life—not much of one, he considered, but the only one he had . . . until he encountered

- the transparent lady in step-ins
- the cocktail that drank itself
- half a mad dog
- and an invisible—but deliciously real—roommate

Topper was out of his rut with a vengeance . . . and he never really wanted to go back in!

D0499146

By Thorne Smith
Published by Ballantine Books:

TOPPER

TOPPER TAKES A TRIP

THE NIGHT LIFE OF THE GODS

*THE STRAY LAMB

*TURNABOUT

*RAIN IN THE DOORWAY

* Coming soon from Del Rey/Ballantine Books

THORNE SMITH

Topper

A Del Rey Book

BALLANTINE BOOKS • NEW YORK

A Del Rey Book
Published by Ballantine Books

Copyright 1926 by Thorne Smith, © renewed 1953 by
June Smith Delaney and Marion Smith Conner.

All rights reserved. Published in the United States by Ballantine Books, a division of Random House, Inc., New York, and
simultaneously in Canada by Random House of Canada, Limited, Toronto, Canada.

Library of Congress Catalog Card Number: 79-55331

ISBN 0-345-28722-3

Manufactured in the United States of America

First Ballantine Books Edition: July 1980

Cover art by Norman Walker

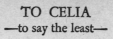

TO CELIA
—to say the least—

Contents

CHAPTER I

No Change

FOR SOME MINUTES NOW SCOLLOPS HAD BEEN GAZING searchingly at Mr. Topper. And Mr. Topper was troubled. Not definitely troubled, but vaguely so, which to some persons is the most troublesome form of trouble. Mr. Topper was one of such persons. In fact he was highly representative of the type. So free from trouble had Topper's days been that gradually he had come to regard with suspicion all creatures not likewise unencumbered. An earthquake, an eruption or tidal wave would mildly move Cosmo Topper, arouse him to the extent of a dollar donation which would later be deducted from his income tax; whereas a newspaper story dealing with bankruptcy, crimes of violence or moral looseness would cause him speedily to avert his eyes to less disturbing topics. Mr. Topper could excuse nature and the Republican Party, but no man. He was an institutional sort of animal, but not morbid. Not apparently. So completely and successfully had he inhibited himself that he veritably believed he was the freest person in the world. But Mr. Topper could not be troubled. His mental process ran safely, smoothly, and on the dot along well signaled tracks; and his physical activities, such as they were, obeyed without question an inelastic schedule of suburban domesticity. He resented being troubled. At least he thought he did. That was Mr. Topper's trouble, but at present he failed to realize it.

He experienced now something of the same resentment that came to him upon being delayed in the tunnel on his way home from the city. Things were going on round him in the tunnel, dreadful things, perhaps, but he did not know what they were. He sat

1

in a blaze of light in the midst of clanking darkness. Surrounded by familiar things he felt stuffy and uncomfortable. Even his newspaper lost its wonted stability. Yes, it was a decidedly objectionable feeling that Mr. Topper had tonight as he gave himself to the solicitous embrace of his arm chair and followed with a dull gaze the rug's interminable border design—a Doric motif, clean-cut and geometrically accurate. Once this design had appealed to his abiding sense of order. Tonight he hardly saw it, although without his knowledge it was wearying his eyes, and had been doing so for several months.

In Scollops' eyes there was an expression difficult to fathom. Mr. Topper held the opinion that the expression was uncomfortably insinuating, making him in some sly way an accessory before the fact. But hang it all, what was the meaning of Scollops' look? The cat had been fed. He had seen to that himself as he had seen to it ever since he had adventurously brought her home from Wilson's, the grocer's, one evening four years ago. Four years. As long as that in this house; and once it had seemed so new. Now it was an old house, an uninteresting house. Perhaps he was old, too, and equally uninteresting. Mr. Topper felt that he was, and for the first time in his life permitted himself to wonder about such things.

His intellectual debauch was rudely shattered by Scollops. The cat yawned and tentatively thrust her nails into her benefactor's thigh. It was rather a plump thigh. Long years of well-regulated commuting had despoiled it of its youthful charm. It was a tight thigh and a fleshy one, yet it still reacted to pain. To such an extent, in fact, that Mr. Topper's sensation of trouble instantly gave way to one of mild reproach as he dropped Scollops softly thudding to the floor.

This faint discord in the domestic tranquillity caused Mrs. Cosmo Topper to look up from her needlework. Mr. Topper, glancing across the table, met his wife's eyes. It was just for a moment, then he looked quickly away, but why, he did not know.

"She yawned," he remarked by way of explanation. "Yawned and scratched."

"I know it," apologized Mrs. Topper, mistaking his words for a direct accusation. "I've been doing it all evening. It must have been the veal."

Topper watched his wife remove her sewing-glasses and place them in their case. With an absorbed gaze he followed her movements as she folded her sewing and wrapped it in a piece of linen, which she then deposited in a basket. At this point his expression became almost desperate, then hopeless. No, there was going to be no change in the nightly routine—glasses, case, linen, basket. If she would only reverse the procedure, or for once forget her glasses, that would be something. Meantime Mrs. Topper, unconscious of tragedy, rose from her chair, came round to where her husband was sitting, and brushed his forehead with her lips. Then, referring once more in a pained voice to the haunting qualities of veal, she left the room.

Mr. Topper listened to her firm step upon the stairs. A certain squeaking of boards apprised him of the fact that she had achieved the landing. For a moment he thought idly about veal in relation to his wife. Then he did an unusual thing. Instead of knocking out his pipe and locking in the cat whose vagrant nature had caused him some rather trying experiences in the past, he gently retrieved that animal from the floor and fell to studying an old atlas which he had plucked from an obscure shelf.

"It made me sleepless, too," murmured Mrs. Topper an hour later as her husband settled down beside her.

And that night Mr. Topper dreamed of eating curried veal in Calcutta. He was surrounded by many maidens, all of whom partook amply of veal, and none of whom complained. It was delicious. He gorged himself.

CHAPTER 11

Scollops Looks Inscrutable

NOT UNTIL THE FOLLOWING AFTERNOON, WHICH WAS Saturday and therefore free, was Mr. Topper able to localize his trouble. The discovery came to him as a shock which gathered intensity as the days passed. It marked an epoch in his life. Even Mrs. Topper, who steadfastly refused to recognize changes taking place around her, detected something new and therefore annoying in her husband. But she reassured herself by believing that all stomachs have their off seasons, and became almost pallidly cheerful when she considered the fact that her stomach's off season was always on— it prevailed the year around. To Mrs. Topper it was an endless source of comfort to be able to trace all mystifying cases of conduct, even her own, to such a tangible and well-established institution as a stomach.

It was Scollops again. . . . Scollops draped on her master's knee with a Saturday afternoon mist swimming in her eyes. . . . Scollops, the inexplicable, narrowing infinity between two orange-colored slits.

This it was that gave Mr. Topper the shock. For the first time in their four years of companionable association Topper realized that the cat saw nothing, that is, nothing immediate. Although her yellow, searching gaze included him, it passed far beyond him down distant vistas from which he was excluded. Caressing and condoning on their way, Scollops' eyes seemed to be roving through the ages, dwelling on appalling mysteries with the reminiscent indulgence of a satiated goddess.

Looking into Scollops' eyes, Mr. Topper discovered that there were things he did not know, colors of life beyond his comprehension, impulses alien to his rea-

son. With his wife's eyes it was different. He knew their
every shade and meaning. Nothing in them lay un-
revealed. He was familiar with the direct gaze denoting
finance, the confidential gaze denoting scandal, the
patient gaze denoting servants, the motherly gaze denoting superiority and the martyred gaze denoting
dyspepsia.

Suddenly Mr. Topper realized what was troubling
him. It was eyes. Old familiar eyes. He felt that he
knew them all. He knew the eyes at the office, from
the president's to the elevator boy's. It was surprising,
he thought, how desperately well he knew eyes. Mr.
Topper saw eyes. Mr. Topper understood them. And
he had an uncomfortable feeling that they understood
him.

Now, however, he was alive to the fact that Scollops' eyes escaped all classification. This both pleased
and shocked him. He realized that in spite of four
years of close companionship he had not the slightest
idea of Scollops' private opinion of him, or of anything
else, for that matter. To what was going on behind
her eyes Topper had no clue.

Mr. Topper found himself thinking that it would be
a relief to have some one look at him in the manner of
Scollops. Preferably a woman. Not that Mr. Topper
was loose, or romantic, or both. He had never loitered
to pluck forbidden flowers beside the marital path, but
had mechanically kept to his schedule with Mrs. Topper to one end and the office at the other.

Once in his youth he had nerved himself to lurch in
reckless pursuit of a shop girl in a skating rink, but the
meeting with her had been so sudden and demolishing
that when he arose from the dust of the floor he
departed with a far sharper pain in his spine than in
his heart. After that he confined his amorous pursuits
to the nice girls of his own set. He never called on
them alone, but always with a jolly company of youths,
which gave him a sense of security. Later he had met
Mrs. Topper, who had already achieved individuality
through smoldering dyspepsia, and he had decorously
followed her through a summer of neat suburban
Sundays, after which he had made the arrangement

permanent in the presence of an orderly gathering of neat suburban property owners. And that ended that side of Mr. Topper.

Now, however, he was getting along. Nearly forty and acquiring flesh. Ten years married. He neither had to stretch to reach the electric light nor stoop to walk under the bulb. His face was unremarkable save for his eyes, which were extremely blue and youthful, as if the fire in them had been banked for the sake of conservation. His features would have been delicate had his appetite not been so good or his habits less sedentary. Had their union been blessed with issue, one of the children, probably Cosmo, Junior, would have been a sandy blond like his father, for Mr. Topper's hair was of an indifferent shade. But there were no little Toppers. Scollops was undisturbed.

He rose, stretched and walked to the window. Scollops merely stretched and resumed her repose, with the austere resignation characteristic of cats when bent on slumber or theft.

"Guess I'll go for a walk," said Topper. "I'm in need of a bit of a change."

"There'll be a roast for dinner," replied Mrs. Topper. "Lamb," she added as he left the room. "You like lamb."

Mr. Topper winced as he collected his hat and stick. Why should he be thus openly reminded that he liked lamb? Couldn't a person creep up on a roast and surprise it some time? As a matter of fact he was not particularly lustful for lamb, or at least he would strive hereafter to dissemble his emotions.

But all he said was "Good!" The exclamation point stuck in his throat.

CHAPTER III

Mr. Topper Pursues the Sun

THE STREET DOWN WHICH MR. TOPPER STROLLED
was a nice street. No one needed to feel ashamed of it.
No one did. And the people who lived on this street
had nice homes; nice, neat homes with well-groomed
lawns, well-shingled roofs and well-stocked larders.
The style of architecture showed a sincere desire to
impress the eye favorably. The effort had been based
more on hope than on inspiration. The houses could
have been—and frequently were—termed "homey,"
"quaint," and "comfortable," but after these terms
had been exhausted little remained to be said save,
perhaps, "sweet."

Mr. Topper and his neighbors were quietly proud
of this street, and had borne their assessments as a
tolerant father bears the extras of an extravagant son
at college. One could bring one's friends from the city
to this street and let it speak for itself; which one
seldom did. Sewerage, real estate and the cost of building were subjects far too fascinating to be left to the
imagination. So the visitors from the city heard all
about these things, and were not amused.

Being on a slightly higher elevation than the rest
of the town, the street was happily called "Glendale
Road." It is rather terrifying to think that the real
estate promoter responsible for this name is perhaps
still unhung and busily engaged in giving equally
stultifying names to other nice little streets in other
nice little towns situated in other nice little localities
throughout the United States.

"You know that swamp?" he is, perhaps, saying
to his wife at this very moment as he lights his cigar.

"Which one, my dear?" she asks. "You've bought
so many swamps."

7

"And sold 'em, too," he replies with a boyish chuckle. "But the one we drove by last week. I pointed to out to you. It was where they found the body of——"

"Oh, yes," his wife excaims, "the rag-picker's wife! They had to vacate their shack, didn't they?"

"Well, that doesn't matter," replies her husband rather quickly. "I've decided to run a drive through it. What do you think would be a good name?"

Deep silence for several minutes. Her husband watches her anxiously. She reads a lot of books. Good things, books.

"Mayblossom Drive," she murmurs at last, with a dreamy look in her eyes. "That would be charming. Let's call it that."

Business of writing name down on back of soiled envelope. Husband departs for development in car and another street has come into being.

Nevertheless Glendale Road was really a nice street. It was wide and well paved. There were trees on it at orderly intervals. And, now that June was here, there were leaves on the branches of the trees and there were birds among the leaves.

For some reason Mr. Topper's mind was not occupied today with thoughts of sewers, real estate or building costs. Community pride was absent from his mood. He heard the birds chirping and listened to them intently. How many of them there must be and what a great to-do they were making. Little birds were always so excited. He had held a sparrow in his hand once and felt its heart beat. Somehow it had made him feel like crying. The little thing had been so excited, so bent on living. Life to the little sparrow had seemed so necessary and important. Topper had released it immediately. How busily it had flown away. Well, these chaps up in the tree were having a good time just the same. They never needed a change. They could come and go as they pleased. A nest here and a nest there. A family hatched and a family fledged. Fresh branches in new lands. Adventurous flights in pursuit of the sun. Not a bad life, that. Be a bird and see the world.

Topper smiled and stopped in front of a public garage. He was now on a side street of the town proper, but Mr. Topper was not altogether sure as to how he had gotten there. He had been flying in pursuit of the sun, and on the following day, after church, two ladies protested to Mrs. Topper that he had looked right through them. What had they done to be so dreadfully treated, and what had come over her husband, who was always so polite to the ladies?

"Sparrows," said Mr. Topper at this point, and walked away, leaving his wife to explain as best she could the meaning of his remark.

Seeing Mr. Topper smiling at him, the owner of the garage rested from his labors and called out an enthusiastic greeting.

"Isn't she a pip?" he asked, pointing to the machine on which he had been working.

Impressed by the man's earnestness, Mr. Topper approached the car and surveyed it with the vague gaze of an amateur.

"A regular pip," he said, looking hopefully at the man. "A regular pip of a car, Mark."

Mark beamed.

"It's the coyest little car in the town," he declared, "and it's carried more than gasoline in its time, though it is only this year's model."

"Bootlegging?" asked Mr. Topper, deciding, now that he came to consider it, the car did have rather vicious lines. Too much nickel and a trifle too low to the ground.

"No, victims," said Mark. "There was a bottle in every flap when they found it."

"Then did the car manage to get lost?" Mr. Topper asked with growing interest.

"Wrecked," replied Mark briefly. "Head on to a tree. I've practically rebuilt it, but the motor's good as new."

"It's had rather a sad life for such a young car," remarked Topper. "Whose is it?"

"Mine," replied Mark with pride. "But it did belong to George and Marion Kerby. You remember. Both

killed three months back. The estate owed me money
so I took the bus in settlement."

Mr. Topper now looked at the automobile with
unfeigned interest. Surely he remembered George and
Marion Kerby, the fastest young couple in town.
At least, they had been. People had always predicted
that they would come to some such end. Kerby had
never worked. No commuting for him. Rich young
devil. And he and his wife had been laid to rest to
the tune of "I told you so." Kerby's wife, a slim girl,
good looking, quick in her actions, a mocking sort of
a creature. Then, like brushing against a cobweb on a
dark woodland path, Mr. Topper's thoughts were
suddenly arrested by little clinging threads of memory.
Marion Kerby's eyes? Ah, yes, he remembered
them. The Kerbys had not belonged to his set, the
solid, substantial, commuting set, but had gathered
round them, from all parts of the country, a group of
irresponsible spirits, who would suddenly appear in a
swarm of motors, riot around the town and coutry-
side for a few days, and then as suddenly disappear
in a cloud of dust and a chorus of brazen horns. No
one had really known the Kerbys, that is, no respectable, accredited member of the community. But Topper had seen them often enough as they darted through
the streets of the town, and once he had met Marion
Kerby at the dedication of the new twenty-thousand-
dollar fire-house.

"Comic operas cost more and are less amusing,"
she had remarked, with a smile, then asked in a serious voice: "Do all white duck trousers have to look
so self-conscious?"

Mr. Topper, being a charter member of the organization, had loyally donned his outfit and joined
the ranks of his fellow fire-fighters. Now, at the question, he looked down at his ducks and blushed. Marion Kerby mingled with the crowd, but she left behind
her the seeds of rebellion in Mr. Topper's mind. He
had never felt in sympathy with white duck trousers,
and now he actually hated them. They did look self-
conscious, but it showed poor community spirit on
Marion Kerby's part to ridicule the uniform. What

would a fire company do without white duck trousers?
Evidently she was one of those modern young women
who had no respect for tradition. Furthermore, nice
women did not talk about trousers on such a slight
acquaintance.

A few days after this he had encountered Marion
Kerby on the morning train. She had nodded to him
and smiled, and somehow her smile had seemed to
convey the impression that they shared between them
an unholy secret of a most delicious nature. Marion
Kerby's smile had caused Mr. Topper to feel much
less married. He had puzzled all the way in that
morning about her eyes. He had found himself unable
to place them. They were never quite the same.
Thoughts danced behind them like fountains in the
sun, hiding their liquid depth in a burst of dazzling
spray.

And now as Mr. Topper stood in the glittering presence of the car in which Marion Kerby and her husband had met their death, he remembered her eyes
and felt dismayed that their light had been snuffed
from the world. A June heaviness settled down on
Mr. Topper and he became conscious of his stomach.
It was too large. Indecent. Yes, he was certainly in
need of a change.

Mark's monologue swam in on his ears.

"They were a wild pair, Mr. Topper," the man
was saying, "but nice people at that. The nicest
couple I ever knew. One minute they'd be fighting
with each other like a pair of wildcats and the next
they'd be guying along like two tramps. Why, the way
they went on would make you think of a couple of
kids. They were always arguing about who was the
best driver and often they'd ask me to decide. There'd
be tears in their eyes, they were so in earnest. You'd
have thought it was a matter of life and death with
them."

"That's about how it was, Mark," said Mr. Topper
thoughtfully. "A matter of life and death. A gay life
and a quick death."

"What's the odds," replied Mark, with a shrug.

"They liked it that way and they got what they wanted."

"I've a feeling they got just a trifle more than they wanted," said Mr. Topper. "They didn't look like a pair that were extremely anxious to die. They were too crammed with life."

"But that's the way it goes," continued Mark, waxing philosophic. "There are lots of people in town I'd rather have seen get in trouble with a tree."

This remark made Mr. Topper feel a little uneasy. He realized that he had never enriched Mark's coffers with the purchase of gasoline or automobile parts. To Mark he was perfectly useless, a fit subject for a tree.

"They had good stuff," Mark went on reminiscently, "and they were generous with it, too. I always had a drink whenever they came in the place. We used to have regular little parties in my office over there."

Mr. Topper walked deliberately to Mark's small office and peered through the door. In his mind's eye he could see Marion Kerby seated at the desk. He had a remarkably vivid picture of her. It was almost as if he had been present at the parties himself. There she sat, her slim ankles crossed, her mad eyes dancing beneath the brim of a smart little hat, and her lips parted in a sarcastic smile. In one hand was a glass which she was holding on high and in the other a cigarette. "Truly an unedifying sight," thought Mr. Topper, and yet he was fascinated by it. He dwelt on the delicate lines of her face, the small impertinent chin and the fine lips curved in a roving, debonair smile. Then he returned to her eyes and became lost in contemplation.

"They were mad," he mused to himself. "They could laugh the devil down."

Fearing that that was what they were probably doing at the very moment, Mr. Topper turned away from the door and looked at Mark, who was in the act of hanging a "For Sale" sign over the radiator cap of the automobile. The deed done, Mark stepped back and surveyed his handiwork ecstatically, head on one side and hands on his hips. "Here," thought

Mr. Topper, "is a master craftsman, one who loves his work for its own sake."

"So you're going to sell it," he said, walking over to the bewitched garage man.

"Sure thing," replied Mark. "And cheap too. Couldn't get any one to believe she's sound. But she is, every nut and bolt in her. The Kerbys themselves wouldn't know the difference except that she's quieter now. They always kept the old bus rattling."

"Well, they rattled their toy once too often," remarked Mr. Topper, looking moodily out at the street. "I hope the next owner will have better luck."

"Lightning never strikes . . ."

"Twice in the same place," interrupted Mr. Topper. "I know, Mark, but an automobile can, and if it isn't the same place it's some place equally unyielding."

With a nod to Mark and a lingering look at the automobile, Mr. Topper left the garage and walked slowly down the street to the main thoroughfare of the town, where he stopped and looked with unseeing eyes into a butcher's window. Behind him a steady trail of automobiles passed by. He was dimly aware of their swift, hissing tires whirling evenly over the smooth road. They were all going somewhere, he thought to himself, without troubling to look around, all out for a good time—a change. Some of them were going to new places, no doubt, places miles and miles away, maybe as far off as the coast. People did such things, camping at night by the roadside or putting up at inns.

Presently he became aware of the fact that he was looking a leg of lamb full in the face. There the thing was, hardly a foot from his nose. Back at home its mate was probably sputtering in the oven by this time. And Mrs. Topper was twittering about preparing new fields for dyspepsia while the cook struggled to swallow her spleen. It was appalling. Mr. Topper considered the lamb with smoldering eyes, but the lamb held its ground, and for a moment they confronted each other like two antagonists. Then Mr. Topper, at last outfaced by his less sensitive opponent, whirled about and walked back to the garage, this time with purpose in his step. But as he approached the garage he became troubled in his mind, and this trouble made him shuffle slightly in his gait. He had no doubt as to the ultimate outcome of his visit, but how to get it over with was what dismayed him, forcing him to drift about uneasily in front of the garage like a criminal released from the gates of durance. The sight of the "For Sale" sign on the glittering object of his quest stimulated him to action. He lifted his head and walked casually up to the car. Mark, emerging from the shadows like a proud but jealous god, greeted Mr. Topper with a slight show of surprise.

"How does the thing start?" asked Topper, without any preliminaries.

"How?" repeated Mark dumbly.

"The automobile," said Topper. "How do you start the damn thing?"

"Oh!" exclaimed Mark, now sparklingly alive to the situation. "Why, it starts like any other automobile. Put your foot on it and off she goes."

"Interesting if true," thought Mr. Topper. Nevertheless he regarded the starter with a contemplative eye.

"Is it hard to learn how to work them?" he continued. "I mean for a person like myself?"

"Why, Mr. Topper," Mark admonished, "there are bigger boobs than you messing up the roads everywhere."

"You shock me," remarked Topper, "but don't let's dwell on it. Now what is this thing for?"

"That's for the ventilator. It lets in the air."

"On what?"

"On your feet."

"An unpleasant inference," murmured Mr. Topper, "but I dare say the thing has its advantages. And this?" he added aloud.

"That lights your cigars."

Mr. Topper produced a cigar. Mark spoke the truth.

"A nice thing," said Mr. Topper, a little more at ease now that his lungs were refining smoke. "A handy thing, that. Very nice. Clever, too, isn't it?"

Mark, becoming more than serious, agreed that it was.

"Yes, yes," continued Topper, sliding into the front seat of the automobile as if he were not thinking of what he was doing. "A convenient little gadget. Adds to the pleasure of driving. Now come here, Mark, and show me what you do to make the old bus go, but first take that invitation off the front of the car. Some woman might come along and buy me. Hot stuff! How about that, Mark?"

"Ha! Ha!" laughed Mark, whose false mirth was arrested by a sudden slap on the back.

"Take the damn sign off, Mark," commanded Topper, a new light gleaming in his eyes.

CHAPTER IV

Mrs. Topper Is Not Delighted

THE FIRST STAGE OF MR. TOPPER'S SECRET LIFE dated from the Saturday on which he purchased the Kerby's ill-fated car from Mark, the ecstatic garage owner. And this stage lasted only a week, coming to a grand anticlimax on the following Saturday. But during that time Mr. Topper, a novice in secret living, was hard pressed to maintain his customary calm either at home or abroad. The fire was no longer banked in his eyes, but seemed to be smoldering through, and occasionally he found himself scrutinizing his friends as if they were total strangers.

His introductory driving lesson was of an anatomical nature. The automobile was discussed to its most intimate parts from which only the finest mechanism could have refrained from shrinking. The lesson completed, Mr. Topper abjured Mark to silence and returned to his home, where he settled his feud with the leg of lamb through the process of absorption. In other words it became one hundred per cent Topper and for

that reason acquired merit while Topper acquired
flesh.

"I knew you would like it," said Mrs. Topper as
though she were addressing a skeptical cannibal who
had just made a meal of a questionable victim. "I've
always said you liked lamb."

Mr. Topper could not deny the truth of her words,
but in spite of their truth they made him wish that he
could uneat the lamb. Not knowing how to do this
decently, he smiled at his wife and said, "I walked
farther than I thought. Worked up an appetite."

The false smile and the black lie quelled the rebellion in his stomach. Without realizing it, Topper was
already far gone in sin.

On Monday morning, after exchanging pennies
with a small Italian child for a stillborn edition of a
New York paper, he greeted his friends with his ha-
bitual placidity. No, he had not heard the new one
about Bill's furnace. He was sorry that Mrs. Thomp-
son was having servant trouble. Too bad. Was that so?
Jennings had made a killing again. Great stuff. Surely,
he'd bring the Missus over first thing. Wednesday evening? Good! Good! His tulips? Doing splendidly! A
whole bed of them—all blooming. No, not brewing,
just smousing about. Is that so! How about your own
cellar? None of that stuff, Jack! The whole town
knows about you. The farmer's daughter and the
tramp? Sure he'd like to hear it. Wait till they got
aboard.

And off went Topper with his boon companions,
all of whom he decided were perfect strangers to him.

At the office Topper treated the president with a
commendable show of tolerance. Cosmo Topper really
and sincerely pitied the man, pitied him from his
heart. He was a good old thing, but out of touch, pathetically inadequate. However, his chauffeur looked
like a keen enough young chap. Funny foreign-looking
mustache, but then a good driver was like any other
real artist. Better in fact. They had to have a little
leeway. Topper would have a word with him one day.
Exchange views on cars. Democratic. That was it. A
man in his position could afford to be democratic. It

went. As for the president, it was too bad. Topper felt
sorry for him.

Now the strange thing about it was that on this
particular morning the president, sighting his world-
weary eyes between the bronze ears of his Great Dane
desk ornament, felt pleased to permit Topper to occupy his gaze.

"A solid man," thought the president. "A good man
and a worker. I can count on him. The others"—and
the president's eyes never flickered—"brilliant, but
they're waiting to cut my throat. To them this bank
isn't home, it's something they want to control through
votes and money and chicanery. Now Topper's different. He's a man, at least. Loyal to a fault."

And the president, rousing his great body, towered
like a devastating sun over the gleaming surface of his
desk, then slowly advanced on Topper.

"You're looking fit, Topper," he said. "This man
from Texas has been in again. Don't want to see
him. . . . Come upstairs. We'll talk it over."

Topper followed.

"Why this?" he thought. "Why have I been selected?"

Topper little realized that there was a new light in
his eyes that set him apart from his fellow men. It was
young and fresh. The president was an old man, and,
like Topper, he had grown weary from watching eyes.
He had peered into them for more than half a century
. . . too deeply.

Topper is speeding through the shadows like a virgin to a forbidden tryst. He is thrilled with secret
alarm. In the close embrace of the night there is something almost personal. It clings to Topper like a
wronged woman, filling him with a desire to be elsewhere.

For nearly a week now Topper had been lying
steadily, mostly to his wife. Once he had stooped so
low as to lie to the garbage man. Topper had come to
that. It was excusable in this case, for the man collected garbage of the better sort throughout the town,
and in order to forget his occupation, he continually
busied his tongue with other people's affairs.

The seal of sin is settling on Topper's brow. He looks healthier and less uninteresting. He suspects everyone and, without being aware of it, he has been having a tremendous change.

At the garage, Mark is waiting for him. Good old Mark. Topper loves the man.

Topper arrives. There is a hurried conversation. Then each through his appointed door slides into the seat and they are off like a pair of conscience-stricken grave robbers. Mark is driving and Topper is doing strange, futile things with the brim of his felt hat. Instead of concealing his face, he succeeds in making himself look like a foppish desperado. He is hoping that he appears both sinister and repulsive so that people will avert their gaze without recognizing him, whereas, in truth, had any of Topper's friends seen him at this moment, they would have been astonished beyond measure, their cherished belief in the eternal sameness of things completely demolished.

The car proceeds down a side street to that section of the town near which no nice people care to build. In this belittered and uncorseted neighborhood Topper feels more at ease. This place which he once considered a reproach to the community, when he considered it at all, has become pleasantly familiar to him, a part of his secret life. It is the hidden door that leads to the open road. The dour houses and dim shops no longer make him uneasy. He regards them with a friendly eye which does not drop disapprovingly at the sight of a woman nursing her child on the least populous step of a front stoop. And when a mulatto maid swings down the street and stops to talk with the technically white youth in the livery stable, the moral responsibility of the race question does not weigh down Topper's heart. "Whose business is it?" he thinks to himself. "People should mind their own affairs." Anyway, she was an upstanding figure of a woman.

Soon the town is left behind and the car spins along an unfrequented road.

"What did you tell her to-night, Mr. Topper?" asks Mark.

"Meeting of the Town Guardians," replies Topper, emerging from his hat.

"Last night it was a Fire Council," continues Mark. "What's it going to be to-morrow?"

"The Assessment Club," snaps Topper promptly.

Mark gives a low whistle of admiration and the conversation languishes.

"They were killed down the road a piece," Mark announces presently. "Want to see the tree? It's on the other end of the old bridge."

"Certainly not," says Topper. "To gaze upon the departing point of my predecessors would hardly add to my skill. I want to shift the gears, not chatter through them."

"All right," replies Mark, bringing the car to a stop. "You take the wheel and turn her around. Drive down the line a bit and then come back. Keep turning, and if anything comes along pull in close to the side and stop. I'll keep an eye out."

Like a dog beneath the caress of an unfamiliar hand the gears shivered nervously at Mr. Topper's touch. They did not exactly chatter, but from time to time uttered cries of protest, like a child aroused from sleep by a convulsive pain in its stomach. Mr. Topper drove wisely but not well. He obeyed all the dictates of common sense, but still there was something lacking. Through no discernible fault of his own he seemed to bring out all the wayward traits of the car. It stopped without reason and started without grace. It darted as if pursued, then loitered alluringly. It displayed all the varied moods of a temperamental woman, one moment purring soothingly, the next scolding petulantly, now running ahead blind to caution, now holding back in virtuous alarm. It strayed from the path and returned again, and it treated its ardent possessor with the arrogant indifference of a beautiful thing. Mr. Topper was charmed. Not so Mark. Nevertheless after three-quarters of an hour of conscientious objecting the car was turned over to Mark, and Mr. Topper, moistly relinquishing the wheel, surveyed the June evening and found it good.

"You'll get by," remarked Mark as he headed the car for home.

And Mr. Topper did get by, what with the influence of Mark and a handful of cigars. Characteristically enough it was not until Mr. Topper held in his hands the official card entitling him to drive that he felt sure of his ability. The card dispelled all lingering doubt. He belonged to the brotherhood of the road. He had been tested and received. He could now speak on equal terms with the boy who delivered the ice. He had something in common with practically all the world.

There were several surprises in store for Mrs. Cosmo Topper on the Saturday following the purchase of the car. The first one came when Mr. Topper, returning from the city, announced without previous warning that he was starting a two weeks' vacation. Mrs. Topper successfully punctured the glory of this surprise by feeling audibly sorry that she was hardly up to going anywhere. Topper, not to be outdone, snatched her fleeting triumph by saying that he was just as well pleased. Of course he was sorry about her not feeling well, but then he was always sorry about that—stoically so, thought his wife.

Her second surprise came when Topper informed her that immediately after luncheon he proposed to attend a meeting of the Defense Society. Mrs. Topper saw scant reason for this, but made no comment until the meal was finished.

"What's this?" she said as he rose from the table. "What are all these meetings about? First it's the Town Guardians, then the Fire Council . . ."

"The other way 'round," corrected Mr. Topper, artistically cherishing his lies.

"Well, it doesn't very much matter, does it?" she replied. "What's gotten into this town? All these meeting!"

"Sparrows," said Mr. Topper as he jauntily left the room.

Mrs. Topper followed her husband with wondering eyes. What a terse and uninforming answer. How unlikc the usually explicit Cosmo. Sparrows. Why that?

A few hours later a third surprise caused Mrs. Topper to emerge with unwonted haste from the house. Topper, abandoning his secret life, was sounding his horn in the driveway. Mrs. Topper, from the front porch, saw a rather flushed and foolish-looking man of middle age gazing brightly at her from the driving seat of a glittering automobile.

"Well, what do you think of us now?" asked the man in a voice which conveyed the impression that Mrs. Topper would never be able adequately to express her admiration in words.

Mrs. Topper did not answer immediately. He had not expected her to. That was partly the fun of it— the dawning of delight, the wonder and unbelief and then the appreciation. Dyspepsia would be forgotten. A new era would start for them.

"You gave me such a start," said Mrs. Topper. "What on earth are you trying to do with that garish-looking car?"

"Trying?" replied Mr. Topper, making a brave effort to retain his smile. "Trying? Why I'm not trying, my dear. I'm actually driving it. I drove it here all the way from the garage. It's ours. Yours and mine. We own it."

"You might own it," Mrs. Topper said, "but we don't. Keep me out of it. I won't be involved. Everybody in town knows the Kerbys' car. Even I recognize it. I've seen it thousands of times. A second-hand car. What a thing to do!"

Topper's smile would not stay fixed. No matter how he strove, his lips refused to respond. Everything was so different from what he had expected.

"I know," he explained, looking down at the wheel. "This is only our practice car. New one next year. Nice though, isn't it?"

"I don't think it's a bit nice," said Mrs. Topper. "Nor do I think it nice of you to sit there and enjoy yourself. Buying an automobile and not letting me know, picking up the most vulgar car in town, coming home at this hour and making noises on the lawn, upsetting my nerves and spoiling the leg of lamb . . ."

Then Mrs. Topper received her last surprise.

"Damn the leg of lamb!" he shouted, embittered beyond endurance by his wife's reception of his surprise. "I'm going for a drive."

An offensive honking of the horn overfilled Mrs. Topper's cup of woe.

"He seems to be able to drive it," she reluctantly admitted to herself as the automobile wavered down Glendale Road.

CHAPTER V

The Nebulous Lap

IT COULD NOT BE SAID OF MR. TOPPER THAT HE WAS in a brown study as he drove away from his wife. He was keenly alive to the fact that he was sitting alone in a moving automobile entirely dependent on him for pace and direction. He alone was now responsible for the safety of the car as well as for his own safety. This knowledge never for a moment left his mind. In spite of it, Mr. Topper was preoccupied, or as preoccupied as a person in his position could afford to be. Violence had been done to his feelings, and a reaction had set in. After a week of tremendous lying, during which time life had seemed to be disclosing new and splendid vistas, Topper suddenly felt that after all life was no whit different. It was as flat and stale as ever. Automobiles were no use, nor were little attempts, nor anything.

"Oh, damn that leg of lamb," he muttered, slowing down with elaborate caution at the sight of a car two blocks distant.

As the automobile passed Mr. Topper, the eyes of the man at the wheel grew incredulous with wonder. He leaned over the side and looked back. He came to a stop and continued to stare.

"That's Hart," said Topper to himself. "Well, damn

him, too. He'll spread the news around. Let him. See if I care."

And Topper stepped on the gas.

Through force of habit he took the same road he had learned to know so well with Mark. This was not the drive he had intended taking—not if she had been decent and friendly about things, but now it did not matter. He drove along, occupied with his thoughts, keeping his eye on the road and paying very little attention to the scenery. Presently he became aware that he had passed his usual limits. Ahead of him was the bridge on the other end of which the Kerbys had met their fate. Topper had never driven over a bridge before and the rattling of planks unnerved him. He stopped on the after-side to regain his composure.

The tree must be somewhere close at hand, for Mark had said it was just at the end of the bridge. Topper got out of the automobile and looked morbidly about him. At the edge of the road stood a stunted tree with a gashed and splintered trunk. Undoubtedly it was the one, the very tree that had caused George and Marion Kerby hastily to withdraw from their questionable circle of friends. Topper surveyed the tree thoughtfully. Two human lives, two warm and vigorous creatures, had been sped into eternity against the age-old bark of that tree. He glanced up. Leaves were out on the upper branches, and wings were flitting though them. Life still went on with the tree. It drank in the moist earth and tossed its palms to the sun. It was made of sterner stuff than mortals. It was more firmly rooted to the earth. Topper had a funny thought. If he had had a son this tree would still be green and filled with birds when the boy was gray and gazing back on life. Topper wanted a son, he felt the need of youth, an enthusiastic, unspoiled soul, to stimulate his ebbing interest in the automobile, someone to admire his daring and to speak favorably of his newly acquired art. Topper was on the point of becoming a shade self-sympathetic.

An observer of character seeing him at that moment would have paused to ponder over his unremarkable

figure. He looked rather small beneath the majestic
reaches of the tree, and his stomach seemed pitifully
brave, thrusting itself out aggressively into a world that
could trump with mountains. The observer would have
noted Topper's stomach and the sturdily planted legs,
and without exactly forgetting these features, would
have really remembered Topper's face. There dwelt
the Prince of Denmark, shadowed and filled with
trouble, an inarticulate prince, perhaps, run to flesh
and bland of mien, but a prince withal, probing the
problem of life and the mystic charm of death, a man
existing reluctantly, unconsciously seeking release.

Mr. Topper turned from the tree and wormed himself into the automobile. And the observer, had he
been endowed with cattish curiosity, would have
noted by the laborings of Topper's body that he had
not long been familiar with the driving seat of an
automobile. Once in he relaxed, then, collecting his
scattered members, arranged his feet and hands as
Mark had patiently instructed him.

"Just the same," thought Topper with an important
feeling of ownership, "these trees shouldn't grow so
close to the road. There should be a law about trees.
A sort of a movement. Something done."

At this particular time Mr. Topper's conception of
the ideal tour was limited only by the skyline of the
Sahara Desert, a wide, unobstructed expanse affording
adequate room for turning. Topper's social instincts
did not extend to motoring. He preferred an unfrequented road where only nature could hear the
neighing of the gears, and where there would be
naught of alarm to galvanize his nerves.

Mr. Topper made the customary movements, and
with delightful regularity the scenery began to slide by.
He became aware of an oncoming line of trees, flashing things filled with shadows, he felt a dip and a
gentle rise and gazed across a sunken plain soft with
grass, scarred by fences and heckled by an astonish-
ingly undecided brook that turned and doubled on its
path. Mr. Topper found himself enjoying this hollow
expanse of green. It was longer than it was wide and it
seemed to extend for miles. Only the woods on the

other side put a stop to its triumphant march. There were dots of trees on the sunken plain, intimate groups of clustering green, but they did not rob the plain of its vastness. Instead they emphasized its majesty like a contentious family huddled beneath the vaulting dome of a deserted railroad station.

"Take those fences down," thought Topper, "and what a space you'd have. Cavalry could charge across those fields."

What a lovely place it was . . . the unexpectedly good road, the sunken fields, the sky closing them in and the occasional farm house bereft of life. The road puzzled Topper. It was as if the world had planned a secret path to nowhere. He felt that he was riding on through an endless dusky solitude. He no longer troubled about the car. It seemed to be running itself. There were trees on one side, green curving space on the other, and an unobstructed road ahead. Topper had become blended with his surroundings. His body was blotting up the landscape and his mind, no longer functioning, seemed to be absorbing the lights and shades and smells along the road. The color of the sky, now churning red with sunset, dropped like a mantle on Mr. Topper and filled the world with stillness.

And out of the stillness a voice spoke to Mr. Topper.

"Topper," it said, "Topper, perhaps you do not realize you are sitting on my wife's lap—or do you?"

Topper's hands grew white on the wheel. He made an effort to stop the car, but as the machine seemed disinclined to stop he abandoned the effort and looked steadfastly in front of him, blindly refusing to admit the fact that he had heard a voice without seeing its owner. The thing just could not be. He, Topper, was at fault, or at least he heartily hoped so. Driving had overtaxed his imagination. The strange solitude of the place and the calm, mysterious beauty of the landscape had affected him. It would have affected anybody.

So Mr. Topper drove on. The behavior of the automobile disturbed him, although he would not admit to himself that it was acting in any way unusual.

Nevertheless it was. It had become a self-propelled vehicle in the fullest sense of the term. It no longer concerned itself with Topper, but obeyed the dictates of its newly acquired independence. It did not hitch and spurt along the road, but progressed smoothly at a speed which the discreet Topper viewed with sincere alarm. Once when the motor slowed down he made an attempt to shift the gears, only to be paralyzed by a voice exclaiming irritably:

"Don't do that!"

After this Mr. Topper withdrew completely from the management of the car and dropped to the rather unimportant position usually allotted to a pig iron image arbitrarily spiked to the front seat of a toy fire engine. And Mr. Topper looked the part. His face was a mask and his arms had become angular and rigid. He was certain of this, however: the first voice had been a man's, whereas the second had been unmistakably feminine. After making a mental note of this Mr. Topper closed his mind. It was better not to think—safer.

"Topper," began the first voice, sounding quite polite and reasonable, "must I remind you again that you are sitting on my wife's lap? Why not squeeze over now and . . ."

"Stop!" cried Mr. Topper, coming to a quick decision, and with an extraordinary effort arresting the speed of the car. "Stop," he repeated, "and for God's sake don't begin again. I can't stand it."

"Come, come now, Mr. Topper," admonished the voice.

"Don't," pleaded Topper. "Let me speak. Please listen. I've bought and paid for this automobile. With great mental anguish I've learned how to make it work, but I'll give it to you, give it gladly, if you'll let me step quietly out, and you then drive on as fast and as far as you can."

Mr. Topper looked earnestly at the vacant seat beside him. He wanted a reply and yet he waited for it with dread.

"Why so tragic?" the voice began. "Why shun our company? Three can sit just as comfortably on this seat as two. We've done it often. Just squeeze over a little."

"You don't seem to understand," said Mr. Topper, with the patience of desperation. "If the seat were a thousand leagues wide I would still feel cramped. Take the car. You're welcome to it. Take it to some far place. Have a nice drive, a good time, but leave me behind. Let me get out. I'm not enjoying myself."

"Still tragic," retorted the voice. "And all the time you are wallowing on my wife's lap."

Topper had a strange and uncomfortable sensation. He felt, or imagined he felt, a pair of arms passing through his body on their way to the wheel. He was almost sure that for some minutes these arms had been playfully hugging him around the waist, and once more he became painfully aware of his stomach. It was indeed an objectionable feature.

"How about my wife's lap?" questioned the voice.

"Hang it all!" Topper exclaimed. "Why doesn't she move over? I didn't sit on her lap, you know. She got it there."

"Topper," rebuked the voice. "You surprise us. I might say, you offend us. I might, mind you, Topper, but I don't."

"Offend you!" cried Mr. Topper. "Great God! What next?"

"Now, taking up the matter of my wife's lap," continued the voice, "I still maintain . . ."

Mr Topper became mentally unfit to hear the remainder of the remark. He passed into one of those distracted calms that precede lunacy. Out of this calm he heard himself saying, with tastefully garnished sarcasm:

"After all, the car really does belong to me. I bought the thing, but not your wife's lap. I'm sorry, but I wash my hands of your wife's lap. You can take the lap or leave it. I'm not responsible. If her lap insists on sitting under me I'm not to blame. However, if you and your wife and her everlasting lap would disappear as speedily as possible, the countryside would not bear witness to my grief. Certainly not."

"We've already disappeared as much as possible," said the voice rather gloomily.

"Not enough for me," replied Topper.

"All right then," said the voice. "Move over, Marion. Topper wants to hog the car."

"Hog the car!" retorted Mr. Topper. "Whose car is it? Answer me that. Answer me fairly that. Whose car is it, I ask you? If your wife's lap were at all lady-like . . ."

"What's this about my wife's lap?" interrupted the voice, a trifle excitedly. "Make one unfavorable reference to my wife's lap. Just one. Let me hear it."

"Now, for God's sake, boys, don't let's have any trouble," put in a woman's voice pleadingly. "Come on, let's get together. That's how it happened the last time. Be sensible, George. Topper seems to be a game old bird."

"Old birds are inclined to be gamey," remarked Topper.

"Ah, there, Topper," said the woman's voice. "Getting common? And still sitting on my lap?"

"Just so," joined in the man's voice. "Don't go any further. Try to remember that you're still sitting on my wife's lap. I don't want any trouble.

Topper's whole mental system was undergoing a revolution. It did not occur to him that he was having a row with space, or that he was being calculatingly nasty to nothingness. So absorbed had he become in the injustice done to himself that, for the moment, the unconventionality of the situation had slipped his mind. Topper was thoroughly aroused.

"Prove to me that I am sitting on your wife's lap," he said.

"Do you understand the fourth dimension?" politely inquired the man's voice.

"Why should I?" said Topper.

"Well, we do," continued the voice. "As a matter of fact you might almost say that we are the fourth dimension. Not of the oldest families, perhaps, but pretty well sponsored at that. It would be a waste of time to attempt to explain it to you, so you'll have to take my word for it. You, Topper, are sitting most heavily, most grossly, on my wife's lap. No man has ever done it, with my knowledge, for the same length of time that you have. I repeat—with my knowledge."

"Don't indulge your jealous nature," said the woman's voice. "Don't irritate me."

"I'm going to leave this car," announced Topper. "I hate bickering."

Topper made an effort to rise, then sank back in his seat. He had an odd feeling. Two arms were holding him round the waist. They were the most material arms he had ever encountered, yet he could not see them. They held him firmly, and made a noticeable depression in his stomach. This impression without the arms was too much for Topper.

"She's holding me," he gasped, sweat beading his lips. "Tell her to take her arms away."

"Not until you promise to be good," replied the woman's voice.

"Let me go," pleaded Topper, "and I'll promise anything. If you'll only take your arms away from my —my—"

"Your stomach?" suggested the woman.

"All right," exclaimed Topper. "Have it your way. If you'll only remove your arms I'll slide over gladly."

Topper drew a deep breath as he felt himself released. Casting a timid glance on either side of him, he slid to the middle of the seat with a movement which for him was voluptuously sinuous.

"At last you've succeeded in getting me between you," he said with spiteful resignation. "Go on now and drive me mad. Finish the job. Smash the car. I don't want it and my wife can't stand it."

"Why can't your wife stand it?" asked the woman's voice.

"Oh, I don't know," replied Topper. "All her reasons are rather obscure. She says the thing belonged to the Kerbys and that's enough for her. It's too notorious."

"Go on, Mr. Topper," said the woman's voice as the automobile gathered pace. "What else did she say?"

Mr. Topper was neither the wisest nor the most

observant of men. His ears were attuned to only one danger signal, Mrs. Topper. The beautiful simplicity of the man lay in the fact that at his age he still thought of his wife as being quite an exceptional woman. His optimistic nature led him to believe that she alone of all her tribe had been cursed with an unfortunate disposition, that she alone was the victim of implacable dyspepsia, that she alone was the only woman who considered herself a martyr and who forced her husband so to consider her. There was only one Mrs. Topper. It was inconceivable that there could be two. Topper clung to this hope. It comforted him a little to imagine that all the other women in the world were different, that they had no small animosities, that they did not spend an hour in saying something that could have been easily stated in three minutes, that they did not take advantage of the fact that they were women and as a consequence nervous wrecks, that they did not spasmodically attempt to please their husbands while consistently endeavoring to crush them, that they were not interested in the puerile mystery surrounding the sudden departure of Mrs. Smith's cook or the Robinsons' trip to Maine, or the fact that the Harts were still in town. Mr. Topper honestly believed that his wife had been especially set aside for him by a kind but casual god. In this belief he accepted her, but not without some mental reservations.

"What else did Mrs. Topper say?" continued the woman's voice.

"I forget," he replied. "She's said so many things."

"For instance?"

"Well, that Marion Kerby was no better than she should be and that her husband was a sot who consumed all his time and money in keeping himself numb with drink."

"That will do," broke in the man's voice. "I've heard enough. Do you happen to know who we are—or were?"

"I had hoped that our acquaintance would never become so intimate," said Topper with the utmost earnestness.

"Well, it has," said the man's voice. "You are speaking to and driving with both George and Marion Kerby. Now how does that make you feel?"

"I ceased to feel some time ago," replied Mr. Topper, "but if I hadn't, your information would be like tossing a paralytic in a blanket."

"The old crow," came contemplatively from the driving seat. "So that somber old moll said that I was no better than I should be. Did you hear what he said, George? Hit him."

"He didn't say it," said George. "Be reasonable. He's not responsible for his wife's remarks. No man is. The race would perish."

"But just the same she said it," the wheel replied broodingly.

At this point Mr. Topper felt forced to interpose an objection. Routine loyalty compelled him to speak.

"In the first place you are a woman," he said, "and in the second you're invisible, and for that reason you're taking a doubly unfair advantage of your sex and lack of substance by calling my wife an old crow and a moll."

Mr. Topper made a mental note of the two expressions. He would never apply them directly to his wife, but it would be quite a comfort to think them at times.

"Say, listen," exclaimed the man's voice, "I'll knock your block off if you begin to pull that first and second place stuff with us. Where do you get . . ."

"Now for God's sake don't let's have any trouble, boys," the wheel pleaded. "Remember, George, we were smashed up the last time."

"Then why did you start things now?"

"Start things? Me?"

"Yes, you, with all your personal injuries."

"I must say you're extremely unreasonable."

"Me unreasonable? Hell's bells! That's a good one."

"Don't be despicable."

Mr. Topper had been watching the casual conduct of the car with increasing anxiety. He thought that it was now high time to enter into the discussion.

"I hope," he said, carefully considering the advisability of each word, "that you won't take it in ill part if I say that at present I have no desire to join your nebulous state. The situation, bad as it is, would be less desperate if I could only feel that someone, no matter how invisible, was paying attention to the car."

Topper was silent for a moment, then his true feelings triumphed.

"I hate bickerings," he said.

He was astounded by hearing a hearty peal of laughter from the steering wheel. Manifestations of mirth encompassed him.

"Stick to the road," he urged.

"Stick-to-the-road-Topper!" the woman's voice exulted. "That's a good name. Let's call him that."

"Only for introductions," replied the other voice consideringly. "Too long for ordinary use. 'Cosmo' is rather crisp. Why paint the lily?"

"What do you mean about introductions?" inquired Mr. Topper uneasily. "Have you any friends? I don't want to meet them. Remember that. Absolutely no."

"I hope you wouldn't embarrass us in case we met a group of our friends," replied the man.

"Embarrass you? Oh, I don't know what I'd do. My God, a group! Not just a friend, but a group!" Topper's voice was distracted.

"Well, how about meeting some of yours?" suggested George. "There are quite a few over here. Not an honest piece of ectoplasm in the bunch."

"Look where you're driving," breathed Topper, reaching for something to cling to, yet unwilling to thrust his arms through the invisible bodies beside him. "I never wanted less to die in all my life."

"Tactful Topper," said Marion.

A slight difficulty with a rail fence momentarily retarded conversation. When the car emerged from the dispute bearing a battered fender Topper voiced his unhappiness by remarking that there was scant comfort to be gained by sitting between two ethereal bodies while one's very soul was being shot through space.

"I have nothing to cling to save hope," he said. "And even that grows dim."

A turn in the road disclosed in the distance the lights of a small town. Mr. Topper gave a sigh of relief. During the course of the conversation he had not actually believed in its reality. He had preferred to accustom his mind to the fact that he had gone mad, mildly mad, and, as he fervently hoped, temporarily so. The best way to combat this madness, he concluded, was to give in to it, to make no effort to regain sanity, but gradually to feel his way back to his normal state like a man delicately shaking a leg that had fallen asleep. Topper felt that a village street, stark and soiled beneath the glare of the lights, and thronged with the usual Saturday night collection of rustics, would do much to restore his mental poise. He would leave the car and mingle with these people. He would not actually kiss and hug them, but he would feel like doing so. Spiritually he would shower them with embraces, and as he absorbed the life of the town the imaginings of the road would fade away and he, Topper, would once more be a full-fledged member of the human race instead of a rebellious participant in an occult phenomenon.

"For the sake of appearance," he remarked to the wheel, "we had better exchange positions as we drive into the town. People have grown accustomed to seeing someone sitting at the steering gear of automobiles. It may seem silly to you, but if we drove down the main street of this town under the present arrangement I would probably be burned for a witch or thrust into solitary confinement."

"You need never fear solitude, Topper, so long as we're around," replied Marion.

"Don't misunderstand me," Topper hastened to explain. "I have no fear of solitude. I yearn for it . . . absolute solitude unbroken by the sound of a voice or the knowledge of a presence."

"All right," said Marion. "Let's change seats. Move over."

"How can I be sure that we are changing seats?" Mr. Topper inquired.

"I'll see that she does," replied George Kerby. "Stop at the nearest garage. We need gas."

A few minutes later Mr. Topper drew up at a garage. He had never before bought gasoline. The situation perplexed him.

"How much shall I get?" he whispered over his shoulder.

"Ten gallons will be enough," Kerby announced. "Get some oil, too."

"Not so loud," Topper pleaded as he got out of the automobile and approached the unenterprising deity of the place. The deity regarded Topper with aversion and his car with disgust. He was almost hostile in his disapproval. Topper could sense it by the angle of the man's hat and the tilt of his cigar. Nevertheless Topper addressed the deity, tactfully suggesting his coöperation in procuring oil and gasoline.

"Bring your car under the pump," commanded the deity, filling Topper's face with smoke. Topper objected to the smoke, but felt that at least it was more tangible than phantoms.

"One moment," he replied, turning round, then he froze in his tracks, his last hope banished. After all he was not mad, not even mildly so. The automobile apparently unassisted was busily edging itself up to the pump. He glanced guiltily at the deity as if to seek comfort in his repellent countenance, but no comfort was there to be found. The deity had momentarily become a mortal. You could tell that by the gold fillings in his teeth twinkling through his widely separated lips.

"How did you do that?" asked the man.

Topper laughed a trifle wildly, as he waved a protesting hand at the car. "Quite a trick, eh? Well, I had her all set, but I guess the brakes slipped."

The man's face cleared, his mouth closed and once more he became a deity. But as he approached the tube to the tank his features again altered. This time his eyes became prominent. As he gazed at the brass cap of the gasoline tank they were much more eloquent with astonishment than the gold fillings. The thing was slowly and mysteriously unscrewing itself. Suddenly it moved through the air, then came to repose on the mudguard of the car. Topper stood by fascinated.

"How did you do that?" demanded the man.

"What?" said Topper wearily, taking out his handkerchief and hiding his face therein. "I wish you'd stop asking me how I do things. I just do them, that's all. Automatic springs. New device. Haven't time to go into all that."

As the man filled the tank with gasoline Topper hurried to the front of the car and leaned in.

"For God's sake stop trying to be so helpful," he whispered. "I'll do everything."

An ineffectually stifled giggle smote his ears.

"Who's laughing?" called the man from the rear of the car.

Topper had not the time to answer. Something was taking place in front that demanded all his attention. A water bucket insecurely balanced on thin air was emptying its contents into the radiator. Topper sprang forward and seized the bucket.

"I'm just giving her water," he shouted. "You must have heard the gurgle. This car gurgles like that. It's a habit."

When the radiator was filled Mr. Topper became engaged in a violent struggle with the bucket, for George Kerby, still bent on being helpful, was trying to take the thing back to the garage. For a few moments the bucket danced crazily in the air, then fell clattering to the ground from which it was seized by some unknown agent and carried swiftly in the direction of the garage. Mr. Topper sped after the bucket, his outstretched hand separated from the handle by several inches of space.

"I'm just returning the bucket," he called over his shoulder. "I'll be right with you." Then under his breath, "Kerby, don't run so fast. Let me at least catch up with the bucket. I merely want to pretend I'm carrying it."

The deity, now transformed into one of the most disturbed creatures that had ever watered gasoline, stood watching Topper's pursuit of the bucket. He saw it describe an arc in the air, and Topper leaping after it with great agility and determination. He saw the bucket rolling rapidly across the floor and Topper,

lost to dignity, rolling after it. Finally he saw Topper
rise triumphantly with the bucket in his hand and
place it under the water faucet, where for a short
space it bounced gaily up and down, then settled to
rest beneath the weight of Mr. Topper's body. The
man did not stay to see any more, but faced about
and hurried down the street. As he did so the automobile began to honk vociferously, a door flew open and
a woman's voice called impatiently to Mr. Topper.
The man increased his pace, then broke into an earnest dogtrot. Still honking madly, the automobile
turned into the road and sped away in the opposite
direcion. But the man did not stop to watch its tail
light disappear.

In the automobile Topper was sitting in silence and
perspiration. George and Marion Kerby were talking
to him at the same time, but Topper refused to
answer. He was a crushed man, a hurt man. The scene
still lived in his eyes, that ghastly pursuit of the bucket.
And it lingered in his eyes until the automobile came to
a stop beside the great tree that had dispatched the
Kerbys. Here Topper began to laugh softly to himself. He was thinking of the amazement on the garage-
man's face. Mr. Topper's laugh gathered in volume.
It was swelled by the laughter of George and Marion
Kerby. The night was filled with their mirth. The old
tree rustled its remonstrating branches above the automobile, but the laughter mocked its rebuke. A farmer
driving home from market warily skirted the glare
of the headlights and clicked to his mare. Down the
road and through the night the wild laughter followed the creaking cart.

"They were all sittin' in the front seat huggin' and
kissin' and carryin' on crazy," the farmer told his
wife at the end of the drive. "I could see 'em as
plain as day. Women smokin' and goin' on scandlous."

"Them townspeople drink too much," replied the
wife as she filled the old man's glass with a generous
allotment of good old Jersey applejack.

CHAPTER VI

Disaster at the Curb

THUS BEGAN FOR MR. TOPPER AN UNUSUAL EXPERI-
ence, to say the least. Not knowing the circumstances,
his friends chastely called it demoralizing. But not so
Mr. Topper. For the first time in his life he consciously, nay, deliberately, assumed a minority rôle.
For the first time he permitted himself to deal with
abstract things without feeling that he had sinned. For
the first time Topper's established routine of living
gave place to a disorderly desire to live. And for the
first time on an evening in June, Topper wonderingly
considered the stars not in their relation to a smart
New Jersey town, but in the relation of the town to
the stars.

This was the second phase of Topper's secret life.
It was in this phase that he came to regard the place
in which he lived as a pool fed by the withering souls
of people who had passed up life. They were usual
people, the people who fed this pool. They had been
accepted and asked out to places. They commuted,
propagated, and entertained with impartial uniformity.
In all the things of life they used the same time-table.
Mr. Topper could not call them vicious. That was the
trouble. Topper bent his brain over an abstract problem. His friends would have been surprised had they
seen the man actually screwing his face into childish
wrinkles over such a time-consuming thought.

And all was not well at home with Topper. He had
cursed a leg of lamb. He had actually damned the
thing. Mrs. Topper could not forget that. Had he
cursed her she might have dimly understood, but to
hurl imprecations at a tender leg of lamb, a thoughtfully selected leg of lamb—oh, no, that could not be

forgotten. Men might rebel against their God, but a leg of lamb, a household deity, a savory roast . . . sacrilege, its very seat and circle!

In spite of her husband's offense Mrs. Topper maintained the brooding sameness of things. It gave her a better opportunity than an open breach to confound him with the seriousness of the situation, the utter hopelessness of it, the black despair. They still occupied their appointed chairs on opposite sides of the sitting-room table. Topper still read his paper while Mrs. Topper did darting things with her needle to a piece of linen. Each dart picked a little fiber out of Topper's nerves. So terrible did it all seem that at times he could hardly restrain himself from dodging as the needle sought its mark. On these occasions Topper clung to Scollops for bodily comfort and moral support. And Scollops with luxurious undulation yawned callously in the face of tragedy. It was not of her making. She was gloatingly out of it. What was important, however, was a good sound sleep. Topper's thigh was a comfortable place for a good sound sleep, though of late, Scollops daintily decided, this erstwhile unimpeachable mattress had been growing a trifle too muscular.

In vain did Mr. Topper try to recapture romance in the eyes of Scollops. Her eyes were closed in slumber. In vain did he seek distraction in market quotations. Industrial bonds no longer inspired him with a feeling of solid security. In vain did he let his eyes shift round the room in search of some object to hold his attention. The room was filled with objects, but for Topper they were bereft of interest. Once, in a fit of desperation, he faltered out an invitation to Mrs. Topper. It was a beautiful afternoon, pervaded with dripping sunlight and carpeted with leagues of green. It would be nice to go driving on such an afternoon. The roads would be almost free from traffic and nobody much would be around to observe them. It would be quite exciting. Mrs. Topper would enjoy it. He imagined that there would be a nice, fresh breeze and that the fields would look quite young and new. They could stop at a roadhouse, a respectable one, the

"Rose-Marie," and have tea. Well, what did she say to that?

Topper looked hopefully at his wife, then looked away. He knew exactly what she was going to say to that. He could have said it for her. But he did not have to. She said it for herself. She was just a little too tired to-day to risk the roads. They might upset her even more than she was already if such an upheaval were possible. Last night had been a bad one—sleepless. A dragging night. Anyway she was not particularly interested in automobiles, but he, Topper, was. Why didn't he go out and take a nice drive? She too was sure there would be a lovely breeze and that the fields would be lovely also. She would stay at home. A sigh. She was better off at home. A look. Home was the place for her. A sigh and a look.

"But," said Topper, his voice trembling slightly as he rose from his chair and confronted his wife, "you haven't even so much as looked at the automobile. You haven't touched one part of it with the tip of your little finger. Aren't you interested at all? There's lots of nice things about it. Come out and watch me light a cigar. You'd be surprised, Mary." His voice grew low with excitement. "I'll teach you how to drive. You could do it. Look at me! It would help you with your dyspepsia."

Mrs. Topper put down her sewing and looked up at her husband's earnest face. What absurdly young eyes he had, she thought. Behind her unsympathetic expression struggled a sincere desire to smile at Topper, to go out and pat the automobile, to marvel over the cigarette lighter, to sit in the front seat and to tell Topper how wonderful he was. Just a little smile would have altered the situation, but the smile was not forthcoming. Topper was making her resentful. He was committing a terrible crime. He was destroying her good opinion of herself. Topper was making her realize how calculatingly cruel and unsympathetic she was, how stubborn as a wife and inadequate as a friend. No man could make her feel like that and gain her forgiveness. No matter how the reconciliation came about she must be the generous spirit and Topper the self-centered. She could not conceive of herself playing any other rôle. Furthermore, Topper was showing himself up in altogether too favorable a light. She was aware of that. She realized that Topper was an exceptionally decent person. This added to her resentment. What right had he to be like that? Was he deliberately trying to emphasize the difference in their characters? Finally, Mrs. Topper had no desire to lose her dyspepsia. It was the very last thing in the world she wanted to lose. Mrs. Topper needed her dyspepsia. She lived in and for her dyspepsia. It took the place of a child. She was tender about it. And in her mistaken mind she hoped that, like a child, her dyspepsia would help her to hold her husband. It gave her an extra claim on him. Mrs. Topper, folding her hands in her lap, spoke to her husband in a dead, level voice deliberately tuned to dash all hope.

"You bought the automobile," she said. "You bought it behind my back. You selfishly robbed me of my pleasure. Selfishly. Yes, that's it. You're so selfish and self-centered, so interested in your own affairs that you don't know I'm alive. And I'm not. I'm not even——"

"I know, dear," Topper broke in. "You're not even half alive. I realize it. That dyspepsia! But really now I wasn't selfish. That is, I didn't mean to be. I figured on surprising you and I worked so hard to——"

"Don't!" commanded Mrs. Topper. "You have told me to my face that I'm not even half alive."

"But I thought that was what you were going to say," hastened Topper. "I just wanted to agree."

"You had better go driving," said Mrs. Topper coldly. "Find somebody who is a little less dead than I am."

Topper drooped his shoulders and turned away without answering. He was thinking to himself that there was more excitement in the company of two completely dead persons than he would ever find at home.

When he had gone Mrs. Topper buried her face in her hands and presently tears trickled through her fingers. "Why am I this way?" she whispered. "I don't want to be. I don't mean to be. But he shouldn't look so hurt. I hate that look."

She started up and ran to the window. Topper was laboring in the driveway. He looked like a man driving to his own execution. Mrs. Topper hurried out on the porch and called to him.

"Let me get my things," she said. "I'll be right out."

Inside she dried her tears on the precious piece of linen.

Topper was radiant as his wife got into the car.

"See here," he said, pulling at the electric lighter. "Too bad I lighted my cigar, but here's how it works. See how red she's getting. Put your finger near it. Feel that heat. Some heat, eh?"

Mrs. Topper obediently approached her finger to the lighter and agreed that it was indeed some heat. However she was not quite satisfied. Topper should say something more. He had not admitted that he was selfish and self-centered. Nor had he drawn favorable attention to Mrs. Topper's generous conduct. She suffered an acute relapse and heartily wished herself out of the car, but Topper was already turning down Glendale Road.

"Now I'm shifting the gears," he explained. "No so hard when you get the knack. I'm not an expert yet, but you don't have to worry. Gee, Mary, it's great you're along," he added a little bashfully.

No, it was not quite adequate. It should have been longer and laden with a deeper appreciation of her character. Mrs. Topper was not mollified. However she kept her peace. She would not spoil the drive—not yet.

Now it was unfortunate that as they crossed the main street of the town Mrs. Topper decided she wanted to shop at the butcher's. It was doubly unfortunate because Topper was not accustomed to stopping on the main streets of towns and had a perilous time wedging himself in between two intimately parked automobiles. It was even more unfortunate that, after Mrs. Topper's departure, Mr. Topper attempted to improve on his position by ramming, with no little violence, the automobile directly in front of him. People stopped and stared at Topper, then stared at the assaulted car. Several examined the damaged fender from which Mr. Topper hastily averted his woeful eyes. Where was the owner? Topper hoped that his wife would hurry so that they could get away as speedily as possible. Topper could never face the man. He felt like pinning a twenty-dollar bill to the fender with a note asking forgiveness. He would sign it "An Unknown Admirer," to make the man feel better about it.

But more unfortunate than anything else was the reappearance of Mrs. Topper in company with Clara Stevens. Mr. Topper little realized how really unfortunate this was. Clara was talking brilliantly and Mrs. Topper was absorbing with gloomy interest.

"And so Harris told him to his face that he would as soon consider buying a second-hand car as oil stock from a third cousin," she was saying as the two women drew near Topper.

The remark did not sound reassuring to Topper. But then, Mary was a sensible woman. Everyone knew how Clara went on.

"Clara was in town last week buying a new car," announced Mrs. Topper, with meaning in her voice, after the customary hypocrisies had been exchanged. "She spent a whole week going from place to place until she was completely satisfied she had made a wise selection."

Topper thought that it was rather remiss of Clara to make no reference to the fact that he was lounging picturesquely over the steering wheel of an automobile, but perhaps he looked so natural that the unusualness of the situation had not occurred to her.

"Clara picked out the car herself," continued Mrs. Topper, "and it's registered in her name. She says Harris was a dear about it, so patient with her and unselfish."

"And here it is!" exclaimed Clara, turning to the victim of Mr. Topper's skill. "Why . . . what . . . has . . . happened . . . to . . . my . . . nice . . . new . . . car?"

Topper thought she would never finish.

"Oh, God," he prayed to himself, "take me out of this. Translate me to the heavens. Make me a fixed star or a shooting star, I don't much care which, but deliver me now from these two women. Let me be somewhere else."

"Whatever will Harris say?" Clara tearfully asked the street.

Topper could see that the girl was moved, that her reputation as a driver was seriously involved. He knew Harris, and he knew that he was neither patient nor generous, nor was he a dear. Topper was also afraid that some helpful bystander would point a denouncing finger at him before he had time to explain.

"I guess Harris will have to talk with me," said Topper quietly. "You see, I did it. I did it with my little car. Fix it as good as new. Stick on another fender in a minute. Sorry. The man behind me just wouldn't budge."

Mrs. Topper was being repaid for her momentary weakness. Before Clara could speak she did, which showed that she had been toeing the mark.

"You should at least have thought of me," she said. "Come, Clara, take me home, will you? I am not feeling well. I knew it would be this way. Cosmo will see that everything is arranged."

"Just a minute," called Cosmo, as the two women entered the other machine. "Aren't you coming driving with me?"

"With you?" said Mrs. Topper, her eyebrows slightly arched.

CHAPTER VII

Topper Calls on a Tree

MR. TOPPER VICIOUSLY PRESSED HIS FOOT DOWN ON the self-starter. In his imagination he was crushing the human race, especially the female branch of it, and in particular Clara Stevens. He had one desire now and only one. He wanted to cut himself off entirely from people and faces and eyes, and from tongues, too. Idle, insincere tongues. He was an embittered man and a confused one. Events had occurred too rapidly. Mentally he tried to catch up with them. There had been a little unpleasantness at home. That had fortunately subsided. Then quite amazingly he had found himself driving off in triumph with his wife. He had talked to her engagingly about gears and electric devices. She had appeared to be interested. After all it was going to be a successful afternoon. Everything was set for it. Then that fatal butcher shop and the accident—a slight thing. Swift on this had come Clara Stevens and exposure, followed by the contained but depressing departure of Mrs. Topper. That was the sequence of events, but Mr. Topper searched in vain for the logic. What was the good of scaling an emotional ladder if only to have its topmost rung yield beneath one's feet? "No good," thought Mr. Topper.

He was driving now with a purpose. He was going back to the tree beneath which nearly a week ago he had taken light-hearted leave of George and Marion Kerby. He was going back to the tree now and he was glad he was going back. In spite of their rather peculiar ideas of a good time Mr. Topper felt that he understood the Kerbys far better than his more obvious friends. And George and Marion Kerby were vastly more acceptable to him than the people who constituted his social circle. He was surprised at this, but not alarmed.

Since his first experience with the Kerbys, Mr. Topper had steadfastly refrained from driving past the tree. Several times he had felt like doing so, but discretion had forced him to master the temptation. He considered communing with spirits much in the same light that he regarded the smoking of opium. It was unnatural. For all he knew it might even be habit-forming. God knows where it might end. If the Kerbys had only been sensible spirits, orderly and law-abiding, and much less active, the situation would have been different—better. Mr. Topper could have created a little club around them. On Thursday nights, for instance, they could have given interesting and uplifting talks to his friends. He, Topper, having sponsored them, would have become famous in a serious and conservative way. "There goes Topper," people would have said. "Psychic devil. He controls two spirits." He might even have corresponded with Sir Oliver Lodge. As a matter of fact there were commercial possibilities in a pair of good tame spirits. Mr. Topper could have incorporated them. But not the Kerbys. They could hardly be trusted. Many of their actions would be too difficult to explain. If they were not quite so willing, so callously unabashed about being dead. A certain reluctance would seem more fitting.

Nevertheless Mr. Topper was strangely attracted to the Kerbys. They were different, refreshingly set apart from the usual run of people. On his modest excursions during the past week George and Marion Kerby had been much in his mind. He had come to accept them without reservation. The ringing quality of Marion Kerby's voice still lingered in his ears. He was able to recall without too great compunction that her arms had quite unmistakably encircled his waist. Mr. Topper's vanity was secretly gratified by the fact that the Kerbys had accepted him in all good fellowship. He knew that they considered the rest of his friends as alien beings endowed with singularly worm-like qualities. But with him they were perfectly natural. Almost too natural.

So Mr. Topper was on his way to the tree, quite definitely on his way. Like a dead eye in a gray face the sun above him gazed starkly through a film of sickly clouds. There was going to be rain or something else equally unpleasant. Topper hoped that it would clear up, and no sooner had he hoped this than it did clear up. The cloud slipped from the face of the sun and the world grew bright again beneath its rays. Mr. Topper became suspicious. There was something ominous in the alacrity of the weather to comply with his wishes. Nothing ever happened the way he hoped. Why should the weather be so obliging? Perhaps through his brief acquaintance with the Kerbys he was becoming endowed with occult powers. To test this alarming suspicion he tentatively hoped for rain. The sun plunged its face into a scum of gray vapors, and Mr. Topper immediately stopped hoping. His credulity was becoming stronger than his nerves. He feared that if he indulged further in this dangerous business of hoping he might innocently commit an entire community to a swift and painful death, Clara Stevens and Mrs. Topper prominently included.

A sudden rattling of planks startled him from his thoughts. He was crossing the dilapidated bridge. Directly ahead of him the old scarred tree shook its vigorous branches. To Mr. Topper this ancient landmark was not so much a tree as a place of residence. And he approached the tree in that spirit. When he came abreast of it he stopped the automobile and waited. Nothing unusual happened and Mr. Topper began to feel a little self-conscious.

"Anyone want a ride?" he moved himself to call. His voice sounded lonely in the branches of the tree. "I say there, Mr. Kerby, would you and your wife like to take a spin?"

"Why, it's Topper!" a voice cried out excitedly. "Hey, Marion! Topper's back. How about a ride?"

"Who's back?" came a woman's voice as if from a great distance.

"Topper is," shouted the first voice. "Wants to know if you'd like a ride. He's waiting."

"If you don't mind," Topper suggested, "I wish you'd stop that shouting. There's a wagon coming. Just run over to your wife and ask her quietly if she wants to use the car. Hold a whispered conversation."

But George Kerby was far too excited at the prospect of a ride to follow Mr. Topper's injunctions.

"Damn it, Marion," he shouted. "Make up your mind. Do you want to go or don't you? Say yes or no."

"Come, George," admonished the woman's voice. "Pull yourself together. Mr. Topper will think you never saw an automobile before. Of course I want to go riding. It was lovely of Cosmo to call. I'd about decided that he had deserted us."

The wagon had stopped beside the automobile and

the driver was gazing at Mr. Topper with obstinate curiosity. Ordinarily this driver was not one easily aroused from his trance-like contemplation of his horses' moving flanks, but these strange voices coming from God knew where gave him an unpleasant sensation. Mr. Topper glanced at the man and winced.

"Come on out of the woods, you two," he commanded. "Where the devil have you gotten to? Why I can't even see you."

"We're picking flowers," called Marion Kerby. "We'll be right with you."

The driver's face resumed its normal mold.

"Nice day," he said to Topper.

"Splendid," Mr. Topper beamed.

The driver settled back in his seat and waited. Mr. Topper, closely regarding the man, decided that from his expression he was prepared to wait indefinitely. It was an unfortunate situation. Mr. Topper got out of the automobile and surreptitiously pinched one of the horses. The offended animal immediately put himself in motion. The driver, as if desiring to conserve his energy, allowed his team to have its head. Mr. Topper returned to the automobile and waited.

"We're so forgetful," said Marion Kerby remorsefully as soon as the wagon was out of earshot. "But George is such a common creature with his great throat."

"Then why are you always moping about?" demanded George Kerby angrily. "If you had any mind at all——"

"I would never have married you," his wife triumphantly interrupted. "And I certainly wouldn't have died with you. When I was alive I put a great deal of faith in that optimistic line 'until death do us part,' but it tricked me."

"May I put in a word?" began Mr. Topper, but Kerby's voice cut him short.

"I know," he recriminated bitterly. "You tried to poison me more than once."

"When the bootleggers failed I tried my hand just for the sake of the experiment," his wife replied, "but your stomach defied all natural laws."

"It seems that you both are defying a few natural laws," put in Mr. Topper.

"Listen to this," said George Kerby hurriedly. "You can judge the sort of woman she is, Topper—the terribleness of her. She claims that we're not married any more and that anything goes just because we were bumped off. How's that for depravity. Not that I care. The line said, 'until death do us part.' Well, as a matter of fact death didn't us part. And so there you are. Tell her how silly she is, Topper."

"It's a delicate point for an outsider to settle," Mr. Topper cautiously replied. "Suppose we go for a ride. It's rather trying to be listening to the pair of you squabbling all over the landscape."

"All right, let's forget it," Kerby agreed. "Come, Marion. Topper's right."

"Just the same it isn't legal any more," said Marion. "I want Topper to understand that."

"Are you both in?" asked Mr. Topper.

"All set," replied Kerby.

"No funny stuff now," warned Mr. Topper as he started the car. "I've had a hard day, a terrible day. I'd like to have a good time."

"You would?" cried Kerby. "Then let me take the wheel. Marion drove last time. I've got a great idea."

"Frankly, I mistrust your ideas," said Mr. Topper, "but rather than be sat on I'll let you take the wheel."

"He's all right," Marion said in a reassuring voice. "Especially when he has an idea. For a fool he's funny that way. Slide over to me."

As Mr. Topper slid over the car gathered speed. Once more he let his eyes wander over the sunken plain. It was smooth and green and peaceful, and it was bathed in a subdued light which recalled to Mr. Topper's mind a certain matchless Easter egg he had once possessed in the days of his youth. It was made of sugar and tastefully decorated with pink confection. The egg was hollow and there was a piece of glass set in a peephole at one end. Mr. Topper had applied his eyes to this peephole and he had never quite forgotten the beauty of the scene on which he had gazed. Never on earth could he catch again such completely satisfying beauty. Never would he meet such a shepherdess or see such lamb-like lambs. The sunken plain had some of the romance of that Easter egg. He felt like running across the dipping meadows in search of his lost shepherdess. Perhaps she was waiting for him in the woods on the other side. The woods looked cool and interesting. They ran away along the skyline like the mysterious fringe of a new life. Mr. Topper keenly appreciated this spot. It had something to do with him. For the moment he forgot that he was sitting between all that remained of George and Marion Kerby. As on the previous occasion, his mind now dropped into a dim repose which was lined with green and tinted by the glowing rays of the sun. Romance was close at hand, but before it could come any closer Mr. Topper's repose was shattered by an alarming report from the automobile and an oath from George Kerby.

"Damn it!" said Kerby. "A puncture."

Mr. Topper looked helplessly about as the car came to a sudden stop.

"What do we do now?" he asked. "I don't know the first thing about changing a tire."

"But I do," Kerby replied briskly. "Don't worry your head about it. You and Marion get out and sit down somewhere. I'll be finished in ten minutes. You've got a brand new spare all loaded and everything."

"Come on, Cosmo," said Marion. "Let's crouch in the grass and leer at George. He's good with tires and corks."

With a feeling of relief Mr. Topper abandoned his car. He felt really grateful to George Kerby. In spite of his reputation there must be some good in the young devil. He did not appear to be afraid of hard work. He was as willing as the next to soil his hands in disagreeable toil. Mr. Topper idly wondered if spirits ever washed their hands. What with, if so? Just the same George Kerby was decidedly helpful in an emergency. To Mr. Topper a punctured tire was an emergency of the first order.

"You'd better follow me," said Mr. Topper, "because I can't follow you. When I come to a place you like just let me know."

"This will do," she announced when they came to a smooth, grassy space near the roadside. "Let's seethe here like a pair of indolent worms. Do you like seething?"

Topper hardly knew. He had never tried it.

"Wallowing is more in my line," he remarked. "I'm afraid I'm not built for seething, as you call it. Too fat."

"It's easy for me to seethe," she went on, and from the direction of her voice she was lying at Mr. Topper's feet. "All I do is wriggle a hole in space and curl up."

This sounded horrible to Mr. Topper, but he made no reply as he lowered himself to the grass, his mind and body occupied with the grace and agility of his descent.

"Do you find it pleasant the way you are?" he began in a conversational voice after he had carefully arranged himself.

"How do you mean?" asked Marion.

"Being a spirit," replied Topper.

"It's rather thin at times," she said, "but fortunately I'm not always this way."

"No?" said Mr. Topper with a rising inflection.

"Oh, no," she answered. "Sometimes I'm quite different."

"How?" Topper bluntly demanded.

"I materialize," she said. "I get thick like you, only not quite so thick, if you get what I mean."

"I'm afraid I do," Mr. Topper replied. "You mean that it would be impossible to achieve my state of thickness. Go on."

"I didn't mean that at all," she said. "Don't be a zug."

"Don't be a what?" he demanded.

"A zug," she replied.

"What's that?" he asked.

"It's my name for a person who doesn't act the way he feels," answered Marion.

"Oh, you mean a gentleman," said Topper. "Well,

if I acted the way I felt I probably wouldn't be here now."

"Why?"

"I'd probably be in jail for wife-beating or arson or poisoning wells," Mr. Topper said thoughtfully. "I've felt like doing all those things to-day."

"I rather suspected you were down on your luck," Marion answered sympathetically. "Poor old Topper."

"If you must be good to me," replied Mr. Topper, "try to be practical about it. Don't get me into any more scrapes like the last time. Don't giggle at people and don't fight with your husband. Emotional people are bad enough, but emotional spirits are impossible. That's that. Now tell me what you meant when you said that at times you were quite different."

"It's like this," she began. "We are what you might call low-planed spirits, George and myself."

Topper nodded appreciatively.

"I can well understand that," he said.

"We are authentic spirits," she continued. "Quite authentic, but still low-planed."

"And no doubt you rejoice in it," put in Mr. Topper.

"We do," said Marion, "particularly after what we've seen of the high ones."

"Death has changed you little," remarked Mr. Topper.

"That's exactly what I tell George," replied Marion. "If anything it's made him worse. You wouldn't believe it if I told you, but that man is actually mad. I wouldn't admit it while I was alive, but now with a lot of space on my hands . . ."

"You were telling me about low-planed spirits," interrupted Mr. Topper.

"Oh, yes," she said. "Well, low-planed spirits to keep well must have a certain amount of ectoplasm. High-planed spirits don't need it, wouldn't know what to do with it, but low-planed spirits must have their ectoplasm."

"Do they serve it in glasses?" asked Mr. Topper.

"All things you cannot be told," Marion replied, "but it's like time with you. We can squander it or use it wisely just as we please. It doesn't matter. We get so much ectoplasm and no more. They're strict about it. Just to show you. George went to the races last month. He'd been saving up his allotment. He loves races. That's why, according to vital statistics, we're officially deceased. Well, this track was down south. George went there and no one recognized him at first. Even when they did they acted as if they hadn't. People are funny that way. They hate to be disillusioned. That's why so few of us ever come back. George cleaned up on the horses. Whenever he wanted to place a bet he faded out and listened to the wise ones. George knows where to listen. But the money got the best of him. He started in drinking and didn't stop until his ectoplasm had run out. About a week later he came back to me with a terrible hangover and a sad story about a twenty-dollar bill he hadn't been able to spend because no one had the nerve to pluck it from the air. He said that he had wandered over several counties with that twenty-dollar bill until he got so sick of it he threw it away. Since then he's been saving his ectoplasm. I've got a lot of it, but I never feel like using it. I'm afraid I'm becoming high-planed, but I might be persuaded to materialize for you."

"Don't trouble yourself," said Mr. Topper hastily. "Some other time. I've had a particularly hard day. Don't upset me."

Marion Kerby laughed. Topper liked her laugh.

"I wonder what sort of a little boy you were," she said, musingly.

"Not much of a sort," Mr. Topper admitted. "A pretty poor type of little boy. I mussed around a lot and didn't go right or wrong. I guess I must have been rather an unofficial little boy."

"And what did you plan to become?" she asked.

Mr. Topper looked uneasily around him. He had a strange feeling that a pair of lovely eyes were floating in the air. It was like being lost in a fog with a strange, but desirable, person.

"I never got so far as planning," he said in a low voice, "but I wanted to be an actor."

"And no one encouraged you?" Marion Kerby's

voice was equally low. There was a deep, feminine quality in it which to Mr. Topper was more intimate than a caress, more tender than a smile. The sound of her voice fortified him against all the perils of life. Everything could go to smash as long as that voice continued. He could sink to the sunless depth of a lonely sea with the memory of such a voice still living in his ears.

"One person encouraged me," he replied. "A drunken uncle. He gave me a book."

"What kind of a book?" asked Marion.

"It was a very thorough book," replied Mr. Topper. "It's old now, of course, and no doubt there are better books to-day, but this one had recitations in it, and photographs that showed you how to do Hate and Fear and Modesty and Surprise and practically all the emotions."

Unconsciously Mr. Topper pressed his hands to his cheeks and did Surprise. The effect was startling, but he failed to realize how startling it was until he found himself staring into the eyes of three seemingly fascinated bystanders who had quietly gathered from nowhere. It was an interesting grouping. Mr. Topper appeared to be leading a class in dramatic elocution. His pupils were registering the most eloquent surprise. Mr. Topper's expression congealed.

"I'm rehearsing for an act," he explained, with a hesitating smile.

The first young farmer looked at the second young farmer and the second young farmer looked at the third, then all three looked at Mr. Topper and Mr. Topper looked away.

"I'm rehearsing," he repeated in an obstinate voice. "Go away."

But the youthful group held its ground. Mr. Topper was on the point of doing Fury with extras when he saw the spare tire of the automobile neatly detach itself from the rack and roll jauntily up to the denuded wheel. Then he saw the flat tire wobble over the ground and with a delicate leap attach itself to the rack. Topper's eyes turned to glass. He was no longer able to register his emotions, but the features of the three young farmers were contorted with amazement. They could find no comforting explanation for the purposefully acting tires. And when they saw a wrench performing masterful revolutions in the air they decided to go somewhere else to think things over. With great speed and with admirable solidarity they departed. Nothing could have separated them. Mr. Topper breathed a sigh of relief as they disappeared in single file formation. Like the three witches in Macbeth, they were destined to appear later at an equally unpropitious moment in Mr. Topper's life.

"You're splendid!" exclaimed Marion Kerby before he could voice his woe. "Prepare to be hugged."

For an instant Mr. Topper presented the appearance of a man with a stiff neck, whereas in reality he was resting his troubled head on Marion Kerby's surprisingly adequate breast. It was just for an instant, but Mr. Topper never quite succeeded in ridding himself of the memory.

CHAPTER VIII

Wayward Ghosts

KERBY'S DESTINATION WAS SHADOWED BY THE WOODS. It was an old abandoned inn, lying far back from the roadway in the arms of its guardian trees. Like a royal drunkard, spent by years of purple debauchery, the ancient structure wearily settled down among the trees and listened to tales of vanished splendor drifting through the branches overhead. Hard days had fallen on the inn. It attracted no longer now the flower of the land. Laughter warmed its heart no more and the silvery chiming of goblets filled with honest liquor was forever stilled. And the great paunch-like cellar of the inn was empty. Gone the bottles that flashed beneath the lamplight. Gone the stout old soul who used to carry the lamp. Even the smell of the place was different. The inspiriting fragrance of old wine had been subtracted from the air, leaving it flat and dead. The spiders, too, had lost caste. There was not a cork to cling to, only empty bins that had once contained the mellow yield of distant vineyards stepping up the hillside to the sun that had given them life.

The inn was built on sandy soil. The sea had once been there. If you looked between the trees at moonlight you could see white patches of sand lying in the woods. And if you stood quite still and listened to the wind thrumming through the pines you could catch an echo of waves falling on vanished beaches. The sea had once been there. The rhythm of its surf still lingered in the air, and the healing tang of its salt blended with the smell of pine. All was silent in the woods. Nobody ever came to them now. No couples flitted across the patches, no whispering voices were heard among the trees.

Mr. Topper stood on the back veranda of the inn and gazed into the woods. A breeze, fresh and soothing, filled with a lonesome fragrance, brought peace and a strange excitement to his heart. He felt happy and almost young. He had forgotten about his stomach. It was as if he had withdrawn from the old life and was digging with his toes in new and magic soil. How unreal and far away Mrs. Topper seemed. How delightfully remote from him was every one he knew. Only Scollops retained her personality. Mr. Topper wanted his cat. Scollops would have loved this place. She would have approved of the rambling old inn with its soft, brown shingles and its long veranda broken by sun-filled angles, ideally arranged for a quiet nap, a warm, sensuous, sun-bathed nap. And Scollops would have found many interesting things in the woods. Mr. Topper unconsciously possessed one of the rarest and most precious faculties of the memory, a graphic and olfactory sense of childhood. He could visualize Scollops stalking between the trees, enter into her little, but intense, curiosities, and smell the things she smelled. There were grasshoppers and ant hills and exciting holes in the trees. What a place for Scollops.

Mr. Topper let his eyes travel along the weather-browned side of the old inn. Far away in the distance the checker-board fields cupped down to an indolent river. Mr. Topper did not know the name of the river. He was equally ignorant of its beginning and its end. These things were matters of small importance to Mr. Topper. He did know, however, that the river added another touch of beauty to the landscape. It garnished the general effect. Curving out in a great leisurely horseshoe, it moved between smooth banks, and here and there a tree or two had crept up to its brink to gaze at its pretty limbs in the flowing mirror below. The sky swept down over the world and dropped behind the stepping hills on the highest of which rose the turrets of a castle dating back as far as 1922. Under ordinary circumstances Mr. Topper would have become involved in calculations regarding the probable cost of building such a place, but to-day he was content to accept it as a part of the scene that was filling his eyes with beauty.

"You sort of like it here," said a quiet voice behind him. "What makes your eyes so sad?"

"I didn't know they were sad," replied Mr. Topper, with an uneasy smile. "Perhaps they've looked too long on desk tops and plumbing and legs of lamb. Perhaps they've looked on loveliness too late."

"Perhaps they've looked on loveliness too late," Marion Kerby softly repeated. "The world does wicked things to us with its success and routine and morality. Topper, it either cheats us with wealth or numbs us with want, steals away from us all the color and wonder of being alive, the necessary useless things. Only savages and children do proper honor to the sun, and children soon grow up into perfectly rational——"

"Toppers," interrupted Mr. Topper rather bitterly. "I know what you're thinking. Those white duck trousers. I never wore them again, not since the day you said they looked self-conscious."

There was a flash of laughter in the air and Mr. Topper felt a small hand brush lightly across the top of his.

"There was something wonderful about those

trousers," she said. "Something pitiful, too. Do you know what I mean?"

"Perfectly," replied Mr. Topper. "The pitiful part was me."

"No," she continued. "I mean that they expressed in a futile way the desire to be dashing and picturesque, the need to slip a little beyond life. They were the starched symbol of rebellion. I liked you the moment I saw you in those white duck trousers. You were shifting from foot to foot, rather guiltily, I thought."

"Don't go on about those trousers," Mr. Topper pleaded. "Try to forget that I ever wore them."

"If it will make you feel any better," Marion said comfortingly, "I'll try to forget that you ever wore any trousers at all."

"You don't have to go so far as that," he replied. "You and your husband have taken my dignity, I have only my decency left."

"Look!" exclaimed Marion. "The sun is sinking behind the castle. How fine it is."

Topper took a deep breath. His very being seemed to merge with the crazy-quilt of colors streaming across the low sky.

"It is fine," he said. "The way it fans out above the towers makes me think of Ivanhoe. I don't know why. There was a girl in it named Rebecca. She was always jumping out of windows."

"Well, the Rebecca living in that castle isn't jumping out of any windows," said George Kerby jarringly, his voice coming from the doorway of the inn. "You couldn't even push the old dame through. She's fat, quarrelsome, and very rich. Always falling in love with her gardeners. That's why she loses them all the time. She's too tough a bud even for a gardener to pick."

"George, dear," Marion remarked in her sweetest voice, "you always sound the right note at sunset. It's a part of your irresistible charm. You're so deliciously low at all times."

"Oh, so that's it," replied Kerby. "I'm not too low to be collecting wood for a fire. While you two have been idling out here detracting from the natural beauty of the scene, I've been looking for stuff to keep you warm outside and in. I've been useful and busy while you've been useless and—and——"

"Indolent, supine or loutish," suggested Marion. "Take your choice."

"You're awfully funny," Kerby retorted.

"Please go away and continue being useful and busy," said his wife.

"All right," answered Kerby in a sulky voice, "but if Topper wants anything to drink he'd better tear himself away from that meager-looking sunset and help me hunt. I've a good idea that the law didn't know all the ropes of this cafeteria."

Topper obediently turned from the sunset. He would much rather have remained with Marion to watch the evening die, but Kerby was a man demanding a man's cooperation in an enterprise that smacked of devilishness. Topper felt that he could not afford to be found wanting. There was something rugged and masculine about leaving a sunset flat to go in search of grog. He would show Marion Kerby that he was as game for a good time as the next one.

"Are you coming, Marion?" asked Kerby.

"Not now," she replied.

"Come on, Topper," said George Kerby briskly, then in a lower voice, "If we find anything to drink we'll jolly well help ourselves before we let her know."

He nudged Topper in the ribs and Topper sprang back, startled.

"Pardon me," he said. "I must have been crowding you."

Kerby laughed.

"No," he replied, "I'm merely over-eager. I'm a dead man parched for a drink, an intangible body with a palpable thirst. Search diligently, Topper. We must find a bottle."

Kerby's voice trailed away across the twilight of the inn. Topper heard things move about, felt clouds of dust descending upon his head, saw empty boxes sliding mysteriously through the gloom, and in the midst of this he stood unmoved. The room had taken possession of him. He looked about like a tourist in a tomb.

The vague, slanting roof extending above his head

was filled with ancient dusk solidified by cross-beams,
great reaching things, rough-hewn and low. High up in
a pointed section of the wall a small window strained
through its dirty panes the departing light of day. The
little shaft of yellow light sifting through the darkness
fingered a yawning fireplace, filled with bits of wood
and dusted white with blown ashes. From where Topper stood the room on either side of him ran on forever
into shadows. Cross-beams and shadows and ebbing
daylight—Topper absorbed these elements, but was
unable to blend them harmoniously in his mind. He
was like a man in a dream, quite willing to accept, but
unable to explain.

And as he stood there, in the great dark room, the
wood in the fireplace suddenly sprang into flame.
Waves of red sparkled over the stones and warmth
carved a pocket in the dampness of the place. The
cross-beams, caught in the glow of the firelight, twisted
and swam in the quivering parade of the flames.
Shadows that had once been dead came back to life
and trembled rhythmically on the floor. The old inn
seemed to sigh and find itself, like a man waxing
expansive after a long period of rigorous domestic
hypocrisy. Topper edged up to the fireplace and absorbed reassurance from its warmth. He had a feeling
that something was taking place in the room, something very near him. An unseen person was breathing
heavily almost at Mr. Topper's feet.

"Topper!" exclaimed a strained voice as a square
section of the flooring flew open. "Topper, my heart's
blood, the world is ours."

Firelight fell into the aperture disclosed by the lifted
boards. Little jets of flame danced redly on deep green
glass. Golden fire-beams trickled through jackets of
spotted straw and girdled the liveried necks of ancient
bottles. A box emerged from the pocket and cut a
swath through the dust. With a business-like snap the
board settled back into place. Mr. Topper gave a
slight start, then smiled nervously in the general direction of his invisible accomplice.

"You've found a lot, haven't you?" said Mr. Topper
with false enthusiasm.

"I've a good mind to materialize just for to-night," muttered Kerby in a preoccupied voice.

Mr. Topper drew a quick breath. From where he was standing he had an excellent view of this much discussed phenomenon. It was, if anything, a trifle too excellent a view to suit Mr. Topper. He would have preferred to have witnessed it from the back row of a crowded hall. "Why," he thought to himself, "should I of all people be privileged to undergo such unpleasant experiences when thousands of spirit hunters would gladly take my place? Why was not Sir Conan Doyle selected? I am not the man."

Mr. Topper stopped asking himself questions. He became incapable of self-interrogation. An appalling thing was taking place before his eyes. George Kerby's legs were appearing, quietly and without undue haste, but nevertheless his legs were quite unmistakably appearing. Mr. Topper began to shiver as if caught in a chill wind. With perfect self-possession and unconcern the legs arched up from the floor. With dilated eyes Mr. Topper followed the ribs in the golf stockings and dwelt reluctantly on the crisscross pattern of the trousers. No detail of those legs escaped him. Years after he could have modeled them in clay. Then, quite suddenly, he realized that another section had been added to the legs. It was the central and after part of George Kerby's anatomy. In a thoroughly detached manner it was flaunting itself in the air. Mr. Topper's feet began to shuffle wistfully. They wanted to go to the door and be let out, but, before they had time to obey this impulse, they clung to the floor like expiring flounders. Mr. Topper was gazing into George Kerby's face, gazing into it, not as Mr. Topper would have liked, but in a peculiarly upsetting way. Kerby's face was oddly suspended between his legs, and it was upside down. Mr. Topper had no precedent to follow. Not even in a sideshow had he ever seen a face placed in such a novel position, but this face seemed to make no difference to the face, for it smiled up at Topper as gayly as if it had been in its conventional location. The wide-mouthed, inverted smile nearly did for Mr. Topper. He found himself unable to return it.

"Oh, dear," he said, moving back, "oh, dear me, is that the way you're going to be?"

"What way do you mean?" demanded the face, its mouth wagging snappily in a manner most horrifying to Mr. Topper.

"The way you are," muttered Mr. Topper. "You know. Is it always going to be like this?"

"Now what the devil's gotten into you?" asked Kerby, rising to his full height and confronting the troubled Topper with a bottle in either hand. "Can't a man bend over?"

"My mistake," replied Mr. Topper, licking his dry lips. "I thought that probably you'd sprained your back in the accident and that . . ."

Kerby cut him short with a laugh and moved over to the fireplace.

"You still believe in ghost stories, I see," he said, good-humoredly. "Well, I'm all here, every inch of me. Never felt better in my life. Shake. I'm glad you see me."

"I'm overjoyed I do," replied Mr. Topper, gingerly accepting the proffered hand. "Would you mind opening one or both of those bottles? A drop of something would help a lot."

"Topper, I love you," whispered Kerby, hurrying away in the gloom.

Topper looked consideringly after the retreating figure. He found it rather hard to accept Kerby in his materialized form after having with great difficulty become reconciled to his voice. Topper felt that there was a lamentable lack of stability in his relationship with George and Marion Kerby. They should be either one thing or the other, but certainly not both. It required too swift and radical an adjustment of the mind to be talking with space at one moment and the next to be shaking hands with a perfectly tangible body. After all, a person could absorb only a certain limited number of shocks in a lifetime. Mr. Topper felt that he had already absorbed his full quota.

With the firelight at his back, Topper, his eyes now

grown adjusted to the darkness, looked about the
room. At one end he saw a gathering of shadowy
tables, one table carrying the other on its back as
though retreating from the field with a wounded
comrade. The legs of the wounded tables formed a
forest in the darkness. At the other end of the room a
huge, many-caverned sideboard flattened its rugged
back defiantly against the wall and waited. It was a
sideboard that would stand just so much and no more.
After the limit had been reached all the prohibition
agents in the world would be unable to make it budge.
One more indignity, another outrageously intimate
searching of its secret recesses might cause it to fly
from the wall and fall on its tormentors. Like the last
of the barons it stood guard over the desecrated inn.
Dust covered its honorable veneer with a delicate pall,
but the old sideboard remained at its post and
guarded the room it had so often seen filled with the
revelers of a freer generation.

George Kerby was standing in front of the sideboard, diligently rummaging through its drawers. As
Topper watched the deftly searching hands he decided
that Kerby was bereft of fear and respect. Certainly,
no ordinary person could thus casually search through
such an imposing piece of furniture. With a low exclamation of satisfaction, Kerby left the sideboard
and returned to the fireplace with a corkscrew in one
hand and two glasses in the other.

"Hold these," he said, giving Topper the glasses,
"but don't make any noise. Marion's really childish
about nature. If we don't disturb her she'll blither
around outside all night and let us peacefully fill our
skins."

With professional skill he extracted the cork from
one of the bottles, then filled the glasses and politely
extended one of them to Mr. Topper, who was extremely glad to receive it. He was honestly convinced
that if any man in the world deserved a drink, he,
Topper, was that man. Kerby emptied his glass at a
gulp and pulled a couple of boxes within range of the
fire's warmth.

"Take it easy, Topper," he said. "This Scotch is

worth a couple of yards of ectoplasm. Do you get drunk?"

Topper, emerging with a brilliant color from his glass, paused before answering the question. A swift, rollicking revolution accompanied by a pleasant tingling sensation was taking place within him. He felt himself growing lighter and less material. Perhaps he was going to disappear altogether. That would be splendid. Then he would be a spirit, too, like George and Marion Kerby.

"Never had much chance," he replied, "but I did get drunk once. No one noticed it, so I didn't have much fun. They were all so stuffy at the party. The kind that know when they've had just enough. Then they become heavily jolly and wink at each other with wise eyes. I went to sleep in a hammock. Mrs. Topper doesn't like drinking. It makes her nervous. I suppose you get drunk most of the time?"

Kerby replenished the glasses before he answered.

"Whenever I get the chance," he said. "Marion says I'm never sober. And she sticks to it, but of course she exaggerates. The moment I take a drink she begins to remind me about the last time and helps me along by autosuggestion."

"It's really too bad about women," Mr. Topper answered sympathetically. "They don't seem to have any sense of proportion at all. If Mrs. Topper should walk into the room right now I'd be forced to speak to her quite pointedly to keep her from raising a row. But I've never beaten her," he went on thoughtfully. "Not yet, I haven't.

"Thanks, Kerby. This Scotch is delicious. Do you feel like dancing?"

Kerby quickly looked up from his drink. Mr. Topper appeared to be perfectly normal. He was sitting solidly on his box and gazing into the fireplace.

"Do I feel like what?" Kerby demanded.

"Dancing, George," replied Mr. Topper in a reasonable voice. "Dancing or singing."

"Certainly not," said Kerby, shortly.

"That's odd," replied Mr. Topper. "I seem to."

"Well, don't do it," Kerby commanded. "You'll spoil everything."

"Then let's each have a bottle of our own," suggested Mr. Topper. "It will seem more abandoned."

"Drink up this one first," said Kerby.

Mr. Topper promptly extended his empty glass.

"Listen, George," he asked humbly, "if I just sit quietly here by the fire and feel like dancing it will be all right, won't it?"

"But don't let your feeling get the best of you," admonished Kerby. "We're all set for a good party."

"I suppose you're a pretty swell dancer," Mr. Topper said rather moodily after a short silence. "I dare say you know all about road-houses and gay parties and the latest steps and everything like that."

"What's gotten into Topper?" Kerby demanded. "Why are you so broken-hearted about dancing?"

"Oh, I don't know," Mr. Topper replied, resting his chin on his hands and staring into the flames. "I've passed up all the good things of life, the dancing and the singing and the drinking. I haven't had any good times at all. I've had a sad life, George. You can't imagine how terribly sad my life has been. I've only one friend in the world and she sleeps all the time. You ought to get to know Scollops, George. She's a good cat."

A tear trickled down Mr. Topper's glowing cheek.

"Open another bottle," he said in a broken voice. "Open two."

George Kerby was a creature of quick sympathies. The sight of Mr. Topper in tears moved him profoundly. In the presence of his companion's sorrow his rude humor deserted him. He was plunged into grief. Getting up from his box, he came over to Mr. Topper and placed an arm round his shoulder.

"Don't cry, Topper," he said. "I've had a sad life, too. At the age of five I lost both my parents. Then I was struck down in the prime of life. Look at me."

Mr. Topper tearfully looked at him.

"Then you're an orphan, too," said Mr. Topper.

Kerby bowed his head.

"By all means make it two bottles," continued Mr. Topper. "The occasion calls for it."

Kerby hurried over to the box.

"That's a funny thing," he remarked, returning with the bottles. "There were twelve bottles of Scotch in that case when we found it and now there are only eight. These two and the one we had make three. Where's the other one gotten to?"

"Maybe you left it about some place," replied Mr. Topper as he wiped away his tears and smiled upon the bottles. "We'll come across it later on. Let's be thankful for what we have."

For several minutes they sipped their drinks in silence, then Mr. Topper suggested timidly: "Perhaps you wouldn't mind if I danced quietly around on tiptoe. You can give me some pointers, seeing we're both orphans."

Fearing that Mr. Topper might once more break into tears, Kerby reluctantly consented.

"Do it nice and easy," he warned. "Don't fall down or knock anything over."

Topper finished his drink and arose with purpose.

"Now this is the way I waltz," he explained, spreading his arms and gliding away in the darkness with surprising agility. "Are you watching me, George?"

A humming noise floated through the air. Mr. Topper was supplying his own music. As he revolved through the firelight on the first turn around the room his body was swaying alluringly from the hips, and his arms, rising and falling airily, gave him the appearence of a large bird in fastidious flight. George Kerby watched Mr. Topper with growing astonishment. Evidently the poor chap's soul had taken wings. It must have been starved for dancing.

"How am I doing?" breathed Topper as he once more passed through the firelight.

"It's beautiful!" whispered Kerby. "Didn't know it was in you."

"Do you like it?" said Topper in a pleased voice, as he circled into outer darkness.

Kerby's spontaneous praise awoke in Mr. Topper a

desire to be worthy of it. Accordingly he redoubled his exertions. His feet flew over the floor and his arms stirred up whirlpools of life in the shadows. A chair got in his way, but he kicked it aside without losing a step. It fell clattering in a corner and Kerby cried out:

"Lay off, Topper. You've danced enough."

But Topper was deaf to Kerby's entreaties. His blood was up. He was both surprised and delighted. It was like a dream in which one found oneself riding a bicycle with the utmost ease and confidence.

"Will you stop ricocheting around the room like the Dancing Faun of Praxiteles?" asked Kerby, threateningly.

Like a blooded horse Topper continued his maddened flight. His veins were quick with Scotch and his imagination fired with a new realization of the rapture of motion. Nothing could stop him now save forcible intervention. This was supplied by the revengeful chair. Mr. Topper still contends that the thing sprang at his legs, deliberately tripped him and hurled him to the floor. However this may be, the chair put an end to Mr. Topper's dancing. Like a spent lizard he uncoiled himself from the courageous piece of furniture and returned to the fireplace.

"That's how I waltz," he said, looking anxiously at Kerby. "How was it, George?"

"The most convincing demonstration I've ever witnessed," replied Kerby. "You deserve a drink."

"It's so good of you to like my dancing," said Mr. Topper with becoming modesty as he swallowed what he deserved. "You know I think I could learn how to live. I can drink all right and I can dance pretty well. Now about singing—let's try a song."

"Let's," said a voice from the cross-beams. "Why not?"

Topper and Kerby regarded each other uneasily, then Kerby hastily took another drink and Topper, with dog-like fidelity, followed his example.

"I was an orphan at nine minutes past eight of a blue Monday in the great blizzard of 1891," continued the voice. "And what's worse, after all the weary years I'm still an orphan."

"It's Marion," groaned George, setting down his glass. "I wonder how long she's been there."

Topper looked up at the cross-beams and became partially sober. On one of the cross-beams an angel, or a woman who gave every indication of being an angel, was reclining. The angel had Marion Kerby's eyes. Topper was sure of this. The angel also had a bottle, the contents of which she was transferring to a glass. As Mr. Topper watched this dangerous operation he shivered for her safety. The angel dexterously sipped her drink and began to speak in a voice that was far from angelic.

"So you thought I'd blither around outside all night," she said, "while you acquired a skin-full, Gentle George, deceitful George, drunken Topper!"

"She's heard every word we said," muttered Kerby under his breath.

Topper took a drink and looked defiantly at the angel. All his married life he had been quietly insulted by his own wife, but in his present mood he objected to being insulted by another man's wife.

"Chase her down, George," he said. "She's calling me names."

"Why don't you come up and get me, you drunken dervish?" challenged the angel, sticking her tongue out at Mr. Topper.

Topper blinked his eyes and looked up as if he were going to bark at her.

"I refuse to be called a drunken dervish," he said with dignity.

"Well, that's what you are," replied the angel calmly. "And George is an unsuccessful little snipe."

"Don't mind her, Topper," said Kerby, with resignation. "That's where the other bottle went. I should have known it all the time. What are you doing up there, Marion?"

"Loathing a couple of orphans," she replied.

"But why the funny disguise?" he asked. "You look awful in that outfit. Why not your usual regalia?"

"I had planned to impress your twin orphan until I discovered how depraved he was," she answered. "His name should be Toper instead of Topper. But

let's see. Topper rhymes with cropper." She began to
laugh, then stopped suddenly and recited in a tantaliz-
ing voice: "Topper, Topper, the big grasshopper, tried
to dance and came a cropper. How's that, Cosmo?"

Mr. Topper was stung to the quick. His recent triumph was being held up to ridicule.

"I don't like it," he said, seating himself heavily on
his box. "It's very poor, very poor indeed. Furthermore, you seem to be drinking yourself, so how can
you talk?"

"Less thickly than you, plump orphan," she replied.

"Kerby," said Mr. Topper in an offended voice,
"I'm afraid I'll have to ask you to request your wife
not to talk to me any more. I can well understand why
you drove her into a tree. With such a wife heroic
methods are the only way out. Use your influence. If
you haven't any, beat her."

"All right, all right," replied Kerby, his resistance
yielding to his alcoholic contents. "Anything for peace.
I'll talk to her."

"Topper wants to sing," he began mildly. "We'll all
sing. Come on down, Marion, and make friends."

Marion looked suspiciously at her husband.

"You'll take my bottle," she said.

"If you think I'm capable of such a trick you can
roost up there all night," Kerby replied haughtily as
he returned to the fireplace.

"But how am I going to get down?" the angel asked
in a more reasonable voice.

"How did you get up there to begin with?" demanded Kerby .

"I materialized here for safety's sake," she said.

"If you were any kind of a spirit," interposed Mr.
Topper, "you'd let go and float down like a zephyr."

"And if you were any kind of a man you'd let me
float down on top of you," she replied.

Mr. Topper accepted the challenge. Swaying
slightly as he walked, he maneuvered himself to a
position directly under the cross-beam on which the
white figure was reclining. As he stood there with
outstretched arms he looked like the statue of a griev-

ing father pleading with his young. Marion Kerby laughed.

"I'm waiting," said Mr. Topper.

George Kerby poured out a drink and regarded the scene with happy detachment. All the parties in his life returned to him. He remembered impossible situations and dwelt lovingly on them. Things as silly as this he had seen, had been a part of, had played, perhaps, the leading role. He shrugged his shoulders and laughed without much merriment. Pageants of past escapades passed before his eyes.

"Hurry up, Marion," he called out. "Topper's waiting."

Without a moment's hesitation, Marion Kerby slipped from the cross-beam and descended on Mr. Topper's aggressively upturned face. After several seconds of Homeric indecision, he decided to give up the struggle and to accompany his charge to the floor. It was hardly a matter of choice with Mr. Topper. Marion Kerby's weight bore him to the echoing planks, whereon he lay concealed beneath a smother of celestial raiment.

"I'm dying," he groaned in a muffled voice. "Drag this woman off."

"A fat man has his uses," Marion Kerby remarked, carefully picking her way across Mr. Topper's stomach.

"Had I known you were going to say that," he managed to get out of him, "I'd have given you the shock of your life. Help me up, George. I'm crippled."

When Mr. Topper had been restored to his seat he looked across at Marion Kerby sitting opposite him on a box near the fireplace. She was clinging to her bottle and looking watchfully about her. There was something in her bearing that reminded Mr. Topper of a defiant child at a party at which none of the other children wanted to play with her. She was prepared for the slightest hostile move. Her little face was filled with resolution and glowing color, and her eyes were bright and darting like those of an inquisitive young bird. The white robe floating about her made her small head, appearing so bravely above it, seem a

little lost and pathetic. Mr. Topper decided that the
robe was not a success. Marion Kerby had never been
intended for an angel. She was far too alert and human, and a trifle too suspicious.

"Well, if I looked silly in white duck trousers," he
announced, "you certainly take the cake in that. It
does my heart good to see you look such a fright."

Marion Kerby gazed at him out of her large, serious
eyes, then most surprisingly her lips began to tremble
and she buried her head in her lap. Stifled sobs issued
from the folds of her robe. Mr. Topper experienced a
strange sensation. It was one of triumph and alarm,
but as the sobs continued with unabated anguish he
began to feel sorry for his unkind remark.

"Give her another bottle, George," he suggested.

"Don't want another bottle," she replied without
looking up.

"Then give it to me," said Mr. Topper. "I can't
stand hearing her make that noise. Do something
about it, George."

Kerby tried to put his arm around his wife, but she
flung it off angrily.

"You go 'way from me," she sobbed. "I never made
fun of his trousers, although God knows they were
funny enough, and now he calls me a fright simply
because I tried to dress up like an angel for him."

"I'm sorry, Marion," said Mr. Topper. "I was only
fighting back, honestly I was. Let's take a drink and
make up. We were good friends this evening."

She raised her head and looked at Mr. Topper's
troubled face. He smiled at her and held out his arms.
More than ever she appealed to him as a small child
recovering from some devastating disappointment.
This impression was heightened when he found her
clinging to him and pressing her wet cheeks to his
face. Mr. Topper swayed beneath this outburst of af-
fection. For a moment he thought he had been attacked, but when he felt two soft lips kissing the lobe
of his ear he concluded that the demonstration was of
a peaceable nature.

"That's all right now," he said, thumping her back
with the flat of his hand. "I was only getting back at

you for calling me a plump orphan. It's true enough. I'll admit it."

George Kerby was regarding the scene with surprise.

"I say, Marion," he remarked, "don't you think that just shaking hands would be sufficiently convincing? This is a party, not an orgy, you know."

Marion laughed and sprang away from Mr. Topper.

"He was such a penitent old sot," she explained. "I just had to hug him. Do you want one for yourself."

Kerby submitted himself to her violence with the polished indifference of a tolerant husband.

"Now that that's over," he remarked, "we can all have a drink."

His suggestion was received with enthusiasm and acted upon several times. The crest of Mr. Topper's wave was on its downward curve. It had been an eventful night for him. He bowed several times in the direction of Marion Kerby and at last in an excess of politeness he bowed himself off the box onto the floor, where he rested motionless on his nose. When he had been replaced by George and Marion Kerby, it was learned that he had been trying to ask Marion for the honor of a dance, but before she had time to accept his invitation he closed his eyes in sleep. Presently, however, he had a confused impression that he was flying through the colors of an evening sunset with an angel clasped in his arms. Two bright stars were looking into his eyes and two red lips, parted in a smile, were thrillingly close to his. An odor of Scotch whiskey filled the sky and made it friendly and stimulating. Mr. Topper breathed deeply. New vigor was returning to his body. The president of the bank was peering at him over the glistening edge of a burning cloud. The old man looked pained and puzzled. Mr. Topper gracefully blew the president a kiss and the venerable financier ducked behind his fleecy barrier. On another cloud, that resembled the platform of his station, Mr. Topper saw a number of commuters. They were holding an indignation meeting and pointing furiously at Mr. Topper, who, as he sailed by, made a vulgar gesture in their direction and laughed down at the angel.

The commuters fell screaming from the cloud and
were lost in the darkness below, their cries of anguish
drifting pleasantly up to his ears. Low down on the
horizon Mr. Topper distinguished the pale eyes of his
wife. They sent a path of reproach across the inter-
weaving colors. He tried to look away, but the eyes
clung to him. His anger mounted and he shook his fist
at the eyes.

"Damn that leg of lamb!" he shouted. "I'm in love
with Kerby's wife!"

"One minute," whispered the angel. "I must take a
tuck in my ectoplasm. This dress is tripping me."

George Kerby, gazing over the rim of his glass into
the dying embers of the fire, was oblivious of his surroundings. So Mr. Topper danced with the angel as
the room grew dark. A visitor standing in the doorway
of the inn would have seen nothing, but would have
heard a soft, humming sound in the darkness and the
scraping of flying feet. And had the visitor listened
very closely he might have heard George Kerby pour-
ing himself a drink and poking the cooling embers
with the charred end of a stick. Little breezes sighed
round the old inn and tiptoed along its rambling ve-
randas. Like a cat closing a watchful eye the last red
spark winked out.

CHAPTER IX

Local Historians Disagree

LATER THAT NIGHT, IN A NEAR-BY VILLAGE, MR.
Topper's automobile stopped aggressively in front of a
cheerfully lighted drug store. This much has been
established and freely admitted, but what follows has
become complicated by a multiplicity of facts, furnished
by various local historians, dealing at white heat with
events still too vivid in their minds to be impartially
recorded. In spite of this it is to these local historians

that one must turn for further information, because, unfortunately, Mr. Topper alone of all the participants is unable to present his version. To be more accurate, it should be known that Mr. Topper had no version to present, his mind having ceased consciously to function some hours earlier in the evening.

The collected data are full of conflicting statements and unconsidered conclusions. Vanity and prejudice have as usual played havoc with the truth, and Mr. Topper's reputation has been tossed into a furnace of frantically wagging tongues. The druggist and his soda clerk are still in disagreement on many important points, and it is doubtful if anyone will ever agree with the chief of police, although many may sympathize with him. On one point, however, all are in complete accord, the point being that Mr. Topper was to blame for everything, and that, had it not been for him, the little village would have continued to lead its tranquil existence to the end of recorded time.

It seems then that around eleven o'clock in the evening, Mr. Topper, after driving with great speed down the main street of the town, stopped abruptly in front of a drug store in which were gathered the flower and youth of the neighborhood. As witness to this fact we have three young rustic wing-singers, who, having finished their evening's singing, were comparing notes in the ruddy glow of the drug store window. It is to be regretted that these three gentlemen were merely the washed and oiled refinements of the farm hands who earlier in the day had been privileged to come upon Mr. Topper by the roadside in the act of doing Surprise. This incident had made a profound impression on their minds, and had only been forgotten for the more serious business of convincing various skeptical maidens that shadows and moonshine do not necessarily lead to perdition. The first wing-singer supplies the prelude. He is speaking to an attentive audience and he does not have to be cajoled to speak. He is saying:

"As soon as he staggered outer the orter I knew his face and I says to Joe, 'Damn if it ain't the same guy and he's still drunk.' Joe laughed right out loud because the guy had fallen down on the pavement and was sprawling there at our feet. Then the guy got up unsteady like and asked in an ugly voice just who had been doing all the laughing, and Joe in that comical way he has said that he had and that he was the mayor of the town and a lot of other funny things. Well, the guy didn't say much for a minute because he was brushing his pants and looking at Joe, and Joe was about to give him a push so he would fall down and we could laugh some more, when the guy asks Joe in a dopy voice how he'd like to get a punch on the nose. At that Joe just laughed in his face, it was so comic, and Joe having such a good sense of humor, but before Joe had laughed much he stopped sudden because that guy had hauled off and hit him on the nose. Then Joe said, 'Come on, boys,' and we all pitched in and showed the guy just where he got off."

From this naïvely significant account of the opening of the hostilities it must be concluded that Mr. Topper's question concerning Joe's nose was purely rhetorical, as Joe was given hardly sufficient time in which to answer and what little time he did have was wasted in ill-advised laughter. In his lust for action, Mr. Topper was perhaps at fault, but a plea for tolerance might be advanced on the ground that after all Joe was such a "comical feller" and for this reason, if for none other, deserved to have his nose punched whenever and wherever the opportunity conveniently offered itself to any public-spirited person.

Thus far Mr. Topper's actions have been traced up to the moment when he was borne down to the sidewalk beneath the combined weight of his opponents. Just what he did there will never be clearly known, for Mr. Topper was, of course, hidden, and the three young rustics refuse to tell. But according to the throng gathered inside the drug store, the cries issuing from the avengers of Joe's deflowered nose were so eloquent with anguish that everyone rushed to the door. It may be inferred then, not without reason, that Mr. Topper did as well, if not better, than could be expected of him under the rather trying circumstances.

The druggist, a person of authority and much unsavory knowledge, adds his contribution to the history of this tremendous fray.

"As I was crowding there in the doorway," he is explaining to an absorbed group of loungers, "the strangest thing happened I ever saw in my life and you've got to admit that us druggists see some mighty queer things."

This being admitted without the slightest opposition the druggist proceeds:

"I'd have sworn on the stand that the automobile was empty. From where I was standing I could look right into it and see every inch of leather on the seats. There wasn't nobody there—nobody. They couldn't even have crouched. But as I was saying, I was crowding there in the doorway just where that dog is now and I was watching this out-of-town drunk getting what was coming to him when right out of the automobile swarm two people, an angel and a guy in golf pants."

"Not a real angel," objects one of the loungers.

"Can't say about that," the druggist earnestly replies, "but she looked the part, flying robes and all. She didn't act like an angel though, except maybe an avenging one, but at that there was something about her different. Nobody but an angel could have been is so many places at once. She was the busiest party I ever saw. She and her friend with the golf pants on sort of took the boys by their legs and just naturally threw them away. Joe went up the street a piece, and Fred went down, and Alf landed up against the hitching post, where he stayed looking quite natural with a sort of gentle smile on his face. Then the angel and her gentleman friend lifted up the drunk and pushed their way into the store, the angel cussing like mad and the man with the pants telling her not to mention names."

"When the three of them came in I was standing behind the counter," proclaims the soda clerk, rudely breaking in on his employer's story.

An imperceptible shifting of shoulders indicates that the center of interest has been transferred to the boy.

"Well, I was that surprised and excited," he continues. "The angel walks up to the counter dragging the drunk with her and asks as cool and sweet as you please for some spirits of peppermint."

"You keep calling this angel her," breaks in one of the loungers. "Angels ain't neither one thing nor the other. That's why they're angels. Was this here angel a woman?"

"Sure," says the boy. "She had black silk stockings, thin ones, and she was a good looker to boot. 'Mix it up, Alonzo,' she says to me, 'and don't stint,' but before I could do any mixing the crowd came surging in."

"Thin ones," remarks one of the listeners.

"And black silk," say another.

"Some angel," puts in a third, rolling his eyes unpleasantly.

"And that's when the man with the golf pants on began to get gay with my siphons," the druggist hastens to explain. "When he saw the crowd coming at him, up he jumps on the counter with a bottle in each hand and lets loose two streams on the nearest heads. Everybody stopped and some went away, and the angel yelled after them, 'Come back here, you boll-weevils, a bath will do you no harm.' While this was going on, the drunk had gotten behind the counter and was playing with the soda taps. You'd have thought he was at a party, he was that pleased and satisfied. 'Look, George,' he kept calling out. 'See the damn thing fizz.' The man jumps down from the counter and says to the angel, 'Get him, kid, we've got to organize.' Then the angel collected the drunk and told him that they'd go somewhere else and have a lot of fun and he suddenly came to life and made for the door, his head down and his arms swinging. And all the time he's yelling something about a leg of lamb he didn't seem to like. The angel and her friend with the golf pants on closed in on each side of him and the three of them charged through us to the street and got into the automobile and then they were nabbed."

It is generally admitted that the three of them were, as the druggist put it, nabbed. The method of nabbing is also a point of local harmony and is acclaimed as being nothing short of a stroke of sheer genius. The method, it must be admitted, was not without its more imposing features.

When Mr. Topper and his companions emerged from the drug store they found that their only means of escape had been more or less surrounded by several and various circles of civic activity. The Quoits Club was staunchly occupying the car. As a club it was none too cheerful. Around the automobile itself, in hushful alertness, marched the local fire brigade. This depressed body of manhood was comfortingly reënforced by an outer circle composed of the more active members of the Security Association. A rotary movement, far on the outskirts, dimly illuminated by a fiery signal, gave staunch assurance that the business element of the town was heartily, if not helpfully, endorsing the procedure. This latter organization was making up in activity what it lacked in actual contact.

In the face of this display of civic coöperation neither Mr. Topper nor the Kerbys were convinced. They continued on. Like a splendid truth they denied facts. It has not been refuted that, on his way to the automobile, Mr. Topper assaulted and felled the chief of police and that the Kerbys scrambled over the body of the stricken man, cursing him vilely the while for being in their way. A submerged and vague-looking person, over whom the chief of police was chief, is responsible for this illuminating addition to the record of Mr. Topper's swift descent from the dead crater of suburban virtue:

"I was practicing away on my clarinet, practicing away like a good one, the Belvedere concert being only ten days off, when in rushes William, little William, you know, he's always rushing in, and he tells me that a riot has broke out in the town and that a couple of guys with an angel were smashing up the drug store. Well, I wasn't much set back by the riot, because I knew that if everybody in the town should get drunk or go mad at the same time there would still be plenty of room on the street for a quiet stroll, but the angel part of it did set me back. It did certainly set me back, that angel part of it."

To make this record strictly unbiased it should be mentioned that the chief of police's staff was not the most popular young man in town. The only thing he could do was play the clarinet and he did not do that badly enough to make him funny nor well enough to win him fame. When not engaged in playing or practicing on the instrument of his choice he had an unfortunate way of making unconstructive observations about life in general and the town in particular, and these observations in spite of their sincerity did not add to the young man's popularity. His casual lack of faith in the town's ability to work up a first-class riot alienated from him even the sympathy of the most tolerant member of the community, and according to the wiser heads of the town his story should not be taken too seriously.

"So I put my music away," his story goes, "and I went out to take a slant at this angel. Up by the drug store it looked like a rehearsal of the 'Covered Wagon.' Everybody was swarming around so and making such important noises. So I edged in and stood there, waiting to look for the angel, when, all of a sudden, I realized that I was the police force. This thought started me edging out, but before I could get away they came through the crowd and I saw them. They looked like nice people to me, and a little drunk. The woman was just beautiful. She must have been an angel because she did queer things to my eyes, sort of made me glad I had them, and that's more than any of the girls round this place ever done. I couldn't make head or tail out of the fight. It struck me as being sort of unfair. I thought of monkeys and lions and dogs and I decided that they wouldn't have acted like that under the circumstances and I sort of felt sorry about it all and a little ashamed. But I felt better when I saw them walking on the chief, although I felt sorry for him, too, realizing all the time that a little walking on would do him no harm. So when these people had passed completely over the chief I helped him up and shoved him in the car. 'You come along too,' he said in

a shaky voice and took me along with him. He seemed
to want me for some reason or other. The car was
already crowded, but I got in with the chief and
watched them all pile down on the angel and the two
men. It seemed kind of silly and overdone to me and I
tried to help the angel a little, but the fire brigade, not
having had any fires for a long time, was wild for
action and did fine, considering that there were only
twelve of them against three, not counting the chief and
myself, and the Quoits Club, and I didn't count for
much of course. Then after a while everybody stopped
squirming and began to get up, and when they looked
at what they had, there was only the drunken man
seeming less drunk, but much more battered. 'Where
my friends?' he says, but nobody could give him the
right answer so they told him to shut up and mind his
own business, and began looking about for the other
two, who just weren't there at all. And that's a strange
thing. I could say something else, but it wouldn't do
any good. So they put the battered man in the lock-up
and stood outside chewing the rag."

What he could have said, but did not say, was
withheld because the boy had been endowed with an
instinctive sense of delicacy, a shred of which still
survived in spite of its unfavorable environment. He
was right. It certainly would have served no useful
purpose had he told his friends that, as he was
walking down the street in the direction of the lock-up,
he stopped beside a hedge to inhale its fragrance.
Vaguely he was aware of the fact that the hedge had
no business to be smelling the way it did at that time of
the year, or at any other time, in fact. It was not
intended to be a fragrant hedge and had never previously laid any claims to fragrance, but to-night an odor
rose from it which stopped the boy and held him
wondering. It made him think of a forest swept by the
notes of violins. He saw a deep cathedral filled with
nude, white figures dancing madly in the radiance of
stained-glass windows. Romance descended on the
village youth, and for the moment carried him away
to realms where only his dreams had dared to dwell.
That was all there was to it, but he knew there was

more. He felt that he had stood very close to some one who was both beautiful and real. The impression perhaps remains with him to-day.

The "battered man" was borne in triumph to the lock-up. An uninformed observer might have mistaken the event for a procession staged in the honor of some honored local deity, so well was it attended as the automobile moved down the street and stopped before the jail. Here Mr. Topper was produced without ovation and disappeared from view without acknowledging the silent tribute of his followers. He was felt, searched, written about in a book, refelt with great interest and thrust into a cell from which he did not emerge until the following morning. When he asked to be allowed to telephone Mrs. Topper, the chief of police refused this request, but agreed to convey his message.

"Tell her I'm well and happy, but that I won't be home to-night."

Nothing loath, the chief aroused Mrs. Topper from a sleepless bed.

"Your husband is well and happy, but he won't be home to-night," said the faithful chief. "Yes, he's safe all right. We've got him safe enough—too safe for him. He's in jail, locked up in jail. What for? Why I wouldn't like to keep you up all night telling you what for. He's done plenty. Yes. It will be held in the morning. You'll hear about it then—all about it."

After a few more words the chief hung up the receiver and sat back, looking pleased. The enemy was his. The village knew how to deal with out-of-town drunks; and he, as chief of police, stood for the village, guarding its dignity, defending its rights, incarcerating its victims. Who could tell? Next year he might be postmaster. He got up and surveyed Mr. Topper, who was thoughtlessly sleeping on his cot. The chief felt grateful to him, but just a little disappointed in him.

CHAPTER X

The Haunted Courtroom

OWING TO THE PUBLIC NATURE OF MR. TOPPER'S various offenses, the trial was held in the Town Hall in the presence of the town's entire population, minors and morons rightfully included. Even dogs were not successfully barred from the trial. Mr. Topper noticed several of them and was favorably impressed by their non-partisan attitude, their utter detachment of mind. On the morning of the trial very little business was transacted in that village, the majority of its inhabitants being either complainants or voluntary witnesses. Instead of opening his hardware and furniture store as was his accustomed wont, the Justice of the Peace arose with unhabitual briskness from the breakfast table, and, surrounded by the numerous members of his family, proceeded with Jovelike mien to the place of trial, where for some minutes the more vociferous members of the community had been impatiently awaiting his coming.

That much was expected of him the Justice clearly realized. And he solemnly promised himself that not even the most sanguine expectant would be left unsatisfied. There was a duty to perform. A public duty in a public place. That was good. In a public place. That was very good. If only the baby would forget to cry. He hoped that the baby would forget to cry, but in his heart of hearts the Justice knew that the baby would not forget to cry. It never did. In vain he tried to prevail on his wife to leave the baby at home, impressing on her the importance of the business before him. "Who with?" his wife had asked quite reasonably, and, rather than participate in a breakfast-table riot, the Justice had refrained from nominating one of his numerous daughters. So the baby, not at all appreciating the fact that it was to be present at one of the most brilliant passages of its father's all too few moments in the sun, was conveyed to the trial of Mr. Topper in its mother's resolute arms.

The Town Hall was a barn-like structure, harsh without and unsympathetic within. Two long rows of benches, now filled with eager spectators, formed a narrow aisle down which the Justice walked a little in advance of his family, as if anxious to leave it behind. It would scarcely have surprised him had his wife and children followed him to the platform and arranged themselves behind him in a proudly silent semicircle. They were forever basking in the luster of his name.

No such misfortune occurred, however, and, after making much noise himself, the Justice succeeded in reducing the village to silence. This was the cue for the chief of police to become active. He responded promptly. With the air of one producing a rabbit from a high hat he pulled Mr. Topper through a side door and modestly displayed him to the multitude. And Topper looked not widely unlike a rabbit, a rather battered rabbit that had nibbled on something more potent than cabbage leaves.

This tableau over, the chief of police pushed his pearl into the presence of the Justice, while the chief's reluctant staff, like a hostage maiden being led naked through an alien street, brought up an unenthusiastic and highly skeptical rear.

"The prisoner, your Honor," announced the chief.

"So this is the prisoner," said the Justice, rubbing his hands juicily and beaming down on Mr. Topper.

Topper felt that had not so many spectators been present the Justice would have kissed him out of sheer gratitude.

"So this is the prisoner," repeated the Justice, his grateful countenance now shedding its rays over the entire room.

Mr. Topper made friendly movements with his features.

"I am," he said. "You're about the first person in this place, with the exception of the chief, who seems really pleased to see me."

The beam was blotted from the Justice's face.

"Silence, prisoner!" he boomed.

Topper stepped back affrighted.

"Sorry," he muttered. "I knew there was a string to that smile."

"He's a tough bird," the chief hastened to explain. "I didn't close my eyes all night. He kept singing. Your Honor, he sang in three different voices, one of them quite girlish and off key."

"That lie alone should discredit him forever," Mr. Topper protested with unexpected heat. "Anyway, his remark is unimportant."

The Justice swooped down over the table like a conventional eagle trademark.

"Prisoner," he said, "it is all important. In fact, it is exactly three times more important than if you had sung in only one voice. I shall make a note of it."

Mr. Topper looked up hopefully. Surely the Justice was exercising his sense of the ridiculous. After all the man was human. But when he met the direct gaze of the Justice, Mr. Topper looked wearily away. The Justice was not human. He was in deadly earnest. He was even making notes. No hope from that quarter.

After a portentous interlude, devoted to the scanning of official documents, the Justice raised his head.

"Your name is Topper," he announced. "Cosmo Topper. Everything is known. Now, prisoner, speak up in a clear voice and tell us where you live and what you do for a living. I am asking you to verify rather than testify, if you can make that distinction."

The Justice felt that he was doing very well. The principal of the Grammar School had laughed out loud. That was a plume.

"But I thought that they didn't do things like that until after you'd been convicted," Mr. Topper replied. "My pedigree comes later, doesn't it?"

"We are trying to save that time," said the Justice.

"But you don't have to hurry so far as I am concerned," replied Mr. Topper earnestly. "My time is at your disposal. As a matter of fact, I'd rather waste a few minutes here than spend several years elsewhere, if you can make that distinction."

"Address the court as 'your Honor,'" put in the chief of police, using an unfriendly elbow on Mr. Topper's ribs.

"You make me feel embarrassed for you," said Mr. Topper. "Try to remember where you are. This is serious, now."

"Stop!" whispered the Justice, a pleading note in his voice. "Don't quarrel. I'll get him sooner or later, chief. Let him hang himself."

"You don't have to let me hang myself," said Mr. Topper in a resolute voice. "Let me say right off that you'll have to make me hang myself. If I killed any one last night I'm sincerely sorry, terribly, terribly sorry, but for all that I deny everything. I'm innocent to the tips of my fingers."

Once more the Justice beamed. The case was shaping up.

"Deny this, then," he challenged, his eyes greedily watching the faces of the spectators. "Deny that you, Topper, struck, attacked and maimed the body and person of one Joseph Williams, and that not satisfied with this unwarranted display of ferocity you brutally assaulted Fred Scafford and Alfred Slides, both of whom together with Joseph Williams are in good standing in this community."

"All right, then, I deny it," said Mr. Topper. "I deny everything so long as you're going to get stuffy about it."

After the night he had put in Mr. Topper was feeling none too well. Standing there, in the presence of the Justice and the hostile throng, a nauseating dizziness swept down on him. He swayed slightly and for support placed his hand on the edge of the platform. Little beads of perspiration gathered round his lips and eyes. He mopped his face with a crumpled handkerchief and tried to look defiantly at the Justice, who was obviously enjoying Mr. Topper's discomfiture. With a swimming head and a morbid sensation in his stomach, Mr. Topper braced himself and waited. The situation was slowly dawning on him. He was beginning to realize that he, Topper, a man who up to the past night had been a respected member of his community, was now actually a prisoner before the bar of justice, that for all he knew he was a murderer and that he was being tried in the presence of a large gathering of hateful people, in a little village very close to his home—too close to his home. This realization still further depressed his stomach and brought dismay to his mind. He thought of the bank, he thought of his wife, he thought of his reputation and fearfully he thought of George and Marion Kerby. And, as if in answer to his thought, Mr. Topper felt two hands fumbling at his bare throat and was petrified to find that the collar which had gone by the board in the course of the evening's activities, was being replaced by a fresh one. The Justice, who had never seen a collar attach itself to a prisoner's neck, can be excused for the interest he displayed in the phenomenon. He moistened his lips with the tip of his tongue and looked fixedly at Mr. Topper.

"The collar," said the Justice. "There's something wrong about your collar. It seems to be getting beyond control."

For a moment Mr. Topper was too busy to reply. His head was being violently jerked from side to side as invisible hands attempted to adjust the knot in a new tie, insisting on getting it just right.

"We're trying to spruce you up a bit," whispered the voice of George Kerby. "How do you feel this morning? There, that's about right. Hold your head on one side so I can see."

"This is no place for a talk," muttered Mr. Topper, pretending to arrange the tie. "I feel like hell. Go away."

Then he glanced up at the Justice and smiled.

"Had them in my pocket," he said. "Thought I'd make myself a bit presentable."

The Justice looked unconvinced. Then his eyes once more grew large with interest. A comb was being passed through Mr. Topper's hair and a washrag was spreading itself over Mr. Topper's face. Mr. Topper became suddenly active. With one hand he attempted

to control the comb and with the other he snatched
at the washrag.

"Don't produce a towel," he whispered. "It would
be too hard to explain."

Again he smiled at the Justice.

"There," he said, thrusting the comb and washrag
in his pocket. "I feel better already. Where were we?"

"Frankly, I don't know," replied the Justice. "You'll
have to stop all this."

The hall was in an uproar. People were asking
questions and standing on the benches to get a better
view of this strangely-acting prisoner. The Justice
banged on the table and the chief of police raised
his voice in admonition. His staff looked sympathetically at Mr. Topper, who, taking advantage of the
noisy interlude, was attempting to explain the situation to his over-zealous friends.

"You've been lovely," he whispered. "Very
thoughtful. I appreciate everything, but don't go any
further. You can see for yourself."

"We're with you, old boy," replied Kerby. "We're
with you to the end."

"But don't be with me here," pleaded Mr. Topper.
"Go outside and wait for the end. It's a lovely day.
Take a walk round the village. It's not half bad. I'll
join you later."

"Marion won't budge," Kerby whispered. "Says she
wants to see that you get a fair trial."

"They'll put me away for life if this keeps up,"
breathed Mr. Topper. "Tell her to go away."

"Not a step do I budge," whispered a voice in his
other ear. "I'm going to stand right here and hold
your hand. Get ready now, old Zobo is going to ask
you something. Brush him off, George. He's all
mussed."

"Righto," said George.

"Please, please," Mr. Topper whispered. "Not so
loud."

As the Justice fixed Mr. Topper with a distracted
eye, Topper felt himself being vigorously brushed and
adjusted. His coat flew back and Kerby's busy hands
yanked his vest into position. The activity was then

transferred to Mr. Topper's trousers, which were spanked and patted with surprising energy. Mr. Topper, attempting to follow the rapid movements of Kerby's hands, looked like a man fighting hornets.

"Prisoner," said the Justice, "I wish you'd stop making such peculiar movements with your hands and body. If you want this case to continue you'll have to give up trying to bewilder me."

"A nervous eccentricity," explained Mr. Topper. "Sometimes it gets the best of me."

"It's almost gotten the best of me," replied the Justice. "Let's get back to business. As I remember it you were denying everything. Were you?"

"It seems to me that I was," said Mr. Topper.

"Very well then," continued the Justice. "Deny these charges if you have the temerity. Deny that you, Topper, Cosmo Topper, forced entrance with your companions into Frederick Schultz's drug store, that there you attacked a body of peaceable citizens, using the most offensive language against them, that you resisted arrest and made possible the escape of your companions, and finally, that you were driving an automobile while under the influence of strong drink. Deny these charges. Did or did you not commit them?"

"I haven't the slightest idea," said Mr. Topper, truthfully, "but I'm glad it's not any worse."

"We shall try to refresh your memory," replied the Justice. "Joe Williams! Step up, Joe, and testify."

Joe Williams was not loath to appear. He hurried down the aisle and stood before the Justice.

"Now look well at the prisoner, Joe," said the Justice, "and tell us if he is the person who assaulted you in front of Schultz's drug store."

Joe looked so long and so well at the prisoner that Mr. Topper thought the young man was trying to hypnotize him.

"He is, your Honor," answered Joe emphatically. "As I was standing there talking—you know, calm and peaceful-like—down the street comes this . . ."

"Later, Joe, if ever," interrupted the Justice promptly.

Joe's face clouded with disappointment as he turned reluctantly away.

"Are you satisfied, Topper?" the Justice asked.

"I am if you are," replied Topper, "but Joe doesn't look so pleased."

"Perhaps then you will tell us the names of your two friends," continued the Justice. "We might try to make things a little easier for you."

"George and Marion Kerby," said a voice unlike Mr. Topper, but apparently issuing from him.

"And where do these two depraved people live?" the Justice asked.

"They're not depraved," snapped the voice. "And anyway they are safely outside your jurisdiction."

"Try to speak in your natural voice," the Justice commanded. "Do you refuse to answer my question?"

"Well, it's mighty hard to answer," said Mr. Topper. "You see they travel about a lot—almost too much."

A note was passed by the chief of police to the Justice, who, after reading it, looked severely at Mr. Topper.

"I have a note here from your wife," he said. "She states that you are either drunk or crazy, because the people you refer to were killed in an automobile accident several months ago. Such attempts to deceive will not succeed with this court. Nor will they materially strengthen your case."

Mr. Topper looked through the hall until he had located his wife. She was sitting with several friends. He recognized Clara and Harris Stevens.

"Thanks," he called out with a terrible smile. "You are very helpful, my dear. The Justice thanks you, too."

"Silence! prisoner," shouted the Justice. "I'll not have you abusing spectators."

"Not even if she's my wife?" asked Mr. Topper.

"Not now," said the Justice. "Later."

"You don't know her," replied Topper.

"That's neither here nor there," the Justice complained irritably. "You're always getting me off on something else. This is a trial, not a conversation. Answer questions and stop asking them."

"All right, what shall I answer now?" asked Topper.

"Were you driving your automobile while drunk? Answer that," said the Justice.

"You'll have to ask someone else that question," replied Mr. Topper. "I can't answer it."

The Justice motioned to the chief's staff.

"Come here, Albert," he said. "Did you smell whiskey on the prisoner's breath?"

"Why, your Honor," answered Albert, in a voice of surprise, "I didn't even try to."

"Answer the question," the Justice commanded. "Did you smell whiskey on the prisoner's breath?"

"I'm not in the habit, your Honor, of smelling perfect strangers' breaths," said Albert with quiet dignity.

"Albert," explained the Justice, "I'm not inquiring into your habits. I'm trying to establish a fact. Please answer the question."

"Well, you Honor," said Albert, "at that time of night everybody's breath smells of whiskey in this town."

A wave of protest from the outraged spectators fortunately drowned the Justice's remarks to Albert. When order had been restored Mr. Topper turned to the Justice.

"If you'll only stop making this public inquiry into the state and nature of my breath," he said, "I'll admit everything."

A cloud of disappointment settled down on the Justice's brow. "Do you mean to say you'll plead guilty to every charge?" he asked.

"Most elaborately," replied Mr. Topper.

At this moment the wailing of an infant filled the hall. The Justice reared his head like a stricken war horse. This was indeed unfortunate. He felt that he was going to have a violent attack of nerves. So far the trial had been a complete failure and now without the slightest consideration for his feelings the prisoner was pleading guilty. It was too bad, the whole affair. And the baby was not making it any better. With a sigh, the Justice decided to put an end to an intolerable situation. He refused to compete with his own child to see whose voice should dominate the hall.

"So, prisoner," he said in a loud voice, a false light of triumph in his eyes, "so at last we have forced you to plead guilty."

"Driven me to it," said Mr. Topper.

"I am glad that you have at least decency enough to admit your guilt after we have clearly established it," continued the Justice.

"I couldn't resist you," smiled Mr. Topper. "Haven't a leg to stand on."

"Don't I get a chance to tell about all the strange things that happened in the lock-up last night?" asked the chief of police in a peevish voice. "Ain't you going to hear about the disappearing clock, and how cigarettes kept smoking in the dark, and matches striking without any hands holding them, and all the funny noises, the hooting and insults and everything."

"It seems that I am," replied the Justice curtly. "But I don't want to and I don't think I shall. Now, Topper, I have it in my power to do either one of two things. I can hold you for the county court or fine you and let you go. I would like to do both. It would give me pleasure to do both, but as I can do only one I am going to fine you and adjourn the court."

"A thrifty decision," said Mr. Topper. "I'm unusually well supplied with ready cash."

"You won't be long," replied the Justice. "Hand over one hundred and fifty dollars."

The Justice thrust the bills in his coat pocket and rose to his feet.

"The court is adjourned!" he shouted. "Clear the hall, chief!"

As the Justice was about to descend the steps leading from the platform he suddenly gave the appearance of a man who had been violently pushed from behind. With an expression of incredulity on his face he flew through the air and landed prostrate on the floor. As the chief bent over to assist him to rise, he, too, as if not to be outdone by his superior, gave a remarkable demonstration of levitation. Without any apparent effort he projected himself through space, sailing lightly over the Justice and stopping with a thud against the base of the platform. The room was filled with wild laughter and the table at which the Justice had been sitting danced crazily in the air. Luckily Mr. Topper could not be held responsible for this disorder. He was standing outside the hall talking with his wife and her friends.

"Why didn't you bring your luncheon with you and make a real picnic of it?" he asked with elaborate politeness.

"You're hardly in a position to be sarcastic," answered Mrs. Topper. "A little common humility would be more becoming."

"I can hardly see that," said Mr. Topper. "I've afforded you more enjoyment than you have me. There will be a tremendous demand for the company of those who attended the trial. You'll be fed free for weeks."

"Come, Topper," put in Harris Stevens. "We were only trying to help you."

"By writing nasty notes to the Justice," said Topper.

"Well, I merely dictated it," replied Stevens. "Your wife thought of it. We didn't want you to get into any more trouble. You've been through a lot. What a time you must have had. Was there a woman in the party?"

"The Follies Chorus," said Topper. "In tights. Pink, blue, red and green."

"Come, Clara," Mrs. Topper interrupted, "we'll be getting home."

"And some of them were in less than that!" Mr. Topper shouted furiously as the party moved off. "Much less than that! Tell everybody I said so."

"May I get a few lines for the local paper?" asked a young man, stepping up to the gesticulating Topper.

"Yes!" cried Mr. Topper, "a few lines in your face if you don't take the silly thing away."

The youth withdrew and Mr. Topper was left comparatively alone. That is, he was surrounded, but at a distance, by an absorbed circle of observers.

"Now where the hell's the car?" he muttered.

As he spoke he heard a loud honking of an auto-

mobile horn and the car, like a playful puppy, came
darting through the crowd. The Justice, standing on
the porch of the Town Hall, witnessed the scene and
shut his eyes tightly. The car was driverless. He could
not stand that. As he leaned against the wall he feared
he was going to lose his mind. When he opened his
eyes again Mr. Topper had stepped into the automobile and was driving off while the people stood about
with panic in their midst.

"Here's the money," said George Kerby. "I
snatched it out of the old bird's pocket."

A roll of bills found its way into Mr. Topper's
hand.

"Oh, my God," he groaned. "Are you two back
again?"

"Sure," said the Kerbys in a breath. "Aren't you
glad?"

Mr. Topper was unable to reply.

CHAPTER XI

Antics of a Hat Stand

THE TOPPERS' HOUSE WAS NOT ONE OF MIRTH. GREAT
quantities of gloom had descended upon the place.
Women had hastened to Mrs. Topper's side as if in
the hour of her bereavement. They sat in subdued
rooms and conversed in subdued voices. Mr. Topper
came to regard himself as a corpse, without, however,
enjoying a corpse's immunity to its surroundings. At
any moment he expected Mrs. Topper to place candles
round him. He had been requested to withdraw from
the Town Council and the honorary residue of the
now professionally organized fire brigade. Why a person had to be moral in order to be useful at a fire was
difficult for Mr. Topper to understand. Nevertheless,
he sent in his resignation and felt better about it. He

was now officially divorced from white duck trousers. That was something to cling to in the ruins.

Twenty-four hours after his release from durance the craving for a smoke had driven him into town. On that trip he had purchased enough cigars to relieve himself of all further necessity of appearing again in public. Topper had only a hazy idea about fallen women, but he imagined he felt very much as they did when adversity had forced them to return to their home towns. Topper had lost everything but his money and because that still remained he was not stoned. He was still a solid man, but terribly soiled. He read about himself in the local press and stopped reading almost immediately. Mrs. Topper displayed no such delicacy. The paper was seldom out of her hands. Topper, observing her absorbed expression, wondered what pleasure she could be deriving from poring over such morbid stuff. Mrs. Topper was deriving a lot of pleasure. Seeing her husband's crimes in print gave her a feeling of security. There could now be no doubt about it. The story was down in black and white. Mr. Topper could not deny it. She was vexed with the reporters, however. They had used altogether too much literary restraint. Now if she had been writing the report—headlines flashed through her mind. It was well for Topper that he could not read them.

Three days had elapsed since Mr. Topper's arrest. Three days passed by him for the most part in the backyard. Whenever sympathetic callers arrived Mr. Topper disappeared. He feared that the women might ask his wife for the privilege of viewing the remains. For this reason he quietly removed himself and his bruises to the backyard. To this retreat Scollops followed him. She was waiting impatiently to resume the repose that had been so rudely interrupted by his unwarranted absence from the house. The man must sit down some time. This tragic stalking about was all very well for a while, but on the other hand something was due a cat, especially such a cat as Scollops. There was little comfort in a peripatetic couch. If Topper wanted to think and be gloomy let him do so in a stationary position. But why think? Sleep was

much more vital. There were a few slight irregularities
in her own life. Scollops remembered, not without
pride, a certain alienation affair in which she had
become involved, but she had no intention of letting
the memory make her haggard. Several times she had
honestly tried to think about the affair, to figure out
if in any way she had justified various backyard ref-
erences, but the effort had made her drowsy. Why was
not this man affected in the same manner? Human beings placed too great importance on the game of
morals. That was why they were constantly breaking
the rules. They really did not want to play and yet
they insisted on giving the appearance of playing. So
Scollops waited while Topper walked. Then Topper
sat and Scollops slept. And in the darkened house
Mrs. Topper delicately arched her eyebrows and was
happy, quite, quite happy in a sane and refined manner.

After three days of morbid seclusion Mr. Topper
came to a decision. His secret life was developing,
growing more complex. When he came to the decision
he was sitting on the lawn roller because it had been
previously warmed by the sun. And what made him
come to a decision arose from a sudden and upsetting
realization that at heart he felt neither grieved nor
chastened by anything that had come to pass. He
found himself actually gloating over his night in the
lock-up—what little he could remember of it. He relished his memory of the old abandoned inn tucked
away among the trees. He felt with pleasure that he
had done some fairly splendid dancing and he was
sure that for the first time in his life he had sung without constraint and fought without fear. Sitting there
on the lawn roller, he was surprised to find that each
little memory brought him some satisfaction and no
regret, and as the indirect rays of the sun sent courage
through his spinal column he deliberately denounced
the town and all its works in terms both round and
rough. His whole past life had been modeled on false
standards which would have to be adjusted at once.
There was only one way to accomplish this. Mr. Topper's fingers abstractly touched one of Scollops' ears

and Scollops with equal abstractness scratched one of
Mr. Topper's fingers. But Topper disregarded the
sleepy rebuke of his cat. He was going away. He was
going quite far away. That was Mr. Topper's decision.
He would drive himself to some great distance from
the town and his wife and her friends. Before he officially proclaimed the new order of things he must first
be alone. He had to think a little. That was quite important. He wondered now how he had ever gotten
along so far with so little thought. He became quite
elated about his brain. It was like a new toy to him.
He had always believed that it had been providentially
arranged for the purpose of making money, acquiring
possessions and paying for legs of lamb. He found that
his brain was quite playful, that it broke rules and was
indifferent, that it entertained the most disreputable
thoughts without becoming panic-stricken. Mr. Topper felt like dancing, but he restrained this inclination.
He realized that if Mrs. Topper saw him making
movements of joy she would immediately call in another mourner for a whispered conversation. And
Topper felt so liberated that he feared he might assault the next woman who heaved a sigh in his house.

So instead of dancing he buried his head in his
hands and held on to himself. It was silly about his
eyes. He did not feel at all like crying. Yet his face
was growing wet.

The next day Mr. Topper went to the city. To
show his indifference to public opinion he took the
usual commuting train. His appearance at first caused
the respectful silence usually accorded to criminals in
transit to the place of incarceration. As he walked
down the platform he felt that life had not been lived
in vain. He enjoyed the situation. Men who had once
greeted him with respect now slapped him on the back
with hands that were moist with condescension.
Friends who had hitherto received him warmly
nodded thoughtfully in his direction and resumed their
conversation. Two representatives of civic virtue were
honest enough to ignore his presence. Harris Stevens,
however, was not to be downed. On seeing Topper he
threw himself headlong into the rôle of official pro-

tector. Stevens' mind was so tolerant that he could
have attended a lynching every day without becoming
critical. He thrust his arm through Mr. Topper's and
led him up to a group of mutual friends.

"If I were handcuffed to him," thought Mr. Topper,
"his happiness would be complete."

Nevertheless Topper made no protest. He was still
enjoying the situation.

"Look out, boys!" cried the jovial Stevens, "he's
dangerous. Wild women and everything. What do you
think of our Cosmo now?"

Of course the assembled gentlemen hardly said
exactly what they thought of their Cosmo now, but
to a man they all displayed a glittering interest in the
mysterious and therefore immoral woman in the case.
Several commuters of the more serious and orderly
type even went so far as to draw Mr. Topper aside
and intimate roguishly that they would appreciate
his confiding absolutely in them. Mr. Topper understood all too well and gave each inquirer a different
name and address. He was thanked by each, nudged
playfully in the ribs, and assured that everything
would be done on the quiet.

"What vile devils they are," thought Mr. Topper
as he smiled knowingly into their eyes, already touched
with the fever of the hunt.

His trip to the city that morning provided him with
much food for thought, each morsel of which was
more unpalatable than the last.

The atmosphere was clearer at the office. News of
Mr. Topper's evil ways had not entered there. Boys
were answering bells, girls were serving the files and
customers were beginning to transact business.

"To what end all this?" speculated Mr. Topper,
making his way to his desk and hanging his hat and
stick on a near-by stand. From his position on the platform he could look down over the activity taking
place on the bank's vast floor. Like a lesser god he
observed with preoccupied eyes the ordered movement
of those below him. What he saw neither pleased Mr.
Topper nor made him feel particularly proud of his
elevated place in this little world. Mr. Topper had al-

ready progressed too far for that, but the quiet briskness of the bank, the crisp little people coming and
going on sure feet beneath the vast dome of the place,
and the massive splendor of the institution's architecture gave him a feeling of permanence. Men and
women were engaged in earning a living here. They
were paying strict attention to their own affairs. Round
him on the platform his brother officers were busy
with callers and correspondence. Here Mr. Topper
felt safe from the oily eyes of his friends. He drew a
sigh of relief and touched a bell. Miss Johnson appeared
with his letters and he thanked her with elaborate
politeness. His secretary was a middle-aged woman
who valiantly strove to draw attention from that depressing fact by decorating various parts of her body
with the tender ribbons of infancy. Mr. Topper's attention was not so easily misdirected, but nevertheless
he was fond of Miss Johnson. He had seen the ribbons
increase with the years and had decided that when
infirmity at last forced the good woman to withdraw
from the bank she would depart under full color like
an aged but fluttering May-pole. In spite of her little
weaknesses Miss Johnson knew her business, or, better, Mr. Topper's business. She knew how to save
him both time and trouble and the more time and
trouble she saved the more tolerant was Topper, the
more he forgave the ribbons. As far as he was concerned Miss Johnson could have appeared in beads
so long as she made up the difference with efficiency.

Mr. Topper's first letter was from a wholesale
grocer in Texas, an old fellow on whom the bank
had been making a decent profit for years. He was
now in trouble. Things were bad. He wanted an extension of credit. As Mr. Topper read the letter he
caught a mental picture of the old man laboriously
writing it from an old-fashioned roll-top desk in Texas.
Mental pictures are not good for banking. Mr. Topper
was well aware of this, but the knowledge did not
succeed in closing his eyes on the man's plight. Instead
he opened them all the wider and dispatched a tele-
gram designed to bring back the courage to a cornered customer thousands of miles away. It was not

an outstanding stroke of business, but on this particular morning Mr. Topper relished it the more for
that very reason.

Up to eleven o'clock Mr. Topper occupied himself
with routine details, then he rose and informed
the president that because of various considerations
due to certain hitherto unknown maladies of both mind
and body an extended vacation was highly essential.
Should such an extension be withheld Mr. Topper's
physician would not be responsible for the conse-
quences. Mr. Topper felt inclined to agree with the
physician, a thing he seldom did. The extension was
not withheld, although its cause was not fully believed. With an unnecessarily spiritless step Mr. Topper returned to his desk as if reluctant to leave it.
Now that his vacation was assured he lingered over
the parting. He had already set his affairs in order,
but he diligently began to reset them now. He dallied
with meaningless papers and dictated meaningless
memoranda. There was a certain satisfaction in
wasting the precious minutes in useless drudgery now
that they were his to waste. In the back of his mind,
however, danced colorful thoughts of golf stockings,
caps and outing shoes, and other equipment necessary
to his trip. Soon he would arise and purchase these
things, going out into the street like a free man with a
new consignment of golden days. For a moment he
delayed, prolonging anticipation. In the middle of
his fifth meaningless memo he was surprised by Miss
Johnson's unusual behavior. Instead of gazing devoutly at her notes as was her invariable custom, her
eyes had become disconcertingly jerky. For a moment
they would remain fixed on the point of the pencil,
then, as if drawn against their will by invisible wires,
they would painfully lift and stare with a fascinated
gaze directly over Mr. Topper's left shoulder. At the
sound of Mr. Topper's voice they would struggle for
a moment before they were able to descend once more
to the pad. Mr. Topper was at first puzzled, then hurt
and at last exasperated. Finally he could stand it no
longer.

"What the devil's the matter, Miss Johnson?" he exclaimed.

"Look!" was all Miss Johnson said, pointing over his shoulder.

There was something in the tone of her voice that made Mr. Topper disinclined to look. In spite of himself he turned in his chair and followed the direction of her finger. He would have been more relieved had he seen a party of bank robbers quietly slaying the entire office force and looting the safe deposit vault. It would have seemed less personal, less fraught with complications. Yet what Mr. Topper saw would not have arrested the attention of the casual passer-by unless he had chanced to be especially interested in hat stands. This particular hat stand was situated in a corner near Mr. Topper's desk. On it were Mr. Topper's hat and cane, or rather, on it they should have been, but the terrible part of it was that they were not where they should have been. The cane had assumed an independent position and was standing unsupported on its own tip. The hat was rakishly poised above it about three feet in the air. As Mr. Topper turned, the hat and cane resumed their normal position as if afraid of being discovered out of place.

At this Miss Johnson gasped and once more uttered, "Look!"

Mr. Topper swung quickly back to his desk. He would look no more. Already he had seen too much.

"I wish, Miss Johnson," he said in a reproving voice, "I do wish you'd stop telling me to look. I see nothing and my time is valuable. What was I saying?"

Training came to Miss Johnson's aid. She dropped her eyes and studied her notes.

"You were saying," she said, "that, owing to your enforced absence, steps should be . . ."

"Ah, yes," interrupted Mr. Topper. "I was saying that."

His voice trailed away and he began to tap on the edge of his desk with the tip of a pencil. Now why had he been saying that, he wondered. Was it possible that the Kerbys had followed him to town? Marion had said that George occasionally ranged abroad, but he could hardly believe that Kerby would follow him to the bank. Miss Johnson's eyes were lifting again. Topper cleared his throat and hastily began to dictate.

"Owing to my enforced absence," he repeated, "I feel that it is important for certain steps to be . . ."

Unable to stand Miss Johnson's eyes he stopped dictating. What was happening behind him? At any moment the hat might thrust itself down over his eyes and make him appear ridiculous. The Kerbys were capable of such an outrage.

"Look now!" exclaimed Miss Johnson.

Mr. Topper turned quickly, and just in time to see his cane and hat retreating to the stand. He noticed with dread that this time they had ventured farther away from their appointed place.

"Oh," murmured Miss Johnson in an expiring voice. "Oh!" she repeated.

"Miss Johnson," said Mr. Topper with fatherly severity, "you must be ill, otherwise you would not be trying to upset me with your wild exclamations."

"Didn't you see anything?" asked Miss Johnson, studying Mr. Topper's face with troubled eyes. "Anything strange?"

"Nothing," lied Mr. Topper. "Nothing strange at all. Now let's try again."

"Then I must be very sick," replied Miss Johnson. "Sicker than I've ever been before."

"It will pass off," Mr. Topper assured her. "Pick up where I left off."

"Certain steps should be taken," began Miss Johnson. "You keep saying something about certain steps."

At this point Miss Johnson capitulated and seized Mr. Topper's hand. The hat stand was swaying from side to side and the cane rattling against its post.

"I'm not as sick as that," she said with conviction. "If you don't see what I see you're the one that's sick."

"All right, all right," Mr. Topper called out, this time directly addressing the hat stand. "I'll finish up at once. Don't worry about that last memo, Miss Johnson. Go home and take a rest. Your nerves are upset. Stay home for a week or so. I won't be needing you for some time."

Mr. Topper got up briskly and swept some papers into a basket. The animated hat stand came to rest. Miss Johnson, her hands full of ribbons, was gazing at it with horror in her eyes.

"See, Miss Johnson," said Mr. Topper, walking over to the stand. "See, it's nothing after all. Only your nerves."

But before he could reach for his hat and cane these articles eagerly sprang from their pegs and presented themselves to his grasp. He snatched them from the air and turned to Miss Johnson.

"Nothing at all," he said with a forced smile. "It was purely your imagination."

For a moment they looked into each other's eyes. There was a prayer in Mr. Topper's. No missionary ever struggled more fervently to implant belief. Miss Johnson was regarding the hat and cane suspiciously, and Mr. Topper realized he had failed.

"Nothing at all," he repeated in a dead voice as he felt himself being gently pushed by some unseen force. "You can see for yourself, Miss Johnson. Go home and take a rest. And if I were in your place I wouldn't speak with anyone. You might be misunderstood."

This last remark was tossed over his shoulder, for by this time Mr. Topper was being propelled with increasing rapidity across the floor. As he left the bank he looked like a man leaning against a strong wind.

"Not so fast," he muttered.

The doorman, thinking the remark intended for him, arrested the speed of the revolving doors.

"That's a queer way for a body to walk," he thought, peering after the slanting Topper. "Especially an officer at this time of day."

CHAPTER XII

A Smoky Lady in Step-Ins

MR. TOPPER WAS IN AN UNSPEAKABLE FRAME OF mind. He shook himself free from the invisible grasp that had made a retreat of his departure, and fumed up the street, escape his one desire. And every time he passed a drug store a slight tugging at his sleeve informed him that he was not alone, that for him escape was impossible.

"Stop doing things to my sleeve," he growled. "Stop pushing."

"But I want you to buy me a soda," came the whispered reply.

"After all you've done to me you ask me that?" exclaimed the outraged man, for the moment forgetting his fear of being caught talking to himself in the streets. "Fiddling with my hat and stick. Giving my secretary a nervous fit. Why didn't you bawl and scream?"

"But you took such a long time in that horrid old place," the voice pleaded. "And that ridiculous woman looked at you so familiarly. I wanted to pull her ribbons off, but . . ."

"Let me understand this," interrupted Mr. Topper, seeking refuge in a near-by doorway. "Am I no longer to dictate to my secretary? Do you object? By what right? I've never compromised you, although God knows you've ruined my reputation—you and your husband. Why don't you torture him and leave me alone?"

"He's left me," the voice replied with just a hint of moisture. "He's gone to sea for a change."

"He needs one," said Mr. Topper. "Haven't you any friends?"

102

"None that I like as well as you. Please don't go on any more. It would be funny to see tears dropping from no place in particular."

The woman was actually hugging him in broad daylight. Mr. Topper swayed forward, then with a supreme effort regained both his balance and his composure.

"Don't do that again, ever," he commanded.

"Let's be glad," Marion pleaded. "I didn't mean any harm. George was gone and I didn't have anything to do so I just went down to the station to see the trains come in and then I saw you and I wanted to go along. It's awfully lonely being a low-planed spirit. You don't know."

Now there had been very little wheedling practiced on Mr. Topper in the course of his married life. Mrs. Topper had arranged everything and Topper had followed the arrangements. On those rare occasions when he had balked Mrs. Topper had instantly assumed the rôle of a martyred woman and in pallid silence cherished her dyspepsia. It was a strange, fearful and fascinating sensation that Mr. Topper now experienced as Marion Kerby clung to his neck and asked him to buy her a soda. He forgot the humiliation of the office out of sheer sympathy for the poor, parched spirit who had been the cause of it.

"But hang it, Marion," he said in a softer voice, "be reasonable. How can I buy you a soda?"

"You can pretend to be drinking it," she replied eagerly, "and when you hold your glass aside to look at your newspaper I can sip through the straw. No one will notice it. Just hold your glass a little to one side and I'll come close to you and sip through the straw— little, quiet sips. But you must only pretend to be drinking it. Don't forget yourself."

"I'd rather risk the chance of a scandal and have you materialize," said Mr. Topper thoughtfully.

"All right," replied Marion. "I'll do that in a jiffy."

"Not here!" Mr. Topper protested. "For once show some restraint. Can't you go somewhere to materialize and then come back to me?"

"How about that store?" suggested Marion.

The store she referred to was a small notion shop which owed its existence to the fact that women, regardless of their means, must be clad in silk or near silk against the ever-present dangers of being run over, unexpectedly married or caught in a sudden gale. The shop seemed suitable to Topper for the business of materialization. He said as much and Marion Kerby departed, declaring that she would be right back in a minute. Mr. Topper waited ten before he became impatient, then he walked slowly past the shop and peered through the door. As he did so a hatless woman came bounding forth with stark terror gleaming in her eyes. She was speedily followed by a small boy, who in turn was closely pursued by a man whose features were working frantically. Before Mr. Topper could recover from his surprise three girls dashed from the store and joined their companions in flight, now huddled compactly at a safe distance from the shop. Mr. Topper felt like running, too, but curiosity overcame his fear. He approached the group and asked questions. One of the girls looked at him and began to cry.

"Mamma!" she gulped. "Mamma!"

He quickly transferred his gaze to the man.

"What's happened in there?" asked Mr. Topper.

"Don't go in, sir," pleaded the man, for the first time in his life discouraging a prospective customer from entering his place of business. "For God's sake, sir, stay here with us."

Topper looked at the boy.

"Little boy," he said, "tell me what frightened all these people."

"I'm not frightened," declared the boy, "but they all started to run and I just got ahead."

"Yes, but why did they start to run?" continued Mr. Topper patiently.

"Because of her," said the boy, pointing to the shop.

"Of whom?" demanded Topper.

"The smoky lady who was trying on step-ins and everything," answered the boy.

At this point the woman who had been the first to seek comfort in flight found her tongue. A crowd had begun to gather and she addressed herself to the crowd.

"She was all smoky," the woman announced. "And you could see right through her. How I first came to notice her was when I pulled back a curtain to show one of these girls some step-ins. There she was, as calm as life, trying on a pair of step-ins, a pair of our best step-ins, and she was all smoky and transparent so that only the step-ins seemed real. When she saw us she got scared and went bounding round the shop so that it looked like a pair of step-ins come to life and gone mad. I started to run . . ."

"And I made a grab for the step-ins," interrupted the man, "but the smoky woman wouldn't let go, so I just decided that, before any trouble started, I'd run out and see what had happened to Lil."

"It was awful," proclaimed one of the girls. "I'll never forget those step-ins dancing around the store."

"Our best step-ins," said the woman.

"A good pair," added the man.

"Perhaps they are not a total loss," Mr. Topper suggested. "Why not go back and find out? I'll buy the step-ins if this smoky woman hasn't walked off with them."

As attractive as the offer was to the proprietor he seemed reluctant to accept.

"Come on," said Mr. Topper. "I'll lead the way."

"But, sir, you don't understand," the man protested earnestly. "Have you ever seen a transparent woman dancing about in a real pair of step-ins?"

"That depends on what you mean by transparent," replied Mr. Topper judiciously. "Anyway it's much better than seeing a real woman dancing about in a transparent pair of step-ins."

At this remark the young lady who had been sobbing for mamma suddenly giggled and looked archly at Mr. Topper. The proprietor seemed unconvinced.

"No, it isn't," he said, with a shake of his head. "Now-a-days you can see that at most any good show, but not the other, thank God. It isn't what I call natural entertainment—not for me at any rate."

"And while you're standing here talking," Mr. Topper reminded him, "the smoky lady is probably trying on every blessed thing in your shop."

"Well, I'm not going back to watch her," the proprietor proclaimed to the crowd. "If any of you gents want to see a smoky woman trying on underwear you can step right in, but I don't budge without a cop—two cops," he added as an afterthought.

Mr. Topper felt a soft, flimsy article being thrust stealthily into his coat pocket. His hand flew to the spot and shoved the thing out of sight. A gentle pressure on the arm indicated that it was time to depart, and a policeman, pushing through the crowd, strengthened Mr. Topper in this belief. He permitted himself to be led away by his invisible guide. After several blocks of silent companionship he could no longer restrain his annoyance.

"Now what the devil do you mean by trying on a pair of those things?" he demanded.

"What a crude question," Marion murmured.

"Your conduct has given me the privilege to ask it," replied Mr. Topper.

"Cosmo," she whispered, leaning heavily against him, "I just love nice things."

"You should leave all that stuff behind you now that you're dead," he answered.

"Even spirits have to be modest," said Marion. "And anyway they frightened me. I was getting along fine until that woman pulled back the curtain. I was pretty nearly completely materialized, but that made me so startled I couldn't finish it."

"That was fortunate to say the least," replied Mr. Topper, "considering the condition you were in."

Topper heard a low laugh.

"You're vile all the way through," said Marion Kerby. "Here's a soda store. Come on in—chocolate with vanilla ice cream."

Mr. Topper felt himself being pulled in the direction of the soda store. He resisted feebly, feeling that he had gone through enough for one day.

"Must you have that soda?" he asked.

"Oh, no," Marion replied in a resigned voice. "I can do without it. I'm used to being miserable. One more disappointment will make no difference. Keep me hanging round your office all morning, then send me in to a place to be scared to death, and after that refuse to buy me a soda. Go on, I like harsh treatment. You remind me of my husband, the low creature."

With the chattering courage of a man being placed in the electric chair, Mr. Topper walked into the soda store and seated himself at the counter.

"Vanilla soda with chocolate ice cream," he muttered darkly in the direction of a white-clad individual.

"No! No!" whispered Marion excitedly. "You've got it all wrong. Tell him quick. It's chocolate soda with vanilla ice cream."

Mr. Topper coud feel her fluttering on his lap.

"Be still," he whispered, then smiling ingratiatingly at the clerk he added, "I'm afraid, old man, I got that wrong. I want it the other way 'round."

The clerk looked long at Mr. Topper, then walked to the other end of the counter and engaged a colleague in a whispered conversation. From time to time they stopped talking to look back at Mr. Topper, whose anxiety was mounting with each look.

Marion Kerby in her eagerness was pinching Topper's hand. He pulled his newspaper from his pocket and hid behind it.

"You and your sodas," he growled. "Why can't you keep quiet?"

"But you had it all wrong," protested Marion. "Look out, here he comes now."

When the attendant had placed the glass on the counter Mr. Topper idly reached for it with the air of one too deeply engrossed in the news of the day to be interested in a trivial beverage. Leisurely he placed the glass to his lips, then held it aside.

"The straws," whispered Marion. "Must have straws."

"My God," murmured Mr. Topper. "Won't you ever be satisfied?"

He procured two straws, plunged them viciously into the soda, then held the glass behind his paper. The liquid immediately began to descend in the glass. From the rapidity of its descent Mr. Topper decided that George Kerby had bought his wife very few sodas during her earthly existence.

"Now dig out the ice cream with the spoon," she whispered. "Pretend to be eating it. I'll nibble it off."

"This is going to be pretty," murmured Mr. Topper with as much sarcasm as can be packed into a murmur. "You'll have to do better than nibble. You'll fairly have to snap it off."

The nibbling or snapping operation required the use of both of Mr. Topper's hands and forced him to abandon the protection of his paper. With an earnest expression, which was perfectly sincere, he endeavored to give the impression of a man publicly lusting after ice cream. The spoon flew to his avid mouth, but, just before his lips concealed their prize, the ice cream mysteriously vanished. It must be said in favor of Marion Kerby that she met the demands of the occasion. Not once did she fail to claim her own. Not once was Mr. Topper allowed to sample that which he most abhorred. When the ice cream had run its course Mr. Topper resumed his paper and waited, with a knowledge bred of experience, for the dregs of the soda to be drawn. He had little time to wait. Hollow, expiring, gurgling sounds loudly proclaimed the welcome ending of the soda. With a sigh of relief Mr. Topper was about to return the hateful vessel to the counter when he met the eyes of the clerk peering at him over the top margin of the newspaper. They were cold, worldly eyes, yet curious, and they fixed themselves on Mr. Topper like two weary suns regarding a new-born star. A nervous muscular reaction contorted Mr. Topper's mouth into a smile.

"Do that again," the clerk said. "Do that trick again without me guessing it and I'll give you this."

He dangled some crumpled bills alluringly in Mr. Topper's face.

"I can't," replied Mr. Topper. "It's hard enough to drink one of your nauseating concoctions, much less two."

"You didn't drink the first one," said the attendant.

"What's your game anyway? I was watching you all the time. Trying to be funny?"

"Not funny," Mr. Topper answered, delicately slipping from his seat. "You're wrong there. That was one of the most serious sodas in my life—one of the worst."

"You're one of those funny guys," said the attendant menacingly. "Come back here and I'll tell you exactly what you are."

But Mr. Topper did not wait to be told. He hurried from the store and mingled with the crowd.

"It's awful to be cut off from sodas," breathed Marion Kerby.

"I have no sympathy to waste on you," said Mr. Topper.

He was hungry, yet he dared not eat. If she had behaved so excitedly in the presence of a soda, what would she do at the sight of food. Mr. Topper shuddered. He was thinking of a plate of soup. No, it would never do. He would have to forego luncheon. This was an overwhelming decision. It left Mr. Topper shaken. Never had he missed a meal save when his adenoids had been surreptitiously removed many years before. Mr. Topper gazed up at the lean cascades of the Woolworth tower through the tragic eyes of a deflated stomach. There was no fortitude in him. He was the abject slave of a passion he longed but feared to indulge. All his friends were eating luncheon now. He wondered what they were having. Menus danced before his eyes. The "blue plate" of the day brought savory odors to his nose. Strangely enough it was in this dismal crisis that Marion Kerby came to his aid.

"Isn't it time for your luncheon?" she suggested.

"Past time," said Mr. Topper, "but how can I eat with you with me?"

"Food means nothing to me," she replied. "I can take it or leave it as I choose, but you're different. You must eat."

"I feel that way about it myself," admitted Mr. Topper. "For once I think you're right, but, frankly, I'm afraid to enter a public place with you. My nerves can't stand it. Too much has happened."

"Come," she said in a changed voice, taking him

forcibly by the arm. "I'm going to see that you get
your luncheon. Don't bother at all about me. I'm different now. The city went to my head at first. I'll admit it. Those step-ins and the ice cream soda got the
best of me. I lost control of myself, but now you don't
have to worry. Just a cup of tea—nothing more."

"That ends it," declared Mr. Topper. "That's
enough. I don't eat. I dare say you fully expect me to
crouch under a table and hold a plate of tea while you
make strangling noises."

Marion Kerby laughed softly.

"I was only joking about the tea," she said.
"Honestly, now, I don't really want it. That's true. I
should want it, but I don't. There was only one person
I ever knew, not counting myself, who couldn't stand
tea, and he was a fine but fanatical drunkard. Graze
with the herd and I'll keep quiet."

So Mr. Topper had his luncheon. It was a tense
luncheon, a suspicious, waiting sort of luncheon, one
filled with false starts and empty alarms. In spite of
everything it was a good luncheon and Marion Kerby
behaved splendidly. Once, when Mr. Topper used the
pepper too violently, a fit of sneezing came from the
opposite chair. The waiter was momentarily startled,
but immediately adjusted himself to the situation. He
realized, as does everyone who knows anything at all
about sneezing, that there are no two sneezes alike and
that most anything can be expected of a sneezer. He
regarded Mr. Topper with the commiseration of one
whose sneezes were infrequent and well under control, and departed in stately search of pie á la mode.
Nevertheless, he considered Mr. Topper as being not
quite the usual customer. He had noticed certain little
things. Nothing you could put your finger on, but still a
trifle different. For instance, why had the tray contain-
ing bread risen to meet Mr. Topper's outstretched
hand? And why had the salt stand behaved so oblig-
ingly? How could one account for a menu tilted in
space? And, if that was perfectly natural, why had Mr.
Topper made such strange fluttering movements with
his hands? Deep within himself the waiter sensed that
all was not well with his table, but the clatter of plates,

the demands of his occupation, and the deep-rooted instinct of all people to deny the existence of the unusual successfully maintained him in his poise of sharply chiseled indifference. The generous size of the tip he washed up in his obsequious hands completely restored his faith in the normal order of things. There had been nothing unusual. Mr. Topper was a man who desired to dine. The waiter hoped he would do so more frequently at his table. The waiter was one of those people whose tolerance increases with the size of the tip. For a ten-dollar bill he would have respectfully tidied up after a murder and made excuses for the toughness of the corpse.

Later that afternoon Mr. Topper was trying on a cap. He was a diffident man about such things, but on this occasion his heart was in his task. The brownish thing that was making his head ridiculous had vague, temporizing lines in it of a nervous blue, but to Mr. Topper the cap was lovely. To a man or to a woman he would have said harshly that the cap "would do," but to himself he had to admit it was lovely. He admired it hugely. It was a good cap. Mr. Topper had no difficulty in convincing the salesman that it was a good cap. With suitable apologies the man agreed that it was a very good cap and that it suited Mr. Topper well. Mr. Topper found himself admiring the salesman. He knew his business, this man—one of the few salesmen with unimpeachable taste. The cap was practically Topper's. All the salesman had to do was to snatch it from Mr. Topper's vainglorious head and wrap it up. Mr. Topper was willing. He had never purchased such a cap in his life. With the eager timidity of a virgin he hoped to demolish the record of years. He was brazen about it, yet he was shy almost to the point of tenderness. The cap was in the salesman's hands. Mr. Topper was reaching for money. The salesman's free hand was politely waiting for the object of Mr. Topper's reaching. Then something happened. A new and different cap appeared in the salesman's outstretched hand. With the instinct of his calling he automatically began to sell the new cap. Then he stopped in confusion and looked helplessly at

Mr. Topper, who was convulsively clutching a roll
of bills. Mr. Topper refused to meet the salesman's
gaze. Instead he glared at the new cap. It was a terrible
cap, an obscene, gloating, desperate cap. Its red checks
displayed the brazen indifference of deep depravity.
Mr. Topper was revolted.

"Take it away," he said. "I don't want it."

At this remark the new cap shook threateningly in
the salesman's hand. He tried to give it to Mr. Topper,
but was unsuccessful. Mr. Topper backed away.

"I don't want it," he repeated. "I don't like that
cap. Please take it away."

The salesman was deeply moved.

"I'm not trying to sell it to you, sir," he said in a low
voice, "but somehow I can't help it."

He stood before Mr. Topper with a cap in either
hand. One cap he held almost lovingly, the other he
clung to in spite of himself, like a man with a live coal
in a nest of dynamite. His lips trembled slightly. He
tried to smile. He was mortally afraid that at any moment Mr. Topper would depart with a bad opinion of
the store. He could never permit that to happen. With
an effort he turned away, but before he had gone many
yards he abruptly swung around and came back at a
dog-trot. To Mr. Topper he gave the appearance of a
man who was being held by the scruff of his neck and
the seat of his trousers by some one intent on motivat-
ing him from the rear. He stopped suddenly in front of
Mr. Topper and, in an attitude of supplication, offered
him the red checked cap. Mr. Topper again refused it.

"I must apologize," the man said rather breathlessly,
"but I really think you had better take this cap."

In spite of his irritation Mr. Topper regarded the
salesman with quick sympathy.

"Why have you changed your mind?" he asked.
"I've already told you that I hate that cap. It isn't a
nice cap. I don't like it."

The salesman was almost chattering. He shook himself like a dog and glanced quickly over his shoulder.
Then he approached Mr. Topper.

"I haven't changed my mind," he whispered. "I've
lost my mind. It isn't the store. It's me. I'm mad."

Mr. Topper was beginning to feel extremely sorry for the salesman. He wanted to do what he could, but he refused to be bullied into buying a cap he utterly loathed, a cap that went against all his instincts.

"It's too bad about your mind," said Mr. Topper, "but I don't want that cap. I won't buy it. And if I do buy it I won't wear it. I'm honest about that."

"Listen," whispered the salesman. "I'll give you the cap if you'll only take it away."

"If you're as anxious as all that to get rid of the cap," Mr. Topper replied, "I buy them both. How much are they?"

"Practically nothing," said the salesman, his face clearing. "I'll wrap them up myself."

He hurried away.

"But I won't wear it," said Mr. Topper, addressing space. "You won't be able to force the thing on my head."

"Here they are," announced the salesman, returning with the package. "You've been very nice about it, I'm sure."

As the elevator bearing Mr. Topper to the ground floor began its descent a low gasp was heard in the car.

"I can't stand these things," whispered Marion Kerby. "They always take my breath."

At each floor the gasp was repeated, whereat Mr. Topper cringed under the curious eye of the operator. Mr. Topper pretended to gasp in order to protect himself. He smiled sickly at the operator and said:

"Did it affect you that way at first? It always does me."

The operator continued to look at him but made no answer. He was glad to see the last of Mr. Topper. He was afraid that the man was going to swoon in his car.

On the train that evening Mr. Topper tried to hide himself in his newspaper, but was unsuccessful. Marion Kerby insisted on turning back the pages and scanning the advertisements. At last Mr. Topper abandoned the newspaper and looked out of the window. Presently he became conscious of the fact that several passengers were regarding the vacant seat beside him with undisguised interest. The newspaper was slanted against the air as though it were being held by unseen hands. Mr. Topper seized the paper and thrust it into his pocket.

"Rotter!" whispered Marion Kerby.

"Fiend!" muttered Mr. Topper.

A heavy personage attempted to occupy the seat, but arose with a grunt of surprise. For a moment he regarded Mr. Topper bitterly, but that distraught gentleman was gazing at the landscape with the greedy eyes of a tourist.

At the end of the trip he hurried home. His day had been crammed with desperate events. There would be nothing for him at home save Scollops, but at present Mr. Topper preferred a sleepy cat to an active spirit. He yearned for repose.

"Good-by," said Marion Kerby as he was turning into the driveway. "I've had an awfully nice time and I want to thank you."

"Why did you make me buy that cap?" demanded Mr. Topper.

"Because I knew it would look well on you," she answered. "George had one once and everybody liked it."

"Well, I don't, and I won't wear it," said Mr. Topper. "Good-by."

Marion Kerby clung to his arm.

"Don't be angry," she pleaded. "I've got to go back now and it's going to be lonely out there without even George to haggle with. Say good-by nicely and call me Marion."

Mr. Topper had a twinge of conscience. He was going away in the morning without even telling her about it. He was running away from her. Although he realized that he was in no way bound to Marion Kerby he nevertheless felt guilty in abandoning her, particularly in the absence of her irresponsible husband. However, if he confided in her everything would be ruined. She would be sure to come along. He knew he would never be able to drive her off. After all why should he not take her along? Then he remembered the events of the day and decided that there was every reason in the world for leaving her behind.

He was going away for a rest and not a riot. With Marion Kerby with him rest would be out of the question.

"Well," he said in a mollified voice, "it's not going to be any too crisp for me at home, but I'll look you up in a few days. We'll take a ride together."

"Good-by," she said, her voice sounding strangely thin and far away. "Don't forget. I'll be waiting for you."

The house had lost none of its funereal atmosphere during Mr. Topper's absence. Mrs. Topper was sitting in the shadows with her hands folded in her lap. She was the picture of resignation.

"Are you feeling better, my dear?" asked Mr. Topper.

"I haven't been thinking about myself," she replied. "There are other things on my mind."

Mr. Topper discreetly refrained from asking her what they were. He sat down and read the paper until the maid announced dinner, then he followed his wife into the dining room, where the evening meal was consumed in silence. He felt like a convict being entertained by a member of a Christian Endeavor Society. Mrs. Topper made it a point to see that he was properly served. She seemed to derive a sort of mournful pleasure in watching him chew his food.

When they were once more in the sitting room Mr. Topper announced the fact that he was going away for a trip. It was a difficult announcement to make and Mrs. Topper was not helpful. She listened in silence until he was through, then she said without looking at him:

"I hope that for my sake you'll try to keep out of jail."

"It's not a habit," replied Mr. Topper. "It was an accident, an unfortunate misunderstanding."

Mrs. Topper bent over her sewing and compressed her lips.

"I'll never forget it to my dying day," she said. "The shame and humiliation of it."

"You could forget it if you wanted to," answered

Mr. Topper. "If you liked me instead of yourself you could forget a lot of things."

Mrs. Topper regarded her husband with melancholy eyes.

"You ask me to forget that?" she asked.

"Come, Mary," replied Mr. Topper in an earnest voice. "I don't know what got into me. I was all wrong, but just the same . . ."

He stopped and, pulling the step-ins from his pocket, began to mop his face with them. They were orchid-colored step-ins heightened in attractiveness by crimson butterflies and lace insertion. They gave Mr. Topper a foppish appearance. As he stood before his wife with his face nonchalantly buried in the silken fabric Mr. Topper looked almost giddy. A new light came into Mrs. Topper's eyes. It was the light of despair masking behind outraged modesty. At the height of his mopping Mr. Topper must have realized the situation, for he suddenly withdrew his face from its tender concealment and peered at Mrs. Topper over the step-ins. Mrs. Topper had risen. As she confronted her husband she was trembling slightly. He tried to speak, but she held up a restraining hand.

"I refuse to remain in the room and have you flaunt your infidelity in my face," she said. "Don't speak to me. Don't try to explain. Everything is perfectly clear."

"But I bought them for you," gasped Mr. Topper. "They were to be a surprise."

"They were a surprise," replied Mrs. Topper, recoiling from the offending garment. "They were a shock."

As she left the room Mr. Topper hurled the step-ins to the table and departed to the garage, where he remained the rest of the evening. Scollops curled up on the evidence of guilt and tried to forget the late unpleasantness in sleep. When Mr. Topper returned to the house the step-ins had disappeared from the table. Upstairs a tear-stained woman was clutching them in her hand. Gradually her sobbing quieted and she looked timidly at the step-ins. Perhaps after all he had bought them for her. But she never wore such things. Mr. Topper knew it. Why didn't she wear such things? She was startled. Perhaps that was the reason. With a feeling of guilt she slipped on the step-ins and looked at herself in the mirror. She thought they were vulgar and pointedly immoral, but in her heart she gloated over them. After all they were quite nice if worn in a proper manner and for an equally proper purpose. Beauty for beauty's sake. She would have to consider step-ins and other things. Absorbed in these thoughts, her eyes traveled up the mirror and encountered her face. After a moment's scrutiny she turned away, her shoulders drooping. She felt foolish and defeated. Desolation filled her heart. As she lay on the bed in her startling attire she looked like a bedraggled doll which some worldy person had dressed in a moment of caprice and then abandoned for other pursuits.

Her outburst of grief expended, she sprang up and, tearing off the offending garment, trampled it under her feet. Then quite reasonably she picked up the step-ins, carefully folded them and put them away for safe keeping. After this she prepared herself for bed and switched off the light. Later, when her husband wearily sank down beside her, she pretended to be asleep.

CHAPTER XIII

Escape

BEFORE THE SUN HAD SET MR. TOPPER HAD left a trail of dust across his native state and carried warfare deep into the heart of Connecticut. Like a floating mine in an ocean lane he endangered the safety and ruined the happiness of all creatures who came his way. His intentions were above reproach had he been able to execute them, but in this he failed lamentably. He was a traveling display of frightfulness, a menace to moving traffic. The curses of his fellow

creatures followed him down the road. He had never
before realized how vindictive, how utterly given to
fury, automobilists were. Sarcasm, insults and jeers,
all were flung at Mr. Topper, and all found their mark.
He shrank within himself and placed his destiny in
the hands of God. But long hours of sustained driving effected a gradual change in his spirits, and towards
sunset it was Topper who was shouting bitter oaths
at passing automobiles. Each oath increased his confidence and self-respect until at last he came to regard
with malicious pleasure the approach of another car,
epithets fairly boiling on his tongue.

"They've tried to ruin my day for me," he thought.
"I might as well get back at them now."

When not engaged in roadside altercations, Mr.
Topper's thoughts strayed back to home. He was
heavily depressed to find that he lacked the thrill of
escape.

In early morning, under the stimulus of the previous evening's scene, he had left his wife, his bed and
the step-ins to settle the dispute among themselves,
and stolen forth to the garage, where the secretly prepared automobile was waiting to carry him to liberty.
As he passed through the sitting room Scollops, abandoned to sleep, was lying in his chair. Lying is hardly
the word. Molded would be more descriptive of the
cat's contact with the yielding upholstery. Given a
sufficient length of time, Scollops might have grown
to the chair, so much a part of her had she made it
already.

It was not without pride that Topper regarded
his cat. She had selected his chair for her slumbers.
Possibly she sensed he was near. Topper's unconscious
craving to be loved made him overlook the fact that
his was the most comfortable chair in the room and
being such naturally recommended itself to Scollops'
practical mind. His knowledge of cats was hardly more
extensive than his knowledge of women. In some re-
spects Topper was more fortunate than he realized.

He had stooped over the sleeping creature and run
his hand along her luxurious side. A short, surprised
bubbling sound signified that although she appreciated

the attention she could do nothing about it at present, complete rest being her most urgent need. However, he could stand there and continue to stroke her if it gave him any pleasure. She rather enjoyed it.

Topper was now thinking of Scollops as he had last seen her. He was wondering whether he should have brought her along. Perhaps she might be forced to suffer vicarious atonement for his sins. That would be too bad. After due consideration he decided that an automobile was as much as if not more than he could well manage, and that Scollops would have complicated things to the breaking point. Yet the fact remained that he was lonely. He almost wished he had taken Marion Kerby along for at least the first stage of the trip, but when he recalled the humiliation of the previous day he felt glad that he had not given in to this weakness—nay, madness.

A slight misunderstanding with an interurban trolley car forced him to concentrate on the business of keeping alive, and when next he had time to glance at his surroundings he found with relief that he was in a town which gave the appearance of being large enough to support life.

The hotel was even more than he had hoped for or expected. It was so self-consciously modern that it wore an injured air. A negro bell boy fairly snapped at his bags and bore them away in triumph down a colonnaded hall. Mr. Topper, hardly less triumphant at having arrived intact at some destination, no matter where, followed at a more leisurely pace. Then it was that the hotel, or at least that part of it assembled in the lobby, received a decided shock. As Mr. Topper approached the desk two books pursued him down the hall. The negro bell boy on seeing the phenomenon dropped the bags and began to look for wires or for any other rational explanation of this unprecedented occurence. Unable to find a comforting solution, he held on to the desk and shivered while looking pathetically at the clerk. Unfortunately for the bell boy the clerk was too much preoccupied with his own feelings to share his moral courage with others. By the strained attention of the clerk's features Mr. Topper could tell that something was wrong. And when the two books thrust themselves under Mr. Topper's arm he knew that all was wrong. He snatched at the books and offered them to the clerk.

"They're not mine," announced Mr. Topper, lyingly. "You'd better take care of them."

"I won't touch them," replied the clerk, withdrawing from the books.

"Well, you take them," said Mr. Topper, turning to the bell boy. "Someone here must own them."

The bell boy shivered himself out of reach.

"They followed you," he muttered. "They didn't follow me. I don't read, boss. Please point those books the other way."

"Damn it, then, I'll throw them here," exclaimed Topper, tossing the books into a chair. "Give me a room and bath."

The clerk, still eying the books suspiciously, reached for a key and handed it to the reluctant bell boy.

"Take him away," he said, briefly.

As Topper turned to follow his bags he cast a swift, pleading glance at the abandoned books.

"Don't follow me," he muttered. "This is serious."

On his way to the elevator he could not resist the temptation to look back. He felt sure that he saw the books fluttering entreatingly in the chair. It was like leaving a dog behind, one that was not to be trusted. Only when the elevator door had closed with a satisfying clang of finality did Mr. Topper breathe a sigh of relief.

Once in his room he endeavored to regain his composure. Looking coldly at the bell boy, he said, "Bring me some ice water and the evening paper, a New York paper if they have them here."

The sound of the closing door synchronized with a terrible scream. Mr. Topper, completely unnerved, rushed to the door and looked out. Two books were coming stealthily down the hall. The bell boy was flattened against the wall, and every time he screamed the books stopped as if undecided what course to pursue under the circumstances. And every time the books stopped the bell boy put his hands over his eyes and replenished his spent lungs with air for further efforts.

Mr. Topper was speechless. He wanted to tell the bell boy not to scream, but he could only speak in a whisper.

"Don't scream, little bell boy," he heard himself saying. "Don't scream and I'll give you a dollar."

But money made no impression on the bell boy. Avarice had been cleansed from his soul. He was purified by fear. And as the books drew abreast of him and made a vicious dart in his direction he sank to the floor. For a moment the two volumes danced wickedly over the fallen negro, then with surprising swiftness flashed into Mr. Topper's room and with an ill-tempered bang deposited themselves upon the table. Mr. Topper closed the door, but not before he had had time to catch a glimpse of the bell boy worming his way in the direction of the elevator.

Still unable adequately to express his feelings in words, Mr. Topper sank into a chair and gazed down on the street. The worst had happened. Nothing hereafter could ever be quite so bad. Had he remained at home with Scollops he would have been far better off. Even Mrs. Topper with her dyspepsia and her sighs would have been preferable to this. He should have stopped at the local madhouse instead of the hotel. What were they talking about downstairs? The long twilight was streaming out and the room was growing dark. Fearfully he let his eyes rest on the books. He cleared his throat suggestively.

"Well," he said at last, "you might as well speak. I know you're here. Why deny it?"

"But I haven't said a word," came a surprised voice from the direction of the wastepaper basket.

"Then don't," said Mr. Topper. "And try to pick out less disturbing places to settle in."

There was no reply, but the window shade rolled down with a sudden snap and the electric lights as suddenly flashed into being. Mr. Topper started nervously.

"You're always trying to be so helpful," he remarked petulantly. "Where the devil are you?"

Like a blind man endeavoring to locate a voice he looked round the room, a baffled light in his eyes.

"For God's sake say something," he exclaimed. "What are you doing now? What are you going to do?"

"For the moment I'm roosting on the chandelier," came Marion Kerby's familiar voice, "but I'll be down presently."

"When are you going for good?"

"Why, I hadn't intended to go," she replied. "I'd decided we'd better take a good long rest and make an early start in the morning."

"We," he said. "How do you mean 'we'? I won't ever go to bed unless you clear out."

"What's the difference?" she asked. "What's so strange about 'we'?"

"You're too depraved to understand," replied Mr. Topper. "Merely because you claim you're not legally bound to your husband don't get the idea that you are to me."

"But there are twin beds here," she protested. "And it's been such a long day."

"If they were triplets it wouldn't change my mind," said Mr. Topper.

"Prude," she jeered.

"Why?" asked Topper. "You seem to think that you should enjoy not only all the privileges of a spirit but also the few comforts that are left to mortal beings."

"Why not?" she answered. "You forget I am quite low-planed."

"Not for a moment," said Mr. Topper. "You never give me the chance."

Marion Kerby laughed.

"I choose the bed by the window," she said. "You can sleep on the inside. You'll be out of the draft."

"That's very thoughtful of you," replied Mr. Topper, "but you don't quite understand. I have a lot of things to do, none of which requires an invisible audience. I must shave and exercise and take my bath, and damn me if I'll have you floating about this room while I'm doing these things."

"I'll hide my head in the pillow," she suggested.

"But it wouldn't be humanly possible for you to keep it there."

"Don't judge others by yourself."

"I can't in this case," said Mr. Topper. "It isn't fair. You're invisible and I can't see you, but I'm quite solid and you can see me."

"Are you making advances?" asked Marion Kerby.

"Not at all!" exclaimed Mr. Topper.

"For if you are," she continued, "I can very easily alter the situation. Just to show you what a good sport I am I'll materialize."

"Don't do that," said Mr. Topper. "Most emphatically not. Get the idea out of your head. There are laws against such things, unpleasant, illogical laws. Do you want me arrested again?"

As Marion Kerby began to laugh at Mr. Topper's consternation there was a knock on the door and a bell boy entered, a new bell boy.

"Stop laughing," commanded Mr. Topper.

"But I'm not, sir," said the bell boy.

"Oh, I thought you were," replied Mr. Topper. "It must have been my suit-case. It squeaks."

A smothered sound descended from the chandelier. Both Topper and the bell boy glanced up.

"That pipe needs fixing," remarked Mr. Topper.

"Anything else, sir?" said the boy, hastily placing the water and the newspaper on the table.

"I hope not," Topper replied earnestly. "I certainly hope not."

The bell boy withdrew without waiting for a tip. Mr. Topper locked the door.

"That sounds interesting," said the chandelier. "I'm so excited."

"Don't be lewd," Mr. Topper snapped. "Do you realize I haven't dined?"

For an answer he felt two arms twining round his neck and two lips touching his cheeks. In spite of himself he was thrilled.

"Stop all this," he said. "I dislike any show of emotion."

A low laugh sounded in his ears and his hair began

to move strangely on his head. Marion Kerby was playfully rumpling her victim.

"Please," protested Mr. Topper. "This is most uncanny."

"I'm just telling you good night," she replied. "You lied to me about going away, but I'll forgive you. Don't worry. I wouldn't sleep in here if you begged me. You go down and have your dinner, get a good night's sleep and I'll be waiting for you in the morning."

"Where?" he asked suspiciously.

"In the car," she replied. "Good night."

Topper suddenly felt himself alone. He could not tell why, but he knew that Marion Kerby was no longer in the room. The place seemed empty. And strangely enough he did not feel relieved. Nevertheless as he left the room he took the precaution to remark aloud:

"I'm not going to read. Leave the books alone."

After a hearty dinner, taken outside the hotel, he returned to his room and prepared himself for bed. For some reason he trusted Marion Kerby. He felt sure that she would not take advantage of his solidity. Yet why had he not taken advantage of her offer to materialize? Topper was not accustomed to sleeping alone. It would have been jolly to have had a companion. A real one. With a backward thought of Scollops and a forward thought of the morrow he switched off the lights and settled into bed. Mrs. Topper stalked his dreams. She was standing at a crossroads gloomily directing traffic, and every time he attempted to go her yellow hand held back his car.

It was after one of these irritating dreams that he awoke to hear regular breathing coming from the bed at his side. He was shocked beyond words. What an outrageous thing to do after her promise. He thrust his hand out in the darkness and shook the bed.

"Wake up," he whispered piercingly. "Wake up. You can't stay in here."

"Oh, let me alone," came the sleepy rejoinder. "Don't bother me. I've had to stand your driving all day long."

"Don't argue," whispered Mr. Topper. "Get up at once and go away. Sleep in the garage."

"Sleep there yourself."

"But, Marion," continued Topper, trying another tack. "This isn't right. Your husband is a friend of mine."

"Well, I slept with him for years."

"How shameles."

"Not at all. One would think I was trying to seduce you."

"I know you're not, but you're making a nervous wreck out of me. I value your husband's friendship."

Marion Kerby laughed mirthlessly.

"It wouldn't be worth a cent if he saw us now," she said.

"When's he due back?" asked Mr. Topper, after a moment's thought.

"You can't tell," she replied. "He might drop in at any minute."

This information contributed little to Mr. Topper's happiness. He looked morosely out into the darkness.

"I could never explain," he remarked as if to himself.

"You wouldn't have time," said Marion.

"Then why not be sensible and go away?"

"Because I'm very comfortable where I am, thank you."

"Oh, dear," he said to the darkness. "I'd rather sleep in the bathtub."

"Go on and sleep in the bathtub. Turn on the water and pull it up over your ears."

Mr. Topper made no answer, but sat hunched up in his bed. Suddenly he jumped. Marion Kerby was yawning in his ear.

"Aw, give us a kiss," she said, "and let's get some sleep."

"This is downright ghastly," he muttered. "Haven't you any morals at all?"

"Hardly any."

"Well, I have a few left. Try to remember that."

He sank back into the bed and gathered the coverings tightly about him. Several minutes of silence passed as he listened to Marion Kerby's regular breathing.

"Won't you please go away?" he said at last.

"If you don't stop waking me up," she replied irritably, "I'll start screaming and get in the whole hotel."

Before this threat Mr. Topper wilted. He buried his head in the pillow and remained silent. His desperate desire to be elsewhere drove him into oblivion, but this time Mrs. Topper did not disturb his dreams. Instead, he was in his pajamas and Marion Kerby was chasing him through the corridors of the hotel. All the doors were open and people were crowding in them. As he sped down innumerable miles of carpet, grinning faces greeted him on either side and ironical cheers of encouragement followed his headlong flight. And the most terrible thing of all was that his pajamas were threatening to part.

"If I trip now," he thought to himself, "I'll be a marked man for life."

CHAPTER XIV

The Singing Shower-Bath

LIKE A SPENT RUNNER BREASTING THE TAPE WITH HIS last stride Topper awoke in the morning. By languid stages he rolled himself to the floor, where his feet unconsciously fumbled the carpet for their slippers. As he stood in the middle of the room tentatively fingering his disordered hair, he allowed his eyes to dwell on the other bed. For some moments he regarded this object with scant interest, then gradually his sluggish faculties assimilated the fact that what he beheld gave every appearance of having been occupied. The coverings of the bed presented a scene of opulent disorder. Once Mr. Topper fully appreciated the significance of this discovery it was but a matter

of a moment for him to act on it. With far greater
speed and decision than he had displayed in quitting
his own bed the dismayed man now returned to it.
There, huddled in the coverings, he considered his
desperate plight, his eyes bleakly searching the room
for some source of comfort.

"Marion," he called at last, his voice softly pleading with space. "Marion, I must get up now. Do be a
good girl and run along."

As if in answer to his words the shower began mer-
rily to prattle in the bathroom. To Mr. Topper's shrinking ears it sounded like a deluge. And out of the rush
of water a slight song came winging through the door.
The words and music belonged to Marion Kerby.
Topper's fingers nervously plucked at the sheets as he
listened to the song:

"I once was a lady as you may divine,
    Though the fact it is hard for to see.
Rare beauty and riches and romance were
        mine,
    Before I ran into a tree.
My husband he did it. The devil would drive,
    The high-flying, low-lying soak.
And that is the reason I'm no more alive,
    For he ran me smack into an oak."

Mr. Topper shuddered at the word "smack" and
sprang from the bed. It was all too horrible. How
could she sing about the accident? And such a song.
"Smack into an oak"—a ghastly picture. Casting his
robe round him, he walked with dignity to the door
of the bathroom, upon which he knocked vigorously.

"Come out of there," he commanded, transferring
his attention to the knob. "Stop that wailing noise.
You're splashing water all over everything."

"You just leave me alone now," came the reply
with unexpected heat. "I'm tired of your airs and
graces. Only wait until you take a shower. I'll raise
hell with you then."

Topper regarded the door with a mixture of fear
and reproach. What a creature of fury she was. And he

had only said a word. The possibilities of her retali-
ations made him thoughtful. There was no telling
what she might do. Then once more the indignity of
the situation overtopped his better judgment. He returned to the combat.

"I'd very much like to know," he demanded, "why
you persist in considering this situation as normal
when obviously there's nothing normal about it. Answer me that. What right have you to become so
threatening and furious? You're haunting me. I'm
not haunting you. This is my vacation. Can't you get
that through your head?"

"Nonsense," came from the shower. "Ladies must
bathe."

"But, Marion, you're not a lady," Mr. Topper protested. "Not any longer. Once you might have been,
although I have good reason to doubt it. You're only
a spirit now and you're supposed to have taken your
last bath. If you overlooked your opportunities when
you had them why monopolize mine now?"

"What low insinuations," the shower retorted. "Just
wait till I get you in here."

"You'll never get me in there," Mr. Topper answered. "Never!"

"But it's such a lovely shower."

"Then hurry up and come out of it. I've lots of
things to do."

"You don't know what you're asking," came in-
sinuatingly from the shower. "You see I materialized
just for the occasion, but if you insist . . ."

"I don't," Mr. Topper interrupted hastily. "Only
please dematerialize and go away."

"Then where are my step-ins?"

"Good God, what a question to ask! I know nothing
about your step-ins."

"You do so. We stole them in New York."

"Oh," he replied, his face clearing, "I gave them
to my wife."

The shower was seized with convulsions.

"She'd look like a staggering sunset in those step-
ins," it gasped moistly.

"Stop saying things about my wife," Mr. Topper replied, shaking the door knob.

"Not unless you try to be more pleasant."

"How about yourself? Will you try to keep within reason?"

"Yes," she replied. "I'll try. I'll do my best."

"And you'll respect my privacy hereafter and get me into no more scrapes?"

"Absolutely, my little chastling."

Mr. Topper thought quickly. He realized the futility of continuing hostilities. Marion Kerby had every advantage in her favor, and she would use it without honor. Perhaps after all it would be wiser to call a truce with this untamed spirit.

"All right," he said. "I'm game. From now on we'll try to enjoy ourselves. This sort of thing is spoiling my trip. What do you say to a truce?"

"I say yes," she heartily agreed.

The flood suddenly subsided and the door flew open. Topper stepped back, but not in time to save himself from the embrace of two fresh though invisible arms.

"Behold," said a voice in his ear, "your instruments of torture have been laid out by loving hands. Come in and see what I've done."

"That's all very nice," replied Mr. Topper. "And I appreciate your thought, but don't go too far. I know all about shower baths. I will join you later."

"Then hurry like everything," she urged as she released him. "Let's prepare for fresh adventures now that we're friends again."

"No more fresh adventures," admonished Topper, thrusting his head through the partly opened door. "Leave fresh adventures out of it. The few I've had with you will never stale."

Topper was one who dwelt lovingly over his toilet. In his blood there was something of the Roman emperor. He gloried in steam and tiles. He was never happier than when allowed to occupy his bathroom unmolested, an occasion which occurred only too rarely in his own household. He made the most of his new-found freedom and soaked himself to his heart's

content. When at last he emerged glowing from the
sweating walls he was both surprised and delighted to
find breakfast already awaiting him. It was appetiz-
ingly arranged on a table, from which a fork was busily engaged in conveying scrambled eggs to nowhere.
To Mr. Topper it was a painful sight. As the fork rose
from the plate and daintily poised itself for the thrust
he watched with fascinated eyes the amazing disappearance of its burden. Marion Kerby's voice interrupted his contemplation.

"Sit down," she said briskly. "Everything is getting
cold. I couldn't wait."

The fork made a quick jab in his direction.

"Don't apologize," he replied, sliding into a chair.
"I'll sit down, but before I begin to eat answer me
one question. How is it that you can put something
into nothing and make it disappear?"

"It's a gift," she explained. "I just gulp it down
into the fourth dimension and there it is changed into
so much extra ectoplasm."

Mr. Topper tried to smile, but he felt that he was
rapidly losing his appetite.

"It's all clear," he said, "but the gulping. Do you
have to gulp when you eat?"

"Don't be insulting," she replied, with the fork
poised in midair. "It's merely that I'm ravenous after
the shower. Absolutely starved. I don't get a chance
to eat very often."

"Then don't let me stand in your way now," Mr.
Topper urged gallantly. "Go right ahead and gulp.
I'm a trifle greedy myself."

For several minutes no sounds disturbed the tranquillity of the room save those occasioned by
eating. Presently, however, Mr. Topper, who had been
glancing at his companion with increasing alarm, was
forced to speak.

"You'll pardon me," he said, "if I seem to turn
away when you gulp your coffee. I can't quite get
used to the sight and it gives me the strangest feeling.
Every time you tilt your cup I expect to see the coffee
splash all over the table."

"Oh, you'll get used to that in time," she answered encouragingly.

"I'm no longer in rompers," he remarked.

"But I never miss," she assured him.

"That's just it," he replied. "It would seem more natural if you did."

In the middle of his next mouthful a new fear interrupted his activities.

"How," he demanded, swallowing quickly, "how did you manage to bring this breakfast into being?"

"I telephoned for it," she answered.

Mr. Topper started from his chair.

"My God!" he cried. "They'll think I had a woman in my room all night."

"Sit down," she commanded, "and don't be so jumpy or I will spill my coffee. I imitated your voice perfectly. In fact, I was quite ladylike."

As Mr. Topper resumed his chair Marion Kerby began to laugh.

"Why that?" he asked.

"Because I made one mistake," she answered. "I told the boy to set the tray down outside the door, but when I went to get it he was still there. Well, naturally you can picture to yourself how mystified he was when he saw the tray slide in, as it were, by itself."

"Only too vividly," said Mr. Topper.

"He did look so upset," she added.

"Don't dwell on it," pleaded Mr. Topper. "I've seen too much tragedy as it is. Was it the first boy?"

"It was."

"Then you have probably killed him."

He poured another cup of coffee and drank deeply.

"If not you have driven him mad," he concluded. "Completely unhinged his mind."

He rose wearily from the table and prepared to depart. Marion Kerby made herself helpful. Combs and brushes, shirts and shaving things moved mysteriously across the room and arranged themselves in the suit-case. Mr. Topper, observing this, felt surprised that he was no longer alarmed. He was becoming accustomed to the situation. Placing the books securely in one of the bags, he strapped his luggage and locked it.

"Remember," he said, "I trust you. No monkey-shines, no helpfulness. If I'm not arrested I'll meet you in the car. Wait for me there."

"I won't do a thing," she promised. "Our first night was delightful."

"Such remarks are better left unsaid," he replied as he closed the door.

Marion Kerby was as good as her word. She allowed him to leave the hotel without further complications. In spite of this Mr. Topper was hardly regarded with warmth by the personnel of the establishment. The bell boys seemed inclined to avoid him, and had he desired to take advantage of his sinister reputation it is highly possible the management would have accepted his absence in lieu of payment. The leave-taking was characterized by a spirit of mutual relief. As no one offered to take his bags, he carried them himself and was well satisfied with the arrangement. Marion Kerby was waiting for him in the car.

"You know," she said. "I'm afraid you'll have to take me shopping. If I'm to go along with you I'll need a few things."

Mr. Topper protested strongly, and it was only after the threat of strange and fearful embarrassments swiftly to follow his refusal that he finally agreed to stop his car in front of the lavishly littered windows of a department store. Here at the girl's dictation he wrote out a list of purchases.

"Not that," he objected after the mention of a certain article.

"Absolutely," she insisted. "You gave my step-ins to your wife. Now you must buy me step-ins. I revel in them."

"Well, you won't revel with me," he said as he mopped his face and made for the store.

Marion Kerby kept close to his elbow and nudged him whenever she had decided on a purchase. In a faint voice Mr. Topper asked for the various articles and stood perspiring until his invisible companion had made her selection. The saleswoman eyed him suspiciously, but he refused to meet her eyes. Had it not been for a disturbing disposition on Marion Kerby's part to possess herself unlawfully of certain small articles by slipping them into his pockets, Mr. Topper would have found nothing radically wrong with her conduct. Whenever he endeavored to replace the things, she pinched his arm so viciously that he was forced to abandon his attempts to remain an honest man. After innumerable purchases he consulted the list, then mutteringly addressed his arm.

"We've bought all the things," he said. "Let's get out."

"All right," she whispered. "I'll go first."

As she did so she succeeded in attaching herself to a red cape and sport hat draped on a near-by model. The model swayed perilously as it was being bereft of its attire. Mr. Topper stepped back and regarded the scene with despairing eyes. Then he looked about for another exit, but could find none. The model, looking rather summery, settled back to rest, and the hat and cape proceeded jauntily down the aisle. At first no one save Mr. Topper noticed the unusual spectacle, but as the hat and cape continued on their triumphal progress the early morning shoppers began to fall back until finally the passage was lined with mute, inquiring faces.

Mr. Topper, vividly recalling his dream of the previous night, refused to follow the retreating garments. He mingled with the crowd and pretended to look surprised. The effect was that of a dangerously ill man.

"I would have bought the damn things," he kept thinking. "Why didn't she give me the chance?"

Finally, a floorwalker caught sight of the animated hat and cape. Perhaps he did not fully understand the situation, but he did seem to appreciate the fact that high-class merchandize was rapidly departing from the store in a new and altogether unauthorized manner. Whether he was an intrepid man or an extremely dull one can never be established. Perhaps he was both as so often is the case. The fact remains that this particular floorwalker uttered a cry of protest and darted in pursuit of the hat and cape. At the sound of his voice these articles stopped and the hat peered back inquiringly over the shoulder of the cape. It was a bizarre effect. A woman screamed and fainted, her parcels rolling over the floor. The hat and cape as if startled bounded down the aisle and, with a final flourish of red, disappeared through the door. But the floorwalker followed no farther. He had completely changed his mind. All resolution had departed from his body. The poised, almost near-sighted expression of the hat as it had looked back over the shoulder of the cape had overcome his sense of duty. He recalled the awful galloping motion of the runaway articles and pressed his hands to his eyes. Before he would involve himself any further in this strange business every stitch of clothing in the establishment could march away in ghastly single file.

For a few seconds after the disappearance of the hat and cape a solemn silence settled over all beholders, then this was shattered by the babble of many voices. Mr. Topper, suddenly realizing that his pockets were bulging with stolen goods and that his arms were filled with bundles, took advantage of the confusion and hurried to his automobile, driving off at full speed. He thought he heard voices, but he refused to look back.

"I would have bought those things," he muttered. "Why didn't you ask me?"

"But you had bought so many things already," Marion Kerby's voice replied. "I didn't want to put you to so much expense . . . and they were so attractive. I've always wanted something red."

"I'd rather be paupered than paralyzed," he retorted, eyeing the road ahead for some luckless automobilist to assault.

A promising candidate came in sight, but at the same moment a red cape swam before his eyes and out of the mist he heard Marion Kerby saying:

"Look at it, old dear. Wasn't it worth the trouble?"

"Put that thing away," he shouted. "I can't see to drive. You'll have us arrested and killed both."

The cape fluttered dejectedly to the floor of the car.

"From the way you fling it about," he grumbled, "you'd think I'd been born in a bull ring."

The cape quivered timidly.

"Stop doing that!" he exclaimed. "It makes me nervous."

Several miles of silence ensued, then Mr. Topper remarked moodily, "I wish I had."

"What?" asked Marion Kerby, unable to restrain her curiosity.

"Been born in a bull ring," he flung back. "I might never have lived to see this day."

At this the cape rose from the floor and sat down by Mr. Topper. Its shoulders were shaking gleefully. He regarded the garment with a jaundiced eye.

"Your sense of humor," he remarked, "would do justice to a hangman."

At this moment an automobile flashed by and Mr. Topper automatically transferred his insults to its driver, but Marion Kerby paid no attention to his mood. She was happily counting the bundles and searching through his pockets with nimble fingers.

CHAPTER XV

Such a Restful Place!

MID-AFTERNOON ON A BACK COUNTRY ROAD. SHADOWS from close-pressing trees cast scrolls across the dust. An automobile snakes gracefully past a farm wagon and disappears round a bend in the road. With a disturbed expression in his eyes, the driver of the wagon gazes after the vanished automobile. Presently he sighs deeply, and gathering up the reins in a preoccupied manner urges his team onward. Little profit, he decides, in idle speculation. What he has just seen he has not seen. That was the only satisfactory way out of it. In spite of this philosophic conclusion the man knew in his heart that the driving seat of the automobile had been unoccupied, and that the machine had performed a difficult passing apparently

unaided by any human guidance. He never spoke of
the incident to any of his friends. The mere thought of
it gave him a helpless feeling. But the memory lay
buried in his heart and to his dying day it remained a
mystifying and inexplicable fact, but nevertheless a
fact.

A few miles down the road the automobile had
halted in a clearing. From the automobile emerged a
red cape and hat accompanied by several bundles.
This singular group, after a moment's hesitation, disappeared into the woods. Presently from the automobile drifted a cloud of smoke. The smoke had in
turn drifted from Mr. Topper. He was smoking one of
his favorite cigars and feeling quite set up about it. In
spite of her momentary weakness in the department
store, Marion Kerby had succeeded in restoring him
to a high state of good humor. So much so, in fact, that
he had permitted her to drive the car. It had been a
secret relief to him. He had sat and rested his nerves.

"I know every road in the state," she had said.
"Let's get off the beaten track."

"By all means," he had answered. "As far off as
possible."

Now Mr. Topper sat smoking and comfortably considering life. He was far off the beaten track and
soothed by a feeling of security. After all, he mused,
Marion Kerby was not so hopeless as at times he had
considered her to be. Unscrupulous she was, to be
sure, and unreliable to a fault, but just the same she
was an amusing companion. What experiences he had
been through since he had first met her. What mad,
unbelievable adventures. And he, the staid Topper,
had played a part in them. Almost too prominent a
part, he thought, as he leaned back with a smile and
fondly eyed his cigar. Then, as if from the sting of a
wasp, he straightened up. Hadn't she told him the
previous night that her husband might return at any
moment? It was an alarming thought. Topper knew he
was blameless, but would George Kerby take a similar
view of the situation? Marion had deliberately wished
herself on an upright man. Any reasonable person
would quickly understand that. However, George

Kerby was not a reasonable person. Anything but that. Charming and generous he might be, but certainly not reasonable. Topper moved uneasily and glanced at the woods.

"Marion," he called in a subdued voice.

"Presently," came the cheerful reply. "Just a minute now."

It was slightly more than a minute before the hat and cape came out of the woods, but Mr. Topper felt well repaid for waiting. The looted garments were now splendidly filled by a sprightly young woman whose disturbing eyes impertinently mocked at Topper from beneath the brim of an exceedingly smart red hat. Mr. Topper, observing her with approval, had to admit that she had stolen with discrimination.

"You look great," he said with eloquent inadequacy.

"Do you think so?" she asked. "I'm just as pretty all over. Want to see? Everything's so new."

"Don't," exclaimed Mr. Topper. "You're always trying to upset me."

"Very well," she replied, getting into the car, "but just the same I am. I'm very pleased with me."

"Then don't be childish."

"I'd like to be," she sighed. "It was so lovely there in the woods."

"And you were the loveliest thing in them," Mr. Topper replied, in spite of himself.

For an answer she violently embraced him, smiting his cheek with a kiss. Topper, highly indignant, managed to free himself.

"Every time I say a kind word to you," he compained, "you practically assault me."

"But I receive so few kind words," she explained. "And I'm terribly impulsive."

"Then try to appreciate my position," admonished Mr. Topper, "and try to respect it. And while we are on the subject, when do you expect your husband back? Last night you said . . ."

"Oh, that was just to frighten you," she interrupted. "George won't be back for months, and even if he did return he'd never find us where we're going."

"Where's that?" asked Topper with interest.

"I'll show you presently."

"Not presently, but instantly," he urged. "Let's go there without delay. I long for peace and quiet."

Marion Kerby took the wheel and, after several hours of what seemed to Mr. Topper to be exceedingly obscure driving, they paused on the crest of a high hill before taking the dip into the valley below. Far across the intervening space, many green leagues away, Topper saw the setting sun sending its streams of colors across a field of deepening blue. The clouds seemed like castles with ramparts edged with gold. There was turmoil in the sky. Cohorts of silver and scarlet charged down the west and assaulted the castle clouds. And in the vast confusion of the sunset Mr. Topper saw, low to the horizon, dim lights drifting behind the trees. Both Topper and his companion watched this kaleidoscopic overthrow of nature with deep, thoughtful eyes, a little touched with the melancholy appreciation of those who look too long upon the sun at its setting. Topper moved a cramped leg and looked at the girl beside him.

"It's quite good," he remarked diffidently. "What do you think?"

"Don't ask me what I think," she replied. Then with a shrug of her shoulders, "I find the damn thing garish."

"It struck me, too, as being a trifle overdone."

She threw him a quick smile and pressed his hand. "Remember the last one we saw together?"

Topper made no reply, but looked unhappily at his shoes. He had a feeling inside of being quite lost. He attributed it to hunger, but strangely enough he was wishing that for once in his life he had fallen desperately and forgetfully in love. It was like trying to trace a vague perfume to its source. Once in the lobby of a hotel a woman had passed Mr. Topper's chair. After she had gone there remained behind a subtle, disturbing fragrance. Mr. Topper had failed to notice the woman, but he had become keenly aware of the perfume lingering in the air. It was floating round him now. Why had he not risen and followed the woman instead of sitting troubled by the faint breath of romance? Why had he always lost himself in the evening paper instead of looking over its edge for possible adventures? Had Mrs. Topper anything to do with it? Perhaps. He remembered that on this occasion he had been patiently waiting for her. Romance? No go, there. She had arrived with voluble dyspepsia and a secret craving for food. In propitiating one and appeasing the other, the desire for romance and adventure had collapsed in Mr. Topper's heart. Instead of following a haunting fragrance he had followed his wife through the tube, while listening to the trials of an unsuccessful shopping day.

With a start he came back to his surroundings and glanced down at the small brown hand resting lightly on his rather fleshy one. At his glance the hand was quickly withdrawn and Topper was surprised to see two spots of pink appear on Marion Kerby's cheeks. He had not believed it possible. Even now he was suspicious. She was probably plotting some crime.

"Don't look at me like that," she said.

"Like what?" Topper asked.

"Like a thwarted pup," she answered. "A pup bereft of milk. I never could stand hungry eyes."

"Are mine hungry?"

"Starved."

"Well, so am I. It's been a full day, but we've succeeded in remaining rather empty. When and where do we eat?"

"Do you see that lake down there?" she asked, pointing to the valley.

"I do now," he replied, "but I hadn't noticed it before. It looks so lost among the trees."

"That's just what it is," she answered. "Years ago that little lake strayed away from its mother, and ever since then these hills have been nursing it here in secret. And every year the mother lake sends the streams and rivers in search of her lost lakelet, but these hills, which are inclined to be barren, consider the foundling as theirs and jealously keep it locked away in the valley."

"Well," remarked Mr. Topper, after a short pause, "now that you've about rung the change on that theme, let's go down and take a look at this lost lake of yours. Perhaps there's some food to be found."

"No doubt there is, you prosaic beast," the girl replied as she started the machine. "There used to be a store at one end."

As the car descended the winding way the road grew deeper in shadows, and when they reached the border of the lake a dim film of daylight still lingered over its still surface as if reluctant to leave this quiet spot.

To Mr. Topper the lake seemed truly lost. And everything about the place partook of the same atmosphere. On its shores he could distinguish only a few cottages and even these had an abandoned look about them. He felt that they must have crept away from some populous summer colony and hidden themselves among the trees to rest. About halfway up the opposite hill a large stone house cut a breach in the trees. A few lights twinkled in the upper windows, these golden specks of life serving only to intensify the solitude of the scene. For the first time in his life Mr. Topper felt really secure from the world and all its works. In such a place as this Marion Kerby could do her worst without disturbing his peace of mind. It occurred to Mr. Topper that it would be a delightful sensation to strip himself naked and go running through the trees, to feel the night on his body and to meet the earth like a free, unabashed creature of the earth. This was a radical thought for Mr. Topper, and happily, some may feel, a passing one. It left him slightly sobered.

"Have you ever been here before?" he asked, sensing the precarious condition of his mind.

"Didn't I just tell you?" she answered. "I've been here lots of times. I used to come here to hide from George when he got on my nerves."

"God grant that we may be as successful this time," Mr. Topper breathed with unfeigned sincerity.

"Don't worry your head about him," she replied carelessly. "He's probably sound asleep in some low café at this very minute. We'll drive down to the other end in search of food and shelter."

"Is there some sort of an inn about?"

"No, but the cottages look deserted."

Mr. Topper did not entertain with enthusiasm the prospect of breaking into a deserted cottage, but as the only other alternative lay in sleeping in the automobile he held his peace.

At the end of the lake they found a small store from which they purchased provisions of a compressed nature. By the time they had completed their transactions under the suspicious eye of the storekeeper daylight had faded from the face of the lake. A world of stars looked down on them and showered the dark water with a spray of golden coins, which danced and sparkled whenever a breeze moved from the shore.

"We'll have to park the car on this side," Marion Kerby said in a low voice. "The road ends here. We can walk round to the cottages by the path."

They arranged the automobile for the night and Mr. Topper, taking a suit-case in either hand, followed his guide along a root-filled path. From time to time he tripped and cursed bitterly, but Marion Kerby urged him on to greater efforts with derisive words of encouragement. After passing two cottages steeped in shadows, she selected the third and more imposing one. Leaving Topper perspiring on the veranda with his luggage, she disappeared in the darkness. After what seemed to him an eternity of time he was startled to hear the door opening stealthily behind him.

"It's all jake," Marion whispered. "I found a reasonable window. Bring in the bags. This is a plush abode."

"It may be plush to you," he grumbled, stumbling in with the bags, "but to me it's far from homelike. We don't even know the owners."

"Would you like to meet them?" she asked from the darkness.

"Not at this minute," he admitted, dropping the bags to the floor. "Light up and let's see where we are."

With the lighting of a candle the house sprang into

terrifying reality to Mr. Topper. Every corner contained a shadow and every shadow contained a
possible danger. But Marion Kerby was delighted.
The house, after a swift investigation, proved to be in
a fair state of order. There were beds and they were
ready to receive occupants. Other equipment was
present. Most gratifying of all there was an oil stove
all ready to fulfill its destiny. These discoveries which,
to Marion Kerby, were occasions for congratulation
were, to Mr. Topper, sources of dismay. As Marion
flitted cheerfully round the place he edged towards
the door.

"Stop chirping like that!" he exclaimed at last. "It's
all clear to me. The owners have just gone out.
They'll be back at any moment. Let's go."

"You'd make a dangerous detective," she answered. "Doesn't your nose tell you that this place
hasn't been open since last summer? Look at this
glass. It's dusty. And the table. I could write your
name on it."

"Don't," said Mr. Topper. "Write yours. I require
no publicity."

"Come back here then and sit down," she replied.
"I'm going to air out the beds in our room."

Mr. Topper looked at her in blank astonishment.

"Do you mean to tell me," he finally managed to
get out, "that in spite of all the beds in this house
you're so depraved as to insist on sleeping with me?"

"I just thought it would be more fun."

"Fun," he repeated. "What has that to do with it?
It might be fun to live in a harem, but right-thinking
men don't do it. Fun fills the divorce courts and digs
untimely graves. Anyway, under the circumstances,
I don't feel funny."

"Why don't you get up on the table and preach
down at me?" she jeered. "Bring me back to the fold.
Point the way to salvation."

"You should know more about the hereafter than
I do," he remarked moodily.

She came over to him and placed her hands on his
shoulders. He stepped back and tried to avoid her
eyes.

"Now don't begin to coax me," he said. "I won't hear a word of it. It was bad enough before you materialized, but now it is utterly out of the question. Absolutely."

"Aw, give us a kiss," was all she said, and she took it.

Topper, though remarkably pleased, remained adamant, and after a certain amount of haggling they arrived at a compromise. They would occupy connecting rooms. Topper thought that that was compromising enough.

"You know," she explained to him, "it's better that I should sleep close by so that I can protect you in case somebody comes."

This last argument struck Mr. Topper with so much force that he was tempted to ask her to disregard his previous objections. His conventional training, however, overcame his natural timidity.

While Marion Kerby was preparing a supper of soup, beans and coffee he watched her with a mixture of admiration and dread. And when at last she placed the provender before him, dread faded away and only admiration remained. Truly she was a remarkable woman for one so loose. He thought of his wife and sighed. Then his thoughts reverted to Scollops. He wondered how life was treating his cat, and whether or not she still slept in his chair. While wondering he ate diligently with the appetite of a famished man. Food had never meant so much to Mr. Topper. Presently he halted and looked up from his plate.

"Do you like cats?" he asked.

Before his companion had time to answer Mr. Topper's jaw dropped, his face changed color, and with dilated eyes he gazed over her shoulder. For a moment she was too startled to complete her chewing. Then she rose from her chair and hurried to him.

"Are you choking?" she asked. "Can't you swallow?"

And with this she began to pound him on the back. Mr. Topper almost fell from his chair.

"I'm not choking," he gasped, "But I can't swallow. Oh, look!"

Marion was too alarmed to heed his words. She stopped thumping and began to tear at his shirt.

"I'll open your collar," she said, "and then you'll feel better."

At this Mr. Topper returned to speech.

"Hell, no!" he shouted. "Don't open my collar. Open a window instead. He's standing in the doorway right behind you."

In an instant the situation was clear to Marion Kerby. Slowly and with great dignity she turned and beheld a rough-looking individual standing exactly where Mr. Topper had said, in the doorway. In one hand he held a lantern, in the other an ugly-looking stick.

"Will you be good enough to tell me just what you are doing here?" she asked in a calm voice.

The man hesitated and looked at her with a surprised expression.

"Protecting the master's property," he replied. "He don't allow squatters here."

"Squatters," she replied in a puzzled voice. "Squatters? Now what exactly are squatters? Sounds like some sort of a pigeon, or perhaps a fish. Are squatters fish?"

"If yer don't understand what squatters is," said the man, "I'll change it to house breakers, trespassers, undesirable people, thieves, loafers——"

"It's quite clear," interrupted the girl. "Don't go on. Now tell me who is the master you referred to?"

"He's Mr. Wilbur," the man replied.

"And where is he now?"

"He's in Europe, that's where he is."

"How odd," she mused. "So is my husband."

"I'm her brother," put in Mr. Topper in consternation. "Her eldest brother. We're nice people and . . ."

The man glared at Mr. Topper and raised his stick threateningly. Mr. Topper sank back in his chair.

"Leave this to me," Marion whispered quickly, then advanced on the unwelcome visitor.

"For some unfortunate reason," she said, "I haven't taken a fancy to you. It might not be your fault. I hope it isn't, but the fact remains that now you must go. Take your little lantern and swagger stick and hop off. If not, God protect you."

"Quit yer bluffing," replied the man, "or I'll use this club on the both of yer."

Then a strange and terrible thing took place. The woman, facing the intruder, crumpled to the floor. Nothing remained of her save an inert bundle of clothing. Even Mr. Topper, as accustomed as he was to unexpected occurrences, sat horrified in his chair. The man looked down at the clothing and strove to collect his wits.

"She's fainted," he suggested, looking hopefully at Topper.

Mr. Topper began to laugh hysterically.

"What's that?" asked the man suddenly as his hat snapped down over his eyes. He raised his hands to his hat, then quickly transferred them to his stomach. As the stick fell to the floor it was seized by an invisible hand and brandished in the air. With great force and accuracy it descended on the now prominent region of his reverse exposure, causing him to snap erect. His face was a study in terror as he fell on his hands and knees and began to crawl to the door.

"Here's your lantern!" a voice cried. "Clear out quick!"

The voice was too much for the man. He staggered to his feet and without waiting for the lantern fled from the cottage; the lantern, following in close pursuit, danced crazily in the darkness. Mr. Topper could trace the retreat of the man by the crashing of the bushes and the cries that disturbed the night. Gradually these sounds subsided and silence settled down. Some minutes later the bundle of clothing began to stir. Mr. Topper saw a confused mass of feminine apparel arrange itself in the air and assume the outlines of a woman. He closed his eyes to blot out the sight and when he opened them again Marion Kerby was standing before him.

"What were you saying about cats?" she asked, seating herself on the table.

"I don't know," said Mr. Topper. "Was I saying anything about cats?"

"It doesn't matter," she replied. "That bird won't be back to-night. I couldn't get him to take his lantern so I was forced to throw it at him."

She slid over to the dejected Topper and, curving an arm round his shoulder, sat heavily on his lap. Too weak to protest, he allowed her to sip his coffee.

"I doubt if he ever comes back," she added reflectively.

"What do you mean?" asked Mr. Topper uneasily. "I hope you didn't kill him or maim him for life. Did you?"

"Not quite," she replied. "Almost though. He called us squatters. I don't mind about myself, but I can't bear to think of you as a squatter."

"I don't mind being called a squatter," said Mr. Topper thoughtfully, "but I couldn't stand that club of his. Every time I looked at the thing it gave me the shivers. There were knobs on it."

Marion Kerby jumped from his knees and squeezed his hand.

"Don't think of him any more," she said. "Let's go outside and contemplate the stars."

"I hope that's all we'll contemplate," replied Mr. Topper.

They sat on the steps of the veranda and Marion rested her head on Mr. Topper's knee. Once more he thought of Scollops. Then he looked down into the girl's eyes and saw that in them, too, there was an expression he could not fathom but on this occasion he was thrilled instead of being troubled.

"You know," she remarked, smiling up at him, "you're not my eldest brother. You're my first and only child."

"Well, from the way you're bringing me up," he replied, "you must be one of those Spartan mothers I read about in school."

"Sure I am," she answered. "I'll make a man of you yet."

"Then keep the door open between us," said Mr. Topper. "I'm feeling far from well. If I dream about clubs to-night I'm likely to die in my sleep."

He lit a cigar and looked down on the lake.

"Nice night," he suggested.

"Swell," she replied, snuggling closer to him. "I'll try a cigar, too."

CHAPTER XVI

Enter the Colonel and Mrs. Hart

A SHAFT OF HAZY SUNLIGHT SIFTING THROUGH MOIST green leaves found its way into Mr. Topper's room. After fingering the bedspread delicately it finally crept up to his strangely innocent-looking face, now lying unprotected beneath a nocturnal gathering of whiskers. Topper stirred fretfully and rolled over on his side. In his heart there was a fierce desire to remain oblivious of life, but somewhere within his subconsicious lurked a painful suspicion that all was not well with the world, or at least, that part of the world which he, Topper, personally occupied. He half opened his eyes and squinted at the room. Had there not been a man with an ugly club? Yes, there had been such a man. And had not Marion Kerby done violence to this person? The fact was not to be denied. Topper was clear about that.

"What a life," he thought to himself. "What a series of calamities. Every morning I wake up in a different place and under more depressing circumstances. It's like a curse."

Nevertheless, when he arose and stretched, he felt within himself a spirit of freedom and buoyancy that had never come to him during his more orderly régime. He liked the smell of the room. The forest had gathered close to the walls and drenched them with the fragrance of its fresh green life. And he liked the way the sunlight sprayed upon the matting. Matting was a pleasant sort of an arrangement. He enjoyed

the way it felt on his bare feet. It made him think of
swimming. Why it did he could not tell, but it did
and that was enough. Topper could swim quite well.
He was satisfied about his swimming. It was his only
accomplishment. Marion Kerby would be surprised
when she saw him in the water. His new bathing things
were in the suit-case in her room. Rather bearishly he
moved across the matting, examining unfamiliar objects and thinking half thoughts. One of these thoughts
was connected with Marion Kerby's room. It occurred
to him that it really was not her room, nor was this
one his. The rooms belonged to someone else. They
were being unlawfully occupied. Topper trod the matting no longer like an aimless bear. His step was more
like the stealthy tread of a criminal, a modest, unas-
suming criminal. He hurried to the open door between
the two rooms and thrust in a frightened face.

"Get up," he said. "We can't stay here forever. The
whole neighborhood will be down on us at any minute."

No answer came from the bed for the reason that
the bed was empty. As he regarded the tossed coverings an alarming suspicion chilled his heart.

"My God," he thought, "she's left me. At any other
time I'd let her go gladly, but not now. She got me into
this fix and she ought to get me out."

With a heroic display of modesty, considering his
overwrought condition, he flung on his bathrobe and
hurried outside. The object of his quest was not in
sight, but he found on the table a partially empty cup
of coffee. The pot on the stove was still warm.

"She's had coffee," he thought bitterly. "She would.
Then she left me without even a word—left me sleeping."

He went to the door and peered miserably out on
the sparkling face of the lake. The scene hurt his eyes.
How could the world look so happy when he felt so
sad? And how could he ever hope to escape in the full
light of day with a suit-case in either hand? He was
reluctant to face the day and was about to withdraw
from it when something resembling a song floated to
his ears. He recognized the voice and was filled with

relief. The song drifted mournfully to him from somewhere close at hand.

> "Oh, I was a daisy and highly adored,
> The boys said as much to my face.
> But now I'm a spirit and terribly bored
> With oodles and oodles of space."

Topper did not care for the words, nor was he impressed by the long-drawn-out plaintiveness of the
voice, but he was overjoyed to know that the singer
was approaching the cottage.

There was a thrusting sound in the foliage, and, after
a few muttered imprecations concerning a certain
blackberry bush, Marion Kerby, wild and disheveled,
appeared at the foot of the steps. Topper regarded
her with thankfulness, but not with approval. That he
could not do. In either hand she held a bottle and
under one arm there nestled another one. Altogether,
Topper decided, it was a convincing display of greed.
Her face was flushed and her eyes sparkled dangerously. She was obviously pleased with herself and expected Topper to be.

"See," she said, wiggling the bottles. "Look what I
brought back."

Topper looked and observed that one of the bottles,
the one under her arm, was not altogether full. It was
nearly half empty. This sorrowful fact did not add to
Topper's spirit of tolerance.

"What do you mean by drinking at this time of day?"
he demanded.

"No harm, old dear," she answered. "No harm."

"Have you no sense of decency?" he continued.

"None at all," she replied with unclouded cheerful-
ness. "Never had. You cornered the market at birth."

"Well, I'll tell you now it's far from decent to be in
your condition at this time of day," said Topper.

"My eye," she replied, leaping up the steps. "That's
simply a question of time. Whether you drink at dawn
or at dusk, you get fuzzy just the same. The earlier the
better, say I. Now, if you'd take a good stiff hooker of
this Scotch, I'll lay you odds you'll jolly soon forget

about being decent. You'll be as happy as a lark, a decent bird, I'm told."

"But I haven't even had breakfast," Topper protested.

"Nonsense!" she replied, with a magnificent sweep of her arm. "Look at the sunlight playing on the windstruck lake. Catch the breath of the morning drifting through the trees. See the young earth sending forth her, her—whatever they happen to be. Feel the world throbbing with new life and impulse. Get wise . . ."

"But I can't eat sunlight and young earth," complained Mr. Topper, rudely cutting in on her poetical outburst. "A cup of coffee and some scrambled eggs also have their decent points."

She looked thoughtfully at his troubled face.

"Take a drink and I'll get you some breakfast," she said. "This is good stuff. I stole it from Mr. Wilbur, our absent host. He has a cellar full."

She filled a glass and handed it to Topper. Feeling the need for courage, he gulped it down and looked startled. The effect was almost immediate. Like the young earth to which Marion Kerby had referred, his blood began to throb with new life and impulse. With a regal sweep of his bathrobe he threw himself down in a chair.

"Did you see our friend, the caretaker?" he asked.

"I did," she replied, splashing some eggs into a pan. "He's still on his feet, but somewhat unsteady. There's a bandage round his head. He limps."

Topper took another drink and placed himself at the table. "On with the eggs," he commanded. "Now that you've crippled him, I'll try to kill him."

Marion Kerby watched him with a kindling eye as he fell upon the eggs.

"That's right," she said. "Eat and acquire flesh. I'll drink and acquire merit, after which we'll both go swimming."

"Great stuff!" exclaimed Topper. "I'll swim clear cross the lake and back in my brand-new suit. It's in your room."

"Braggart," the girl replied. "I'm going in to dress."

"Just wait and see," said Topper, refilling the glasses. "Throw me out my rompers."

"Hand me in a drink," she called back, flinging his suit through the door. "I'm Eveish all over."

She thrust out a bare white arm and wiggled the fingers impatiently. Topper placed the glass in her hand, then, seized by a sudden impulse, bent over and kissed her smooth, cool arm. Marion gave a little gasp of amazement.

"If I wasn't afraid of spilling my drink," she said, "I'd come out and smash your face."

"You'd do nothing of the kind," announced Mr. Topper, straightening up and looking proud. "Nothing at all of the kind. I'll kiss you as much as I want."

He finished his drink and walked unevenly to his room. At the door he uttered a triumphant laugh, which ended ingloriously in a hiccough.

"Merciful heavens," came Marion Kerby's surprised voice. "What has come over our Cosmo? He's actually getting aggressive."

"Make no mistake," he shouted back, desperately weaving his legs into his trunks. "I'm the master in this house. From now on I rule."

Marion Kerby dashed into the room and Topper began to scream.

"This isn't fair," he protested. "Wait till I've gotten my shirt on."

Marion refused to wait. Like a white flash the slim figure darted around Topper, raining blow after blow on his well upholstered body. Fighting his way into his shirt, he attempted to defend himself, but his efforts were futile. She closed in on him and tickled his fat ribs. With a series of girlish squeals he sank panting to the floor, whereupon she danced on his stomach and uttered a cry of victory. Like a jovial porpoise Topper rolled from side to side, sweating profusely from too much Scotch and exertion.

"Who's the master of this house?" she demanded, digging a toe in his side.

"You are," he gasped. "Stop tickling me before you give me a stroke."

With a final kick she withdrew from combat and stood looking down at the vanquished male.

"Get up, you tub," she said. "From now on I rule. Get up and swim across the lake."

"You're a fiend in a one-piece bathing suit," Topper muttered in a husky voice. "Go get that bottle. I'm all in."

"Keep a civil tongue in your head," she warned as she hurried from the room.

When she returned with the bottle they sat down on the edge of the bed and eyed each other suspiciously. Topper gratefully swallowed his drink and sighed deeply. Then he reached over and clumsily patted his companion.

"You know," he announced rather thickly, "I haven't been so happy in years. Take me out and show me the lake. Something seems funny about my legs."

She threw an arm round his shoulder and together they left the room, their voices raised in song.

"My husband he did it. The devil would drive,
        The high-flying, low-lying soak.
    And that is the reason I'm no more alive,
        For he drove me smack into an oak."

"I can't get used to that word 'smack,' " said Mr. Topper. "Otherwise the song's good."

Throughout the uneven progress of the journey Topper was more helped than helpful. He had a decided tendency to a starboard list, which the girl bravely endeavored to offset. Once she failed and the great weight of Topper bore down on her with full force. For a moment there was a threshing of arms and legs emerging from a cluster of deep-seated grunts. Eventually she succeeded in extricating herself and Topper was helped to his feet.

"Don't trip me again," he panted. "It's not at all funny."

Marion felt her bruises and laughed sarcastically.

"Do you think it's my idea of a good time to be crushed to earth by a hulk like you?" she asked.

"Then why didn't you dematerialize?"

"Because you'd have broken every bone in your gross body," she answered with heat.

"Hadn't thought of that," Topper apologized. "Very much obliged."

"Don't mention it," she replied. "What's a little fall between friends? Here we are at the landing. It's your first move."

Topper swayed dangerously on the edge of the landing, then with surprising agility rose in the air and disappeared neatly into the water. As soon as he reappeared he stroked out with a tremendous show of purpose for the opposite shore, about a quarter of a mile away. As the space grew wider between them, Marion Kerby watched him at first with anxiety and then with admiration. His arms flayed the water rhythmically and a trail of foam followed his churning feet. Topper was swimming as if possessed. Everything was in his favor. He was unable to fall and too fat to sink. When Marion had eased her mind as to his ability to keep above water, she arched her back in a businesslike dive of her own. Like a water sprite she played around the landing, not troubling so much about swimming as creating a great confusion. By the time that the aquatic Topper had achieved the other side she had exhausted the possibilities of the lake. Like a fretful child she stood on the landing and stamped for Topper to come home. The keen morning air was not the warmest of blankets. She raised her voice in a long cry.

"Come on over," she shouted. "I'm going back."

Upon the reception of this message Topper placed an admonishing finger to his lips and with his other hand swept the surrounding hills. He was partially sober now and wholly fearful.

"Why does she have to arouse the neighborhood?" he muttered as he watched her dancing form.

Ceasing from this activity, she threw her head back and, thrusting her thumb into her mouth, gave an eloquent but vulgar pantomime of drinking. Then she turned and ran up the path, her white legs flashing in the sunlight. The effect was registered on Topper. He plunged back in the lake and put forth his best efforts.

"She has no conception of honor," he thought gloomily as he wallowed along. "She'd cheerfully drink while I was drowning."

A little surprise in the form of a tall, distinguished-looking gentleman was waiting for Topper when he reached the landing. Upon seeing this stranger, Topper's first impulse was to sink forever beneath the protecting surface of the lake, but there was still enough Scotch in his veins to give him the semblance of courage.

"Good morning," said the distinguished-looking gentleman in a suspiciously friendly voice. "You seem to be enjoying yourself."

"I am," replied Topper. "I deserve to."

"I'll not dispute that," said the man on the landing, "but I doubt if you could prove it."

"My own enjoyment is proof enough," Topper answered.

"And how do you arrive at that conclusion?" asked the other.

"I've already arrived," said Topper.

"That I see, but how I don't," the distinguished-looking gentleman pursued.

"By the simple process of reason," Mr. Topper explained as he laboriously trod water. "Any creature, man or beast, who has the capacity and desire to enjoy life deserves that enjoyment."

"You preach hedonism," replied the other, briefly.

"Whatever that means I doubt it," said Mr. Topper, "but whether it is or isn't, I'm not going to drown myself to discuss the point further."

"And that's quite sensible," the gentleman answered. "Come out and I'll give you a lift."

Stooping over, he firmly seized Mr. Topper's extended hand and helped him out of the water, after which he continued holding the hand, shaking it cordially the while. Topper feared he was captured.

"Delighted to meet you," said the distinguished-looking gentleman, beaming down on Topper. "I greatly admired your skill in the water."

"Thanks," replied Topper, weakly, "but before we go any further let's settle one point. You are not by any chance remotely connected with the law, are you?"

"I am afraid not," said the stranger.

"I'm glad not," declared Topper.

"As a matter of fact," the other continued, "I've devoted most of my life to breaking the law. I have been a soldier, a legalized and official killer, a person beyond the law."

Topper drew a sigh of relief and rose to his feet. For some reason he had taken rather a fancy to the distinguished-looking gentleman. It occurred to him that he had not spoken to a man for several days. He had been too long in feminine company. He would cultivate this stranger.

"If you are beyond the law," said Topper, "you'd probably not balk at a glass of Scotch."

"I'd do more than balk," the gentleman answered. "I'd actually lie down to it."

"Then come along with me," Topper said, turning up the path.

"One moment," the man called. "I happen to have a wife about somewhere. Would you balk at her?"

"By no means," answered Topper. "Although convention prevents me from going to the same extremes as you, I should be delighted to meet her."

"The opportunity is at hand," replied the gentleman.

Topper looked up the path and saw a tall, fair-haired woman approaching. There was something engagingly rakish in her bearing. He placed her age as a good-humored thirty-five. She was carrying some early flowers in her hand and puffing a cigarette.

"My dear," called the man, "this gentleman has been so good as to ask us to share his Scotch."

My dear dropped her flowers and flooded Mr. Topper with a delighted smile.

"He is heaven-sent," she exclaimed in a rich voice. "Let's hurry before he drops dead or changes his mind. Watch the roots. He might trip and lose his memory."

"Truly," thought Mr. Topper, as he led them up the path, "this is a frankly thirsty pair."

The gentleman began to whistle and call the name of Oscar. Topper looked back in surprise, but seeing no new arrival, ascribed the gentleman's conduct to a spirit of fun caused by the prospect of a drink.

On arriving at the cottage Topper hurried up the steps and looked inside. Marion, still in her bathing suit, was sitting at the table with a glass in her hand. She was smoking one of Topper's best cigars.

"I'm bringing some friends," he announced under his breath. "Are you sober enough to receive them?"

"Trot 'em in," she replied brightly. "But are you sure they're friends?"

"Positive," said Topper. "Good sports."

Marion went to the door and greeted the pair.

"I am delighted," she said sweetly, "to meet any friends of my husband. Come right in."

The gentleman thoughtfully removed the glass from her hand and, bending low, ceremoniously kissed it, after which he waved to his wife.

"We are Colonel and Mrs. Scott," he said. "And I am sure we are all happily met. Lie down, Oscar."

"That's a joke of his," whispered Topper.

Marion laughed agreeably and took Mrs. Scott's hand.

"Why, you're so beautiful, my dear," she said, "that I can't keep my eyes off you. Come in and give me a cigarette. I'm tired of my husband's cigars. Cosmo, do the honors."

She took the glass from the reluctant Colonel and led the way indoors.

"And you," said the Colonel, "look like a creature from another world—the spirit of the lake, the priestess of the woods."

Marion threw him a narrow glance, then bowed gravely.

"Sit down, Arthur," said Mrs. Scott in a calm voice. "You'll get your drink anyway."

"My darling," exclaimed the Colonel, "what a cynical remark. Down, Oscar."

Both Topper and Marion laughed politely, thinking that this was expected of them. Then Topper distributed the drinks and the party sat down at the table.

"This seems," announced the Colonel judiciously,

after he had sampled the Scotch several times, "this seems to be prime whiskey. Of the best."

Topper, who as a result of his long swim and liberal hospitality had been showing a decided disposition to slumber, opened his eyes at this remark and squinted at the Colonel.

"It seems to me," he said unpleasantly, "that you do a devil of a lot of seeming."

"I do," agreed the Colonel with winning affability. "Because things are not always as they seem."

For a few moments Topper concentrated on this reply. To him it was fraught with meaning. It covered his whole life.

"You're right, Colonel," he said at last. "You're dead right there. To you I seem to be a sleepy man in a bathing suit, whereas I'm a fat banker running away from his wife."

The Colonel elevated one eyebrow just sufficiently to betray surprise.

"Then the present arrangement, I take it, is not permanent," he suggested with a delicate inflection.

"Neither permanent nor tangible," Topper answered, solicitously filling his own glass.

"I see," replied the Colonel thoughtfully, showing equal solicitude for himself. "Then, indeed, we are happily met as I have already remarked. Neither is our relationship of a lasting nature. Mrs. Hart and myself are just visiting each other. Regards!"

Slightly scandalized in spite of the liberalizing influence of the Scotch, Topper mechanically raised his glass.

"Regards," he said absently. "Happily met."

"Isn't it too funny for words," exclaimed the newly discovered Mrs. Hart, leaning over to Marion Kerby. "Give that man a few drinks and he becomes as frank as a fool. I never do."

"I'm sure I don't know what's happened to Cosmo," Marion replied. "Usually he's the world's worst hypocrite."

"Not at all, my love," he protested. "Usually I'm the world's best hypocrite—and that in spite of you."

"Down, Oscar!" the Colonel irritably interrupted. "Damn it, go to sleep."

At this point Topper sprawled back in his chair and laughed uproariously, while the Colonel watched him in dignified silence.

"Tell me," asked the Colonel, when Topper had subsided, "why do you always laugh when I call my dog?"

Topper wiped his eyes and looked admiringly at the Colonel.

"You're a scream, Colonel," he said. "And you say the funniest things. Why I thought you wanted me to laugh. You haven't any dog."

"But I have a little dog," declared the Colonel. "Want to see him?"

"Don't be silly, Arthur," interposed Mrs. Hart.

"Nonsense," said the Colonel. "I'll show him my little dog. Come here, Oscar. Do your stuff."

Topper glanced down and saw a vague stirring in the atmosphere around the Colonel's feet. Then gradually the rump of a small, shaggy dog appeared. Its tail was wagging excitedly.

"That's the boy!" cried the Colonel. "Keep it up, Oscar. Make a whole dog for the gentleman."

A few more inches of dog appeared, but evidently Oscar had exhausted his talents. The tail continued to wag as if asking to be excused from further endeavors.

Topper rose unsteadily from his chair.

"Please, please, Colonel," he pleaded, "don't make him do any more. He's done enough already. Ask him to go away."

"Very well," agreed the Colonel reluctantly, "but he can do much better than that. Sit down, Oscar, like a good chap."

Apparently forgetting the condition he was in, Oscar, or rather the rear end of him, settled to rest. The tail gave a final wag, then came to repose on the floor.

"I feel in need of a little fresh air," Topper remarked in a strained voice. "This has been a very unusual occurence."

He turned to the door, then took a step back. Three

large men were crowding in it, and in the background stood the caretaker.

"We're surrounded!" Topper exclaimed, turning back to the table.

But Topper found no comfort there. The table was empty.

"God," said one of the men, "they're all gone but him."

"He's enough," replied the caretaker. "Go in and drag him out."

The men advanced and Topper automatically retreated.

"And when you get him," continued the caretaker, "give him a few for me."

This sent Topper shivering to the wall. It was at this stage in the proceedings that the command, "Sic 'em, Oscar!" rang through the room. Immediately a low growl was heard and Oscar's hind quarters became involved with the legs of the bewildered attackers. Thus began the Battle of the Lake, one of the few decisive engagements on record and one which Mr. Topper did not linger to witness.

Out of the din and confusion that filled the room Topper heard Marion's voice shouting, "Break for the car, old thing. We'll bring the luggage along."

Topper did not wait for further bidding. Stepping on the face of a prostrate man, he fought his way to the door.

"Don't forget my trousers," he called back. "They're on the chair in my room."

"Hell, no," grunted the Colonel. "Run for it, man."

Topper dodged past the crippled caretaker with the agility of a fawn and darted down the steps. As he raced along the lake path cries of anguish followed his flying feet.

"I don't hold with this at all," he thought to himself as he sped over the roots. "Is my life to be one mad pursuit, all summer long?"

As he rounded the bend two suit-cases flashed past him at a dizzy speed and these in turn were followed by a carefully poised bottle and a bundle of Marion's clothing.

"Speed, O lout," a voice panted, and Topper redoubled his efforts.

The rear was brought up by Topper's trousers, snapping in the wind and Oscar following after, his rump low to the ground and his claws kicking up dust.

Few persons have ever lived to witness such a remarkable sight—Topper and half a dog chasing a pair of runaway trousers, not to mention a flying bottle and a couple of bounding suit-cases. Even at the moment Topper was impressed by the novelty of the situation.

Like a rallying standard in a headlong retreat, Topper's trousers danced in the morning breeze. And Topper followed his trousers with his last spark of energy. Far behind him he heard shouting voices, but he kept his eyes to the front and a trifle raised. He could not bring himself to look at the contortions of Oscar. The impatient honking of a horn urged him onward, and with a final burst of speed he reached the car and flung himself into the front seat. Oscar was sitting beside him, his invisible section panting audibly. The automobile was already in motion, hurtling down a branch road that led through the valley. Mr. Topper collected himself and moved a little away from Oscar, whose hind leg was busily engaged in dislodging an unseen flea.

"Well, Topper," came Marion Kerby's calm voice, "we got you out of that fix."

"You got me into it, too," replied Topper. "Why didn't you tell me they were all spooks?"

"Didn't know it myself," she answered, as the car lurched round a bend.

"I suspected something all the time," said the Colonel, "but I wasn't sure of Topper."

"Yes," put in Mrs. Hart. "What's the matter with him? Isn't he a low-plane?"

"No," replied Marion. "He's solid through and through."

"How very, very interesting," continued Mrs. Hart, poking an inquiring finger into Topper's shoulder.

"Make her stop," said Topper to Marion.

"Stop tickling my boy friend," she called back. "He's so bashful."

"Here, Topper," said the Colonel, passing the bottle forward, "take a drink, my buck. You need it."

Like a greedy baby Topper closed his fingers round the bottle and brought it to his lips. It was difficult drinking, what with the speed of the car and the condition of the road, but Topper refused to remove the bottle until he was convinced that he felt better.

"Don't forget the driver," said Marion Kerby.

"And don't forget that we are still your guests," Mrs. Hart suggested sweetly.

"That's the last bottle," said the Colonel. "We'll have to do something about it."

"Well, you go ahead and do it," replied Topper. "I've done enough for one day."

"Trust me," agreed the Colonel. "I never fail. Stop at the next town and I'll visit a few of the best houses, guided by my unerring instinct."

"In the meantime do you want your dog?" Topper asked. "I'm afraid he's crowded up here."

"Not at all," the Colonel answered. "Don't worry about Oscar. He loves the front seat."

Topper closed his eyes and let the rushing wind cool his face.

"There are three of them now," he thought, as he clung to the side of the car. "Three spirits and half a dog. I'm as good as done for already."

"Colonel," he called, continuing aloud, "give me another drink. I'll have to keep myself numb until I've gotten used to the situation."

"Eat, drink and be merry!" cried the Colonel, "for tomorrow . . ."

"Don't finish it," interrupted Mr. Topper, hastily reaching for the Scotch. "I am intimate enough with death as it is."

"I won't," agreed the Colonel, "if you don't finish that Scotch."

Topper did his best.

CHAPTER XVII

The Colonel Orders Dinner

IN THE COOL OF THE EVENING FOUR FLUSHED FACES peered from Mr. Topper's automobile at a rain-washed sign bearing the legend: "The Sleeping Fox." After a whispered conversation within the machine, the four flushed faces once more emerged. Topper now was completely clad and his companions had neatly materialized. To all outward appearances they gave the impression of being four quite normal persons bent on an evening's pleasure.

"With our thirst and Topper's money we should do very nicely here," remarked the Colonel, casting an anticipatory eye at the road-house.

"Don't frighten him before we get him inside," Mrs. Hart said warningly. "This looks to me like a lovely layout."

"Fear is my constant companion," replied Topper. "Don't consider me."

He was standing in need of a little judicious propping and the women were furtively assisting him. They were endeavoring to give the appearance of two ladies being escorted to dinner by a prosperous and dignified gentleman. In carrying out the deception Topper was of little value. With the most casual regard for dignity he ambled up the path.

"You women are so good to me," he murmured, and, as if overcome by his effort, sank heavily back in the supporting arms.

"For the love of Pete, stand up," Marion tragically whispered. "Remember, everything depends on you."

"I know it does," he gloated. "I know damn well it does. And you remember this, from now on I rule. No more foot-racing, no more queer dogs, no more disorderly parties. Remember all those things."

"Of course we will," the Colonel hastened to reply in a mollifying voice. "Didn't we throw Oscar away half a mile down the road?"

"Half a mile is a short distance to throw that dog," observed Mr. Topper.

"I know," continued the Colonel, "but it showed that our spirits were in the right place."

"Don't mention spirits to me," Topper retorted. "The very word is revolting. And furthermore you're not in the right place. If you were you'd be far, far away."

"Ah, Topper, how cruel you are to us all," Mrs. Hart protested. "I'm sure you don't mean that."

He looked scornfully at the women, then plunged free from their grasp.

"Stand back, the pair of you," he commanded, "and I'll show you how a gentleman takes his ease at an inn. I am weary of your arms."

He squared his shoulders belligerently and with heavy dignity began to mount the steps. As if he were performing an acrobatic sensation his companions clustered watchfully round him, ready to spring to action at the slightest show of weakness. An immaculately clad individual, appearing in the door of the road-house, stopped with surprise on seeing Mr. Topper, then hastened forward with a smile of welcome.

"Why, Mr. Topper," he said. "This is an unexpected pleasure. How are things at the club?"

At the mention of the word club, Mr. Topper swayed perceptibly on his feet.

"Club," he repeated thoughtfully. "Club. Why is it I don't like that word? Ah, yes, I remember, Williams. I have just recently escaped from the most terrifying of clubs."

"And Mrs. Topper?" asked Williams, tactfully changing the subject.

"And Mrs. Topper, too," replied Topper. "I've just escaped from her."

As if cheered by this reflection, he turned his back on the astonished Williams and beckoned to his com-

panions, who were hovering like hopeful orphans at
the head of the steps.

"It's all right," he assured them. "Williams is an
old friend. Knew him when I was a respectable member of the country club. He was our steward then.
First-class steward."

More for support than friendship he turned to Williams and extended his hand.

"Don't mind my friends," he continued. "They're
thoroughly low. And remember this, Williams: silence
is crisp and green. Here's a little silence now."

Williams, who had hitherto considered Topper as
being rather a painfully proper man, was both surprised and delighted at this lighter side of his
character. He deftly pocketed the money and with a
murmured expression of gratitude ushered the party
to a table where he spoke impressively to the waiter.

"Hear what he said," gloated Topper. "He told the
waiter to bring us anything we wanted. That's because
I'm along."

"Then tell him to bring us some cocktails and we'll
be even more impressed," Marion remarked.

"I'll boost it one," put in Mrs. Hart.

"And I'll double it," said the Colonel promptly.

"Bring them double cocktails," Mr. Topper explained to the waiter. "And bring me one, too."

"Any particular brand, sir?"

"Dry Martinis are more business-like," the Colonel
suggested. "It would be wiser to stick to them."

When the waiter had departed the Colonel set himself the task of planning the dinner, and in this he
displayed such a lack of self-control that finally Mr.
Topper felt called upon to interrupt.

"Don't look upon this as a barbecue, Colonel," he
remarked. "Regard it rather in the light of a quiet
little dinner. Don't stint yourself, but at the same time
don't stuff. Perhaps you once saw service in a famine
district. There is no danger here."

Marion Kerby turned on Topper with venomously
flashing eyes.

"Are you trying to humiliate me in front of my
friends?" she demanded.

"Not at all," replied Mr. Topper. "I was merely trying to introduce a little reason into this sordid discussion of food. It's not humanly possible to consume at one sitting all of the things he's planning to order."

"You forget that we're not human," Marion replied briefly. Then, turning to the Colonel, she continued with a sweet smile, "Go ahead, Colonel. Order the whole damned card. Don't mind him.". .

"Let's see," said the Colonel blandly, as if the interruption had never occurred. "Where were we now? Oh, yes, here we are. We'd gotten down to the fowl."

"The fowl," breathed Mrs. Hart, clasping her hands in delight. "I'm a perfect demon with a duck."

"Well," remarked Mr. Topper, with weary resignation, "you're the most material-minded spirits that ever returned to earth to drive a mortal mad."

"Why, the more irregularly I live the more regular I feel," said Mrs. Hart, taking Topper's hand. "Aren't you that way?"

"I am not," he answered shortly, withdrawing his hand from the table.

"The cocktails are among us," Marion announced as the waiter arranged the glasses. "Cheer up, everybody. I propose a toast to Topper, our reluctant and respectable host."

She rose from the table and raised her glass.

"Here's to Topper," she said. "A good sport in spite of himself. I know him by the back."

"That's about the only way anybody knows me now," observed Topper. "I'm always running."

"You poor old dear," she said, and, bending over, quickly kissed him. Topper grew red in the face and looked guiltily about him.

"The last shred is gone," he remarked. "Nothing remains but blackmail—blackmail, divorce and disgrace."

He tossed off his cocktail at a gulp and gazed solemnly at his companions.

"From now on," he announced, "I cast decency to the winds. Let's strip ourselves naked and run around screaming."

"Hear! Hear!" cried the Colonel. "That was spoken like a man. Waiter, another flock."

And another flock was brought. Nor was it the last flock. Nor even the next to last. Great execution was done that night at the inn, prodigious eating and lavish drinking, the Colonel leading the way by example and encouragement. Topper danced with Marion until his collar became a rag and his feet two nests of blisters. When finally, through a combination of complications, he was forced to retain his seat at the table, he lived happily in the memory of his dizzy flights through space. Marion Kerby sat close to him, whispering surprisingly pleasant words in his ear, and Topper, being in too expansive a mood to be suspicious, sweated in his seventh heaven.

This state of things was suddenly demolished by an unexpected arrival. The Colonel and Mrs. Hart were engaged in a highly enterprising type of dance when the unexpected arrival occurred. And the unexpected arrival was none less than Oscar, or at least that portion of Oscar which he had chosen to show to the world. Topper was the first to see that portion, and at its appearance his happiness vanished. Oscar dragged himself wearily through the door of the inn, displayed an undecided rump to the assembled guests, then set off patiently to follow his master's exuberant heels.

Unaware of this singular attachment, the Colonel continued to dance with the blissful Mrs. Hart. And even the other dancers appeared to take no notice. It was at that stage of the evening when one would rather not see such things. Without a shadow of doubt there were many diners and dancers who really did see Oscar in his unfinished condition, but those who did see him refused to report the fact, fearing that it might be a serious reflection on their own sobriety. So Oscar followed the Colonel until the Colonel passed Topper's chair. Here his gyrations were interrupted by Topper's hand on his sleeve.

"Oscar's back," whispered Topper. "For God's sake do something about it. I knew you hadn't thrown him far enough away."

"But, my dear man," the Colonel expostulated, "there's a limit to my strength. I can't chuck him back into the fourth dimension the way he insists on going about."

"Then sit down," said Topper, "and get him under the table. Some of these people might throw a fit. I'm sober myself already."

"If they don't like my dog," fumed the Colonel, "they can throw as many fits as they want."

"It's not that they don't like your dog," explained Topper, "it's merely that they don't understand your dog. Oscar to them is not quite clear. Please get him out of sight."

"I'll agree with you there," replied the Colonel, seating himself at the table. "Oscar is no ordinary brand of dog. There's more to him than greets the eye."

Oscar crawled under the table and Mr. Topper drew in his feet.

"That's just what I'm worrying about," he remarked. "Does the invisible part of him bite? If it does it is sure to bite me."

"Have no fear about Oscar," said the Colonel. "He never harbors a grudge. He was kicked around too much in life for that."

"I'm sorry," declared Mr. Topper, sincerely. "Perhaps he's hungry now. I'll give him this bone to gnaw on."

He held a bone under the table and it was instantly snapped from his hand.

"He is hungry," Topper continued, quickly withdrawing his hand. "Very hungry. Listen to that."

The bone was rattling on the floor and from beneath the table came the busy sound of crunching. The waiter, who had just arrived with coffee and ices, on hearing this small commotion, raised the tablecloth and peered down at the massed feet in the center of which lay Oscar engaged in appeasing his hunger. The waiter dropped the tablecloth and leaned down to Mr. Topper.

"Don't tell the ladies," he whispered, "but the funniest thing is going on under your table. Half of a dog is messing around with the leg of a duck, so help me God."

Topper glanced under the table, then looked stonily at the waiter.

"You might be right," he said, "but I don't see it. One of the ladies has dropped her fur piece and I myself dropped that duck leg. Bring the check and say nothing more about it. No one will know you've been drinking."

"Sorry," apologized the waiter. "I hadn't realized it myself, but the Colonel kept on insisting."

"Then don't abuse his liberality," advised Topper. "Hurry with the check."

"Yes," put in Marion Kerby, "hurry with the check. This place begins to irk me. I'm dying to take a stroll."

The waiter hastened away and Topper leaned over to Marion.

"Collect that dog," he told her, "and keep him under your cape until we get out of here."

"Only for you," she replied, "would I do such a thing."

She reached down and after a little scuffling succeeded in gathering up Oscar. For a moment his tail waved frantically above the edge of the table, then flashed from view beneath Marion's cape, which from time to time thereafter became suddenly convulsed with life. The waiter arrived with the check and in his preoccupation handed it to the Colonel, who, upon scanning the total, promptly disappeared. It was like the flashing out of a light.

"There isn't that much money in the world," floated through the air.

Only the check remained, still poised above the table. It was trembling slightly as if the invisible holder were shaken by an attack of nerves.

"The shock was too much for him," whispered Mrs. Hart. "I've seen it happen before."

"He's gone," said the waiter, looking inquiringly at Mr. Topper. "He's not here any more."

"Of course not," laughed Mr. Topper. "He never was. Pass that check to me."

Before the waiter could reach it the check moved

across the table to Mr. Topper's outstretched hand.

"You're welcome to it," a voice murmured.

The waiter moved away from the Colonel's empty chair and stood close to Mr. Topper.

"Mr. Topper," he pleaded, "please don't say he wasn't here. I could never bear that. Why his cup is still half full of coffee and there's his smoldering cigarette."

In the face of this undeniable evidence of the Colonel's recent presence, Mr. Topper was forced to alter his bantering tactics. He opened his wallet and selected several colorful bills.

"Take this money away," he said, "and stop asking questions. Let us admit that the Colonel was here. What of it? As you accurately pointed out, he isn't here any more. He slipped away somewhere as all of us must do at times. If I were in your place I wouldn't press the investigation any further."

"I certainly wouldn't," remarked Mrs. Hart. "It has gone far enough."

"I'm sorry," replied the waiter, "and I'm very much obliged. As you say, Mr. Topper, he must have just slipped away in a hurry like."

Marion Kerby burst out laughing and patted the waiter on his back.

"That's it," she said. "That's exactly it. He slipped away in a hurry like, or, to put it differently, with all possible speed."

The waiter smiled nervously and bowed, then emulated the Colonel's example to the best of his ability. Mr. Topper, despite his eagerness, was forced to be more leisurely in his retreat. With earnest but wavering dignity, he followed the women from the room. Oscar lent distinction to their departure. Every time he kicked his legs Marion Kerby suddenly bulged out in the back in a most grotesque manner, an occurrence which caused Mrs. Hart to burst forth into hysterical laughter to the greater humiliation of Mr. Topper. Once safely outside in the darkness he mopped his face and gave vent to his feelings.

"After eating and drinking his fill," he complained,

"he plays a trick like that. And he calls himself a soldier."

"A Colonel, no less," said Marion Kerby, "and he allows me to protect this unlettered hound."

She dropped Oscar to the road and readjusted her cape.

"He couldn't help it," Mrs. Hart defended. "The check was too much for him. I'm sure he didn't mean to do it. At the size of the figures he lost control, and anyway, think how much he drank."

"I never saw a man do better," admitted Marion, "and for that reason I forgive him. We all plays tricks in our cups."

Without paying attention to their direction they wandered down the wooded road until they came to an open field, a meadow slanting off in the darkness. In the distance, above the trees, an old battered moon was sailing low in the sky. The night was quiet and peaceful around them, filled with secret rustlings and a thousand fragrant smells. The Sleeping Fox seemed miles away, its brilliance vanished and its orchestra stilled. Without knowing it they were soothed and subdued by the quiet beauty of their surroundings. And out of the quiet beauty of their surroundings a singing voice, deep and undaunted, came storming towards them down the road.

"It's the Colonel," exclaimed Mrs. Hart. "He has a splendid voice. Listen!"

Marion and Topper listened without enthusiasm to the following chanty:

"Oh, dark and stormy was the night
    When last I left my Meg.
She'd a government band around each hand
    And another one round each leg.

"Yo ho, my boys, yo ho,
    And a-sailing we shall go.
We'll said no more on England's shore—"

"A splendid voice," remarked Mr. Topper, sarcastically interrupting the booming flow of the old sea song. "Caruso must be fairly spinning in his grave."

"What's this about Caruso?" asked the Colonel, looming large in the darkness. "Why, I taught him his do, re, mi's."

"So you are once more with us," said Marion Kerby. "What was your hurry to go?"

"Couldn't help it," explained the Colonel. "The size of the check destroyed my resistance. There were no such figures in my days. But I've brought along gifts as a show of atonement."

He slipped his hands into his pockets and produced two large bottles.

"In view of the size of the check," he continued, "I took the liberty to remove these from the pantry. I have still another."

The gifts of atonement proved more than acceptable and the Colonel was reinstated with full honors and privileges. With a bottle circulating freely between them they wandered off into the meadow until wandering no longer suited their mood. Mr. Topper insisted on demonstrating the fact that he was rapidly becoming a spirit himself. With the utmost conviction he would throw himself into the air, but being a little heavier than that element he invariably returned with great speed to the earth, from which his companions would lift him and once more set him in motion. It was a night of magnificent distances and headlong enterprise. They sang and danced and made patriotic speeches and pursued each other across the meadows to the intense delight of the gamboling flanks of Oscar. To Topper, it was like a dream, one in which he was liberated and given tremendous strength. His steps seemed as light as feathers and as long as leagues. The field was filled with dancing forms that swirled in wild abandon until they left the earth and went circling around the moon. And through the darkness he heard shouting voices as the party searched for one another. The Scotch with which the Colonel plied them became transmuted in their brains into the glory of the night. Nature became intensely beautiful and their bodies madly alive. It was such a night as comes seldom to a man and which fortunately for his peace of mind is seldom remembered after it has gone. Topper remembered but little when he awoke the following morning on the bank of a slow-moving river. Oscar's bushy tail was draped across his chest, and that was all that remained of Oscar. He had lost ground during the exhausting activities of the night. Topper slid cautiously from under the tail and looked down into the clear water of the river. His body was feverish and his head an aching weight which he balanced with the greatest difficulty. Several yards away Marion Kerby was sleeping sweetly in Mrs. Hart's lap. The Colonel, deep in slumber, was sitting erect as if he had forgotten to lie down. Topper turned his eyes away from his companions and looked longingly at the river. His body craved to feel the soothing flow of its cool waters. Unable to stand the temptation any longer he crept away into a clump of bushes and divested himself of his outer garments. With a last timid look at his sleeping friends he slid down the bank and insinuated himself into the water, his hot blood leaping with gratitude as the river closed around him. But Topper was not alone. A flaunting tail had followed him to his tryst. Round and round it circled, splitting the water neatly like the periscope of a submarine. Topper was hardly pleased with the presence of Oscar, but he was enjoying the river too thoroughly to leave it undisturbed to the dog. His enjoyment was interrupted by a greeting from the bank.

"Good morning," the Colonel called to him. "Will you join me in a drink?"

"That's all I ever seem to be doing," replied Topper, swimming over to the Colonel. "But just for once I will. After this I'm going to swear off for a while."

The Colonel passed down the bottle and Topper refreshed himself.

"My dog seems to have grown less," observed the Colonel, watching the sportive tail. "I'll have to do some hard work on him to-day."

"If you make him disappear altogether you'd be doing me a favor," said Mr. Topper, holding up the bottle.

"The creative spirit is too strong in me for that," replied the Colonel. "I must make him a whole dog or bust."

His head was withdrawn from the bank and in a few minutes he reappeared accompanied by Mrs. Hart and Marion Kerby, very sketchily attired in improvised bathing suits. With little screams of delight they plunged into the river and swam friskily round the dismayed Topper, who, submerged up to his chin, was modestly treading water.

"An auspicious beginning to a new day," cried the Colonels. "This will set us all up splendidly."

"This and a good breakfast," added Mrs. Hart.

"What a night it was, Cosmo," said Marion, swimming up to him and resting her hand on his shoulder. "Did you ever have so much fun?"

"It was fun," admitted Topper, "but whether I should have enjoyed it or not I am too vague to remember. What did we do with the automobile?"

"It's still at the road-house. We'll get it presently and move along."

"I don't move along an inch," replied Topper, "until all of you have cleared out of here."

"I'll get them out," said Marion. Then, turning to the others, she said, "The last one out forfeits a drink. Only three are left in the bottle."

This announcement was immediately followed by an undignified scramble up the bank of the river, the Colonel doing his best to block Mrs. Hart's progress. With great good humor Mr. Topper watched the three pairs of legs speeding over the grass. Marion Kerby was leading the way, running like a frightened deer, her flimsy draperies streaming in the wind. After a final turn in the water, Topper emerged from the river, and, casting a cautious glance about him, sought concealment in the bushes, his eyes still filled with the grace and beauty of Marion Kerby's flying form.

CHAPTER XVIII

Mr. Topper Does Not Celebrate

IN THIS CONVIVIAL MANNER BEGAN ONE OF THE MOST
active and interesting periods of Mr. Topper's incredible vacation. He had originally decided that he
needed a change. Now his needs were more than
satisfied. No man's life could have undergone more
radical alterations. The Colonel and Mrs. Hart garnished his trip with their misconduct, lending to an
automobile tour the atmosphere of a raiding party.

For three weeks the four of them cruised perilously
about the countryside, upsetting the entire New England States and leaving ruined and shattered nerves in
the wake of the hard pressed automobile. At night
they slept wherever they chanced to find themselves
and frequently they found themselves in strange and
unaccountable places. To-night it might be a roadhouse, on the following one a field. And there were
moments so fraught with danger that they retreated to
the woods until the hue and cry had subsided.

Despite the many discomforts of this open-air existence, Mr. Topper accepted his lot for reasons of
economy, Mrs. Hart and the Colonel being rather
fastidious in their tastes. Whenever the party put up at
an inn they loudly demanded the best of accommodations, for which they graciously allowed Mr. Topper
to pay. That neither of them had been asked to
become permanently attached to Mr. Topper never
seemed to occur to them. They were childlike in their
faith that they were wanted. Topper occasionally wondered about this, reflecting that his invitation to the
Colonel to share his Scotch had turned out to be one of
the most costly acts of hospitality he had ever performed.

Nevertheless, Mr. Topper appeared to have profited by his outing. His body had grown lean and alert, ready to run at a moment's notice, and his skin had been tanned by constant exposure to the elements. His character had also toughened considerably and his drinking capacity enlarged. True, he was hardly what one would call a desperate and reckless man, yet he had learned to accept danger with fortitude and delinquency with tolerance. Nor did his reputation weigh too heavily on his mind. By day he flaunted it in the face of the world and at night it dangled in jeopardy. And strangely enough Mr. Topper, in spite of his disorderly life, or rather, because of it, had become a better member of society; more self-reliant, more capable and far more interesting. He discovered in his heart the first faint whispering of pure Christianity, and in some way he continued to keep his virtue intact by keeping his vices active.

After the swimming party in the river he had eschewed strong liquor, and Marion Kerby had followed his example. Of course there had been a few slight lapses, but these had been such trifling affairs that they no longer counted with Topper. The Colonel and Mrs. Hart, however, were implacable in their thirst, to the quenching of which they devoted most of their energy and thought. For several days at a time they would absent themselves from the company of Mr. Topper and Marion to revel in more congenial surroundings. From these little side trips they invariably returned in a state of moral collapse; Oscar, more or less visible, close on his master's heels.

During the absence of this unedifying couple, Topper and Marion dwelt together in comparatively quiet and peaceful companionship. On one of her flights from his side she had acquired, without cost, a copy of the "Odyssey," and this brave tale they read together throughout the long, still, summer days.

For the first time in his life Topper came to realize that loose living and large thinking could get along quite comfortably together, that they were in fact boon companions. Under the influence of Marion Kerby he developed along altogether new and improved lines. But whenever the Colonel and Mrs. Hart returned from their excursions, Marion reverted to her former ways and joined them in a conspiracy to destroy Mr. Topper's tranquillity.

On this particular occasion there were good reasons for rejoicing. Oscar at last, after a tremendous burst of concentration, had succeeded in materializing up to the ears. This was the farthest north the dog had ever achieved, and as a consequence the Colonel was bubbling over with gratification and pride.

"Just mark my words," he went about saying. "I'll make a whole dog of him yet."

Oscar, rather dizzy at his unexpected success, swaggered aggressively in his gait and danced incompletely around. Up to this time he had shown but little interest in his personal appearance, being satisfied to remain at whatever length of dog he happened to find himself. On some days he was only an animated tail, on others a leaping rump, and on several occasions he appeared simply as a leg and let it go at that. Mr. Topper had never grown thoroughly accustomed to Oscar because of his continually changing appearance, but the man's natural love of animals gradually overcame his first decided objections. To-day he shared in the joy of the others and complimented Oscar on his brilliant showing, saying that he hoped some day to see his face.

"If ever there was an occasion that justified a celebration that occasion is now at hand," declared the Colonel with conviction. "I know of a first-rate hotel near by and I strongly suggest that we put up there for the night."

"You're a particularly ingenious person in finding occasion to justify a celebration," replied Mr. Topper, "but on this one, Colonel, I'm with you. I'd do anything in my power to encourage that dog of yours to go one way or the other, preferably the other. Let us descend on this hotel."

"Never have I seen such an improvement in a man in all my life," exclaimed Mrs. Hart in rapture. "Marion, you've done him a world of good."

Topper cast her a critical glance. "You look terrible," he remarked. "You should cut it out for a while."

"But our visit is nearly over," she replied with a little sigh. "Let's all raise hell while our ectoplasm lasts. You don't have to worry, Topper."

"What a tough baby she is," Mr. Topper mused to himself. Then he added aloud, "Is your husband still alive?"

"Yes, thank God," she replied with fervor, "and I wish him good health and a long life."

"Amen," said the Colonel piously.

"Beautiful characters," remarked Mr. Topper. "What about this celebration?"

To deprive the hotel of its legitimate profit it was decided that Mr. Topper should engage a large room and that the others should, as the Colonel tactfully phrased it, "join him there."

"The idea is good," agreed Mr. Topper, "but for one consideration. What about Oscar?"

"We can cram him into the trunk on the back and cut an air hole in it," replied the Colonel, proceeding to act on his words.

"If Oscar can stand it I can," remarked Mr. Topper. "What's to prevent him from dematerializing and joining us at some ill-chosen moment?"

"I hardly think he'll do that," said the Colonel. "He's so pleased with himself as he is that he wouldn't lose an inch for the world."

"Let us devoutly hope so," said Mr. Topper, as he watched the Colonel and Mrs. Hart unceremoniously cram Oscar into the trunk.

The hotel lay far back on a deep green, floor-like lawn which supported the weight of many trees, large trees whose generous limbs showered the benediction of shade upon the opulent persons who sat beneath them discussing golf, bridge and gin and appraising the new arrivals. The hotel itself was a rangy structure, having been added to in various styles of architecture as its popularity spread abroad. However, through sheer massiveness, it succeeded in presenting a harmonious whole, being sufficiently antique and modern to appeal to the comfortably artistic.

Around dinner time the front of the hotel afforded a striking study in modesty. Some of the ladies dressed directly in front of their windows, some dressed a trifle removed, but no lady, it seemed, ever dressed entirely out of sight. It was around dinner time when Mr. Topper arrived and so naturally he had no eyes for the blue sea that swept away to the horizon nor for the tent-like sails that slanted against the sky. As he followed the bell boy down a dark corridor along which trunks were parked like so many automobiles, a tinkling sound of an unmistakable nature issued from every door. Patriotic Americans were paying their evening tribute to the sacred laws of the land.

"If it were not so confounded hot," thought Topper, "I'd think I was on a sleigh ride. That tinkling makes me thirsty."

With the foresight bred of experience he halted the bell boy at the door and took the key from his hand.

"I can do very nicely now myself," he told the boy, giving him a generous tip. "Don't bother to come in."

It was well that he took this precaution, for, when he entered the room, he found his companions in varying stages of incompleteness. The Colonel was practically present, but Mrs. Hart and Marion Kerby were still sufficiently vague to have given the bell boy a decided shock.

"Sorry to have kept you waiting," he remarked, dropping the bags to the floor. "This is a decidedly musical hotel, isn't it, Colonel?"

"It is," replied the Colonel. "And our room alone is silent. What do you say to my taking steps?"

"Under ordinary circumstances I'd say no," said Mr. Topper, "but as this is a celebration, and incidentally a hot evening, I quite agree with you. Steps should be taken; but step, Colonel, with the utmost caution. Don't, for God's sake, stumble."

"Leave everything to me," replied the Colonel as he swiftly faded from view.

"I don't have to," remarked Topper. "You'd take it yourself anyway."

In a few minutes a gleaming cocktail shaker was seen to float through the open window. Without taking the time to reappear, the Colonel poured out a small drink and tasted it.

"Terrible," the voice remarked. "I'll take it back and throw it in his face."

The shaker floated away and after a short wait another one, accompanied by a bottle of gin, appeared at the window and, drifting across the room to the table, settled there with a silvery tinkle. The Colonel emerged from obscurity and sampled his plunder.

"Excellent!" he exclaimed. "Excellent! Now we can all have a drink."

From down the hall came the babble of excited voices mingled with the sound of running feet and slamming doors.

"Somebody seems to be upset," remarked Marion Kerby.

"It sounds so," said Mr. Topper. "How did your victims behave, Colonel?"

"Very nicely," replied the Colonel. "As is usual in such cases they were too confused to realize what had happened until after it had happened. The man was standing with the shaker held aloft, poised for the downward shake. I snatched it from his hand, seized the bottle of gin and fled, casting back a fleeting glance at the petrified company. The man was still holding his hand in the air like Ajax defying the lightning or Liberty bereft of her torch. One woman, I believe, had fainted. That was about all."

He knocked the shaker against the table and made a slight dent in it.

"In case of a search being instigated," he explained, "we can identify our property by this mark. All gin looks alike, but to make assurance doubly sure we had better drink this up as speedily as possible."

"Justifiable inebriety," Mr. Topper suggested.

"Exactly," agreed the Colonel. "Telephone for some glasses, ice and a few oranges."

When Mr. Topper went down to dinner half an hour later he was in a state of high good humor. Marion, the Colonel and Mrs. Hart had elected to remain behind, the Colonel judiciously pointing out that the dinner hour was the ideal time for looting, so many guests

being absent from their rooms. Moreover, there was
still some gin left to be turned into cocktails. Mr. Topper, relieved to escape from his boisterous companions,
was delighted with this arrangement.

"Don't hurry back," said Marion as he was about to
leave. "We can manage everything. Stroll about and
amuse yourself."

With a grateful look Mr. Topper innocently departed and made his way to the dining-room. Here he
was seated at an enviable table occupied at the moment by a handsomely gowned woman. She was plump
and pretty and appeared to have been in this life long
enough to have learned how to enjoy it without too
many qualms. Mr. Topper bowed and the woman
smiled, and before the end of the dinner he had
gleaned the information that the woman's name was
Mrs. Brewster and that her husband had died some
years ago of Bright's disease as she had repeatedly
warned him he would. On leaving the table she favored him with a particularly promising smile and in-
timated that there were many beautiful walks about
the place if one cared for that sort of thing. That sort
of thing, Mr. Topper said flatly, was exactly what he
cared for most. She smiled again and undulated away,
Mr. Topper following her departure with glowing eyes.

When he had finished his dinner he repaired to the
general assembly room of the hotel and mingled
complacently with the guests. A tall, perspiring gentleman was raffling lace garments for the benefit of some
worthy cause, and round this gentleman the ladies
were milling, their ears eagerly attuned to catch the
numbers he called out as he drew small bits of paper
from a hat.

As Mr. Topper was standing there enjoying this
little flurry of excitement, the woman directly in front
of him gave a most undignified start and rubbed herself tenderly. Then she turned and glared at Mr. Topper, whispering a few words to the woman next to her
as she did so.

"Why, what a thing to do!" exclaimed the woman,
looking indignantly at Mr. Topper.

This was too much for Topper. He shrank guiltily

away to the other side of the circle, where he stood wondering what it was all about. But here the same thing happened, only more publicly. A woman, brushing past Mr. Topper, suddenly stopped and, uttering a little cry of pain, looked at him with a shocked expression.

"Sir," she said, "if you do that again I'll have you ordered from this hotel."

"But what have I done?" asked the bewildered Topper.

"You know very well," she replied significantly. "If you were a gentleman you wouldn't even ask."

Before the disapproving glances of a number of guests, Mr. Topper abandoned all hope of clearing himself and fled to the smoking room. Here he sat down on a sofa beside an elderly gentleman who was snoring with childlike candor, his half-smoked cigar still held in his hand. Topper produced his handkerchief and mopped his flushed face. When he looked up the eyes of the elderly gentleman were fixed reproachfully on him.

"Why did you do that?" he demanded.

"You were snoring," replied Mr. Topper for lack of a better answer.

"That was no way to stop me," said the gentleman. "Don't do it again or I'll call for help."

Topper, at his wit's end, thereupon decided that his room was the only safe place for him. Taking the precaution to stay as far away as possible from any one, he made for the stairs, but here his retreat was cut off by the charming Mrs. Brewster. He was on the point of hurrying past her when she gave a sudden little cry of surprise and looked coyly at him.

"Why, you naughty man," she said. "I don't know why I'm not angry. Just for that you must take a walk with me."

Mr. Topper, too alarmed to inquire what "just for that" signified to Mrs. Brewster, obediently followed her from the hotel. She led him to a gathering of boulders overhanging the beach and gracefully arranged herself thereon, using Mr. Topper's hand for support and forgetting to give it back to him.

Mr. Topper's mind was in a state of siege, unhappy thoughts attacking it from all sides, as he vainly strove to figure out what curse had overtaken him. He was convinced that Marion Kerby was in some way involved in his predicament, that she was, in fact directly responsible for it. Mrs. Brewster's cooing voice interrupted his moody reflections.

"I was such a lonesome girl until you came," she said. "There's not a single man in all this hotel that's half alive."

"But I'm not a single man," Mr. Topper replied cautiously.

"Oh, I don't mean that," she laughed. "And anyway I hate single men. They always propose marriage."

Not feeling quite sure as to what proposals were expected of him, Mr. Topper made some pleasant reference to the character of the night.

"It's delicious," murmured Mrs. Brewster, moving closer to him and extending one hand to the sea.

Then a strange thing occurred. A white arm suddenly darted from the night and the hand at the end of it, seizing Mrs. Brewster's, shook it violently up and down. With a cry of terror she fell back into Mr. Topper's arms, and when he had succeeded in propping her up, a headless dog was sitting calmly before them on the rocks. Mr. Topper recognized Oscar immediately, but Mrs. Brewster had never met the dog. Nor did she stay now to be introduced. With little moaning noises she rose unsteadily to her feet and scrambled over the boulders with goatlike agility. The sound of maniacal laughter bursting in the air above her hastened her departure. Mr. Topper turned back to the ocean with thoughts of suicide, only to find that Oscar had vanished and that Marion Kerby was standing in his place.

"So that," she began in a voice of cold fury, "so that is the way you make use of your liberty. Picking a woman up at dinner and taking her out on the rocks. You love walking, don't you? Yes, you do not. I know. I know everything, heard every word you said, saw every look you gave her. Sitting here holding hands and expecting me to go rustling up grog for your fat paunch. Quite a ladies' man, aren't you? Having a grand time and me hanging around like a dope. Well, let me tell you one thing, I'm through. I quit now, but if I ever catch you with that moth-eaten old troll again I'll scare the living lights out of her. Of all the nerve. Sitting here on the rocks. Disgusting. Don't talk to me, you're too low for words. Come along, Oscar, and I'll shove you back in your trunk. We've intruded too long already."

Oscar appeared from the shadows and followed Marion Kerby's swiftly retreating form. Topper, awaking from his daze, sprang to his feet and cried after Marion.

"Don't go away," he pleaded. "Give me a chance. I can explain everything. Come back, Marion."

"If this damn dog only had a head," she furiously shouted back, "I'd sick him on you. Don't dare to follow me or I'll make the scene of your life."

Through a side door of the hotel Topper sneaked up to his room only to find it depressingly empty. Squeezed oranges and empty gin bottles bore silent witness to the success of the Colonel's endeavors. Topper walked wearily to the window and looked out over the lawn. Had Marion Kerby permanently left him? That question was uppermost in his mind. He had never before seen her so angry or unreasonable, yet with all his heart he wanted her back. For a long time he walked restlessly up and down his room. Several times he whispered her name, but received no answer. Finally he undressed, switched off the light and, getting into bed, lay there wondering what his vanished companions were doing.

"A lovely celebration," he muttered bitterly to himself, rolling over on his side and seeking forgetfulness in sleep.

CHAPTER XIX

Oscar in Toto

FERVENTLY HOPING THAT HE WOULD BE LESS EASILY
recognizable in a bathing suit, Mr. Topper on the following morning took a solitary breakfast in his room,
then hurried down to the beach. Here for an hour or
so he reclined torpidly on the warm sand, too dispir-
ited even to attempt the water lapping invitingly at his
feet. Under happier circumstances he would have
been secretly thrilled by this broad expanse of ocean,
but to-day the old spell was broken. Topper was a
lonely man, longing for Marion Kerby.

With gloomy eyes he watched the early bathers and
reviled them in his heart. Their carefree outbursts of
enterprise depressed him. One young chap he particularly disliked. He was tall and blond and beautifully
tanned, clean-cut, varsity manhood every inch of him.
A slim girl and shapely was watching this cute giant
with her soul in her eyes as he carried a canoe, as if
it were a straw, down to the water's edge. And when
Mr. Topper saw this happy couple go paddling off
over the deep blue sea he earnestly hoped that a large
wet wave would rise therefrom and mightily smite
their budding romance.

"He smokes a pipe," thought Mr. Topper, jeeringly,
"and that's just what he would smoke, a pipe, man-
fashion."

Nor did the children playing round him appeal to
his better nature. He thought they all looked bold and
unpleasant and wished they would go somewhere else.
The beach was no place for them. Why couldn't they
keep to their rooms? As a matter of fact, why couldn't
all these people clear out and leave him alone? Take

that man for instance, romping with his little son. Could anything be more revolting?

Mr. Topper turned away from this disturbing scene and gazed idly down at two small bare feet, one of which was impatiently tapping the sand. Automatically his eyes traveled up an attractive length of slim limbs until they found themselves squinting into Marion Kerby's face—a set, unfriendly face.

"If I catch you in the company of that woman," said the face with suppressed conviction, "I'm going out and drown her."

"You won't catch me," he answered meekly. "Sit down."

Mrs. Hart and the Colonel joined them at this moment and allied themselves with Mr. Topper in urging Marion to be seated. Ungraciously she flopped to the sand and favored Topper with a sneer.

"If it hadn't been for these two," she told him, "you'd never have seen me again. As it is, I doubt if I stay."

"But I hope you will," said Topper.

"Don't speak to me now," she snapped. "I can't stand your silly voice. It's 'yam, yam' this and 'yam, yam' that until I'm nearly mad. Keep quiet."

"All right," replied Mr. Topper with even greater meekness. "I won't say a word."

The Colonel's voice broke in on their happy reunion.

"You should have been with us last night, Topper," he said. "We had a splendid time."

"What did you do?" asked Topper, not greatly caring now that he had Marion back.

"Made friends with the proprietor," the Colonel replied, "and got him squiffed on his own grog. It was wonderful stuff."

"Wonderful stuff," Mrs. Hart echoed with deep feeling. "Wonderful!"

"He wants me to stay all summer," Marion remarked casually. "Room and board free. He says I look all run down as if somebody had been terribly, terribly unkind to me. I just laughed in his face, but I haven't told him whether I would or wouldn't. Not yet."

"You could do much worse, dearie," Mrs. Hart said, furtively eyeing Mr. Topper's face. "At least he doesn't seem to be the flighty kind."

Topper cast her a look of loathing, but discreetly held his peace.

"Well, Topper, shall we take a dip?" suggested the Colonel, rising from the sand.

Not knowing what else to do, Topper followed the Colonel's example.

"Sit down!" flared Marion Kerby. "What are you trying to do, make a show of me on this beach? Sit down before I knock you down."

In his eagerness to obey, Topper almost fell to the sand.

"All right," he said. "All right."

"Now get up," she commanded, "and we'll all take a dip."

"Don't let her get away with it," whispered the Colonel. "I wouldn't. They're always meanest when they know they're wrong. They want to break you down."

"What chance have I?" said Topper. "She has every advantage in her favor and no scruples at all. She's got me where she wants me."

But before the swim was over friendly relations were once more established between Mr. Topper and Marion Kerby. From the way she treated him it seemed as if the unpleasant incident had never occurred. Topper, exalted to the skies, frolicked like a dolphin and lost all memory of the harsh words she had hurled at him. Exhausted at last by their flounderings, the party returned to the beach where they wallowed in the sand and went over the events of the past night, Mr. Topper listening with such an envious expression that Marion Kerby took his hand in hers and promised him a bigger and better celebration.

It was then that from down the beach came the terrified yelping of a dog. They looked in that direction and saw a large collie in the act of going mad. As he approached them his terror increased. He snapped at the air, spun round on his feet, arched himself in a desperate circle and rolled over in the sand. Nurses snatched up their charges, women screamed and the bathers fled to safety. During all this commotion the Colonel sat watching the actions of the collie with purely professional interest.

"Doesn't look mad to me," he observed. "Looks more as if he were fighting something."

"Oscar," breathed Mrs. Hart.

"Possibly," replied the Colonel. "I forgot to mention that when I brought him his chow this morning, Oscar was not in the trunk."

"Oh," said Mr. Topper slowly. "Oh, dear me."

At this moment the collie decided that enough was enough. He rolled over on his back, thrust his legs in the air, and let his tongue hang out. He was unmistakably through. Then above the vanquished dog appeared Oscar's bushy tail, which was quickly followed by his hind quarters. Gradually the dog progressed until he had reached his ears. Here there was a hesitation, a noticeable wavering, then like the final shove at the goal line, Oscar's head swam into view.

"By God! He's done it," exclaimed the Colonel.

The collie took one horrified look at Oscar, then turned his head away and closed his eyes. This was indeed too much. Oscar, as if forgetting his victim, trotted over to the Colonel and looked him square in the eye with an expression which eloquently conveyed the meaning that from now on he would take no more nonsense from any one. He was a whole dog now in his own rights, and his rights were to be respected. With a nasty look at Mr. Topper he sprawled out in the sand and began to police his newly acquired hide. Meanwhile the collie had dragged himself away.

For some moments the Colonel studied his dog with puzzled and considering eyes, then presently his face cleared.

"I know what it is," he said. "He must have forgotten his spot. He had a little spot in real life right on the side of his nose, the left side, but in the excitement and all I fancy he must have overlooked it."

"That's merely a detail, Colonel," put in Mr. Topper. "Don't send him back for his spot now. He can pick it up later."

The Colonel agreed to this and the party reentered their bath houses, Oscar's performance having attracted to them rather unpleasant publicity. Some time later, when they foregathered on the lawn of the hotel, the Colonel was the last to appear, and when he did appear he was exploding with excitement.

"Don't ask me where I got the news," he began, "and anyway it doesn't matter. George Kerby is back and is looking for you, Marion. He's heading this way and he seems to have heard something."

Topper looked for a chair, but finding none, braced himself on his legs.

"You're not joking?" Marion calmly asked the Colonel.

"Credit me with more tact," he replied in an injured voice. "This isn't a trifling matter."

"Did they say," Topper painfully inquired, "did they say that he seemed to be angry?"

The Colonel laughed sardonically and Topper winced.

"Not at all," replied the Colonel. "He's just crazy to see you, Topper."

"I wish I could say as much," said Mr. Topper. "What, oh, what shall we do now?"

"Clear out," answered the Colonel. "Vamoose plenty pronto."

"I know just the place," exclaimed Mrs. Hart, with a wild light in her eyes. "What a lark!"

"Try to take things seriously," said Mr. Topper. "If you mean the lake I won't go back there. I'm a marked man in that vicinity."

"No," Mrs. Hart explained. "It's a deserted beach in Connecticut. No one ever goes there. It's been left vacant through a family quarrel ever since my father died. What a family. I'm glad I'm out of it."

"This is no time to be abusing your family," Mr. Topper retorted. "Let's start for this beach at once."

"Not so fast," said Mrs. Hart. "We'll have to stop somewhere to buy some tents and provisions and things——"

"And I'll have to loot without delay the proprietor's private locker," interrupted the Colonel. "Oscar can sit with us and I'll fill the trunk."

Marion turned to the impatient Topper and placed a soothing hand on his arm.

"Don't worry, old dear," she told him. "We'll take care of you. Hurry now and pack your things. We'll be waiting in the car."

"Won't you come with me," Topper pleaded. "For some reason I hate to be alone."

Thus was the flight planned and right speedily was it executed. Twelve hours of high pressure driving, relieved only by an interlude of hectic buying, jostled them to their night-shrouded destination.

"What a devil of a place this is," said the Colonel, sloshing about in the weeds and darkness. "The entire world is deserted."

"You don't know the half of it," Mrs. Hart replied. "Wait till the morning comes."

"I won't even wait for that," said Mr. Topper, who had been diligently applying himself to the bottle throughout the entire course of the trip. "Here and now I sleep."

"In spite of my remarks I'm still desperately engaged with these damn prehensile weeds," the Colonel called. "This isn't a beach, it's a jungle."

"The beach is farther on," explained Mrs. Hart. "This field leads down to it."

"Then be kind enough to put a cushion under me and place a bottle in my hand," said the Colonel. "Then kiss me a chaste good-night. Like Topper, I sleep here and now."

Some hours later, when the nice, clean, freshly starched sun rose and favored the field with its light it looked down on four untidy figures plus one rumpled dog stretched in various unpicturesque attitudes of slumber. Presently the figures stirred and sat up. They yawned, stretched and rubbed their eyes with frank disregard of each other's presence. The dog unwound himself and snapped wearily at a fly. Mr. Topper was the first to speak.

"Are we safe?" he asked.

"So far, it seems," replied Marion, fluffing out her hair, "but you never can tell about George."

"The bottle, Colonel," said Topper promptly. "Already I scent disaster."

The bottle went the rounds, then the figures shook themselves and rose to their feet. Mrs. Hart led the way to the beach, the others straggling through the weeds beneath the weight of the tents and provisions. And the sun, as if to register its disapproval of their morning salutation, caused them to perspire freely.

The beach was a narrow yellow band, about one hundred yards in length, pocketed away in a wooded cove filled with cool, green water. Far out against a wall of billowy clouds a single sail stole gracefully along. Gulls were in the air. The smell of clam shells, salt and shrubbery gave a distinctive fragrance to the place.

"This is more than a deserted beach," said Marion Kerby, appreciatively. "It's a little pocket in nowhere. No wonder your family fought for it. I could live here the rest of my life, if I had a life to live."

The smile she gave to Topper had lost a little of its old-time impertinence. Something about it troubled him. For a moment he tasted the savor of the end of things and caught a glimpse of an empty landscape. The very stillness of the place, its hushed, watchful solitude, the fanning out of the green, flat water and the clouds out there beyond conspired to make him feel that so much beauty could only end in pain. More than ever before he realized Marion Kerby's keenness of feature and the world of untouched wonder that lay behind her eyes. Some subtle influence emanating from her at that moment made him begin already to miss her. He wanted to go over and stand close to her side, but, in his self-consciousness, the few feet separating them were as difficult to achieve as the Sahara Desert on stilts. All that he could say was:

"You've lived enough for two already."

Apparently not hearing this remark, she walked away and sat down on a rock close to the water's edge. The Colonel and Mrs. Hart were wrestling with the tents, the Colonel booming directions and assur-

ing Oscar that if he did not go somewhere else he
would speedily kick him back into the fourth dimension. Topper followed Marion and sat down at her
feet. They were happy as they were, with silence and
space around them, the deep blue sky above and the
green water murmuring along the beach. There was a
remote expression in Marion's eyes as she gazed away
from the shore. She seemed somehow to have withdrawn a little from Topper and her surroundings.

"Listen to me, Topper," she said at last. "Are you
any happier now that you've lost your stomach and
your smug commuting ways?"

"I've lost more than that," he replied, his eyes
riveted on her face.

"What a coy devil you are," she answered. "Do you
mean to imply delicately that you've lost your heart
to me?"

"You know it," said Mr. Topper. "You know it with
hateful complacency, but it's true and so here we
are."

"Yes," she answered with a little shrug of her shoulders. "And so here we are, but we won't be here long,
at least, I won't."

"What do you mean?" he asked.

"Something is happening to me," she replied. "I
seem to be losing interest in all things—all except you.
Perhaps I'm getting high-planed."

"Don't do that," he pleaded. "You never could
be so lovely as you are right now."

"Do you think so?" she said with a thoughtful
smile. "For that you deserve a kiss. Come closer."

Topper took her in his arms and pressed her to him.

"Make it snappy," she exclaimed. "I didn't ask
you to strangle me. Hurry and help the Colonel. He's
swearing abominably at that poor woman."

Topper was unable to analyze his emotions. Sen-
sations were confused within him, happiness and sorrow, triumph and defeat. To work off his feelings he
joined the Colonel's staff and became desperately involved with a tent to the amusement of Mrs. Hart, who,
upon Topper's appearance, immediately sat down and

gave up the struggle. The Colonel regarded her with a brutal eye.

"Get up," he commanded, "and collect some wood and I'll show you how to cook breakfast in case you don't know."

"I don't know," admitted Mrs. Hart, "and I don't know that I care to know, but I will get some wood. The stomach of me is raging at the very thought of food. Teach Topper to cook. He looks enterprising."

Under the Colonel's skillful direction the camp was eventually arranged. During this interlude he showed himself to his best advantage, his military training coming to the fore. Topper became his chief assistant and Mrs. Hart the camp drone, her disinclination for work manifesting itself by her absence whenever there was any work to be done.

And now began one of the quietest and most peaceful phases of Mr. Topper's vacation. The nearest village was five miles off and this they very seldom visited. Topper drove over once and came back with a canoe and some fresh provisions. The canoe was received with delight, the Colonel immediately going fishing in it, taking a bottle along. Some hours later he came back with nothing more useful than a tendency to stagger and to curse at the fish he had almost caught.

The days slipped by tranquilly, almost unnoticed, and gradually the fear of George Kerby's arrival faded from Mr. Topper's mind. Some one was always in swimming and there was always ample Scotch or some other equally heady beverage, the Colonel being a splendid provider. At night they gambled for Topper's money and cheated him when they could, Mrs. Hart being the most successful and persistent, making it a point never to play an honest hand unless driven to it. Topper took Marion paddling whenever she would let him and he fell more deeply under her spell, although no further demonstration occurred. And the Colonel succeeded at last in making Oscar retrieve his spot. Sometimes it would be in the wrong place, but the Colonel was not particular. Topper became thoroughly attached to Oscar and told him about his cat, Scollops, the dog listening with his head on one side and an ear politely cocked.

It was Mrs. Hart's surprising suggestion one Sunday that they should all go to church. They did this and Marion Kerby established a local miracle by slipping away in the middle of the sermon and materializing angelically directly above the preacher's head. Mrs. Hart laughed so hysterically that she had to be helped from the church, but from that time on the preacher began to believe a little in the truth of his own sermons. The news of this event spread throughout the country and brought much fame and many visitors to this little country church which hitherto had been content to remain in bucolic obscurity.

The following night, just before dawn, Topper awoke with a feeling of profound depression which was not relieved by what he saw as soon as his eyes had grown accustomed to the darkness. A figure was standing at the flap of the tent. That was all. It was motionless. It just stood there and seemed to be examining Topper with calculating interest. When Mr. Topper moved the figure laughed unpleasantly. Most unpleasantly, Mr. Topper thought.

"Topper," said the figure, "Topper, I've got you now, and, God, how I'm going to make you sweat."

Mr. Topper was sweating already. His tongue clove to the roof of his mouth and his hands trembled on the coverings.

"Who's speaking?" came a sleepy voice from the other bed. "Are you awake, Cosmo?"

The figure at the flap of the tent raised its hands to its head and clutched its hair.

"By all that's holy!" it cried. "Living together in open shame."

"It's all a mistake," said Mr. Topper in a despairing voice. "I didn't even know she was here. She must have sneaked in after I went to bed. For heaven's sake, George, wait until I explain."

"And if I believed that," replied George Kerby more calmly, "you'd probably tell me another one, wouldn't you?"

"Why, if it isn't George himself!" exclaimed Marion,

rising from the bed. "And he's in one of his most play-ful moods. Welcome home, honey."

"Shameless woman," he cried. "Put something over your shoulders. God, won't I make him sweat for this! Leave this room, Marion."

"It isn't a room, it's a tent," she replied. "Do try to be accurate, and while we're on the subject of ac-curacy, I might mention the fact that Topper was right. I did sneak in here after he fell asleep. My tent is some yards away, but the Colonel was snoring so violently I came in here."

"The Colonel?" said George and Topper at the same time.

"Yes," she explained patiently. "His tent is close to mine."

"It won't go with me," George Kerby replied. "Lies, lies, lies, a tissue of lies from beginning to end. Oh, but won't he sweat for this."

"Don't keep telling me how much I'm going to sweat," put in Mr. Topper. "I've lost five pounds in the last five minutes. Let Marion explain."

"Yes, George," said Marion. "Don't be tragic. I can explain everything. Topper's as innocent as a lamb. He doesn't know any better. Don't jump at con-clusions."

Once more George Kerby laughed unpleasantly.

"I'm hardly jumping," he retorted. "Conclusions are forced down my throat."

Topper shivered and pulled the bed clothing round him.

"You talk to him, Marion," he suggested. "Take him away somewhere and tell him everything. Maybe he wants a drink. It's such lovely Scotch. Will you have a drink, George?"

Topper's voice trailed away to a wistful nothing-ness.

"I'll go," said George, "but don't think you're go-ing to escape. I'll keep my eye on this tent and in the morning you'll answer to me. Understand? In the morning you'll answer to me. You'll sweat then."

"Why must you repeat everything?" complained

Mr. Topper. "Take a good drink and lie down. You're all upset."

"Not so upset as you are going to be," George Kerby replied. "Not nearly so upset. Now I'm going, but I'll be back at any moment."

"Good-night," said Mr. Topper in a cloyingly friendly voice. "Good-night, George. I hope you'll feel better in the morning after you've had a nice talk with your wife."

"Never felt better in my life," George answered. "I'm fit all over and that's more than you're going to be."

Marion threw on a bathrobe and led her belligerent husband away, but sleep was murdered for Topper. In the pale dawn he sat hunched in his bed and wondered what George was going to do to make him sweat so much. Not until it was well on to breakfast time did he have the courage to leave his tent. The whole camp was astir and George Kerby was sitting on a log in dignified aloofness.

"Here's where the sweating begins," thought Topper as he looked fearfully at George's grim face.

When the Colonel saw Topper he greeted him with unusual impressiveness and led him aside.

"Topper," he said, "I'm sorry, but Mr. Kerby demands satisfaction. There's no way out of it. If you don't fight him he'll kill you."

"He'll kill me if I do," replied Mr. Topper.

"Perhaps, but there's always a chance," said the Colonel. "Now this is what I propose and Kerby seems to agree."

The Colonel's proposition was unique. It was nothing less than a duel with clam shells at twenty paces, each principal to have three throws apiece.

"Why I never threw a clam shell in my life," said Topper, "but I understand they're very dangerous. Isn't there some other way? Some more reasonable way?"

"I can't answer for the other way," replied the Colonel. "He is waiting for your answer. If you refuse, may God be with you."

"May God be with me anyway," breathed Topper.

"Make him agree to one throw apiece, won't you, Colonel?"

"I'll do whatever I can," said the Colonel, walking with great dignity to George Kerby.

Marion brought Topper a cup of coffee and looked at him sympathetically.

"He's a bum shot," she whispered. "Don't worry. It could be much worse."

"Can you do anything with him?" Topper asked. "Get him drunk or something?"

"Not until after the duel," she answered. "He insists on satisfaction. I've pleaded with him for hours."

"I'm so thrilled!" exclaimed Mrs. Hart, joining them. "When is it going to be? Think of it, a duel, and we'll be here to see it. It's just too wonderful."

The Colonel left Kerby and approached the group.

"Be ready then at five o'clock," he said. "Kerby agrees to two shots apiece and intimates that he will need only one."

Kerby had left the log and was arranging a target on the beach. Then he collected some clam shells and began to hurl them at his imaginary foeman with all his might. At first the shells went wide of their mark, but gradually he began to get the range of the target. Patiently, deliberately and earnestly he practiced all morning until he had developed murderous control. Everywhere Topper went he heard the clam shells striking the target with increasing frequency and force. The sound got on his nerves. With fascinated eyes he watched George Kerby at his grim occupation. After a brief rest for luncheon Kerby returned at once to the target and put on the finishing touches. Topper, unable to bear the sight, retired to his tent. Once he emerged and endeavored to do a little practicing on his own part, but when he saw George Kerby sardonically watching his futile attempts to hit a tree, he dropped the clam shells and stole back to his tent.

Slowly the hours dragged by until five o'clock, when the Colonel promptly appeared and solemnly conducted Topper to the beach.

"Gentlemen," he said, "take your places at the

proper distance and when I drop this handkerchief start firing."

At this little announcement, Mrs. Hart, who had been drinking a trifle in anticipation of the event, clapped her hands enthusiastically.

"Atta boy!" she cried.

Topper looked at her with disgust, then turned his eyes to Marion. She smiled back at him encouragingly, but remained silent. George Kerby beckoned to the Colonel and made a few hurried remarks, after which the Colonel approached Topper with a troubled expression on his face.

"Topper," he said, "Mr. Kerby insists on his privileges as a spirit. He demands to be allowed to dematerialize as that is, he claims, his natural state."

"Tell him not to be childish," said Mr. Topper. "How can I see to throw at him?"

"I mentioned the fact and he replied that that was your worry, not his," answered the Colonel.

"Ask him if he would prefer to murder me in cold blood," Topper remarked bitterly. "There's a razor in my tent."

"Do you agree to Mr. Kerby's proposition?" continued the Colonel.

"What else can I do?" cried Topper. "If I don't agree he'll chase me all over this place with clam shells anyway. Let's get it over."

"Very well," replied the Colonel. "Here are your shells, and good luck."

Topper looked miserably at the clam shells the Colonel placed in his hand.

"Give him little ones," he whispered to the Colonel. "Don't forget, Colonel pick out two small ones, small and light."

"When I drop the handkerchief," the Colonel once more announced, "you gentlemen can begin to fire."

"At what?" called Mr. Topper as George Kerby faded from the scene.

"I can't see as that makes much difference," replied the Colonel. "But if you want a mark fire where you last saw him."

The Colonel raised his arm and the handkerchief fluttered in the air.

"One minute," called Mr. Topper. "Suppose he sneaks up behind me? Tell him he shouldn't do that."

"Don't interrupt me again," said the Colonel impatiently. "Of course he wouldn't do that."

"Oh, wouldn't he!" answered Topper. "That's just what he would do."

He looked at the spot where he had last seen George Kerby and saw a clam shell poised in the air. To Topper it looked neither little nor light. It was a brutal clam shell, the great-grandfather of all clams.

"Are you ready, gentlemen?" called the Colonel.

"I am," answered Mrs. Hart. "What a lark. Topper, you'll soon be with us, old boy."

The handkerchief dropped to the ground and Topper, aiming at the poised shell, missed it. Then the poised shell aimed at Topper and did not miss. It met Mr. Topper just above the eye and sent him speedily to earth. As if the shell had struck her, Marion gave a little cry and ran over to him, lifting his head to her lap. George Kerby reappeared and stood looking down at Topper rather guiltily. The Colonel was bathing the wound.

"If you've killed him," said Marion Kerby, "he'll be over on our side and then the triangle will be complete."

"I hadn't thought of that," replied Kerby, bending anxiously over Topper. "I didn't mean to throw so hard. Pull him through, Colonel."

Mrs. Hart was crying softly to herself and sipping a glass of Scotch.

"He was such a nice man," she sobbed. "Such a generous host."

The Colonel and Marion worked swiftly and silently as they skillfully bandaged Topper's head. Then the Colonel took him in his arms and carried him to his tent, Mrs. Hart following after them with tipsy lamentations.

CHAPTER XX

The Return to the Tree

WITH AN EXPRESSION OF CONGEALED SOLICITUDE George Kerby was holding a glass of Scotch to Mr. Topper's lips when next the stricken man opened his eyes on a world he had elaborately resigned himself to leave forever. The Colonel was making bandages with professional detachment and Marion Kerby was sitting on one side of the cot. Mrs. Hart, in an attitude of florid grief, was untidily draped over the foot of it. As he took in the serious group Topper was reminded of wax figures.

"Are you trying to poison me," he asked, "now that you've got me down?"

"Oh, dear me, no," Mrs. Hart pleaded moistly. "Please take a little drink. It will do you a world of good. It's already helped me tremendously."

Mr. Topper looked with surprise at her tear-moist face.

"What's this?" he asked. "Tears? Don't cry, my child, he'll get me the next time."

"Yes," she answered dramatically, "they're tears if you want to know. Ask them all. Tell him, Marion. Ever since that clam shell knocked you out I've been crying as if my heart would break. And I do believe it will unless some considerate person gives me a little something to tuck up my nerves."

Kerby bent over Topper and looked contritely into his eyes.

"Listen, old man," he said. "Tell me that I'm forgiven. I'm terribly ashamed of myself for getting you all messed up. The honors are even now."

"But not the injuries," Mr. Topper replied with a tired smile. "You put the gory in glory, George, but

I don't mind. Give me that drink and let's call it a duel. There's one thing, though, I'll never forgive, not to the end of my days."

"What's that?" asked George Kerby.

"You've eternally ruined clams for me," said Topper. "You don't know what that means. Clams were my only vice once upon a time—a secret craving I kept to myself. Even my wife didn't know I loved them. That's all over now. Hereafter whenever I see a clam I'm going to duck and run like hell."

"How droll he is," murmured Mrs. Hart. "Let's all have a drink."

They all did, all save Marion Kerby, who held a moist cloth to Mr. Topper's head.

"Do you want me to send these ruffians away?" she asked him. "Perhaps you had better rest."

"Let the ruffians stay," he answered. "The situation pleases my vanity. Never before have I been such a center of attraction."

The Colonel turned to Kerby with one of his most disarming smiles.

"Now that the storm is over," he said, "I want to tell every one that it's been a real pleasure to have met George Kerby. We have thought so much about him."

"Thanks," acknowledged Kerby, "but if it hadn't been for Marion's playfulness in that church you might never have had the pleasure. You can't imagine what a great to-do her misplaced sense of humor has created. By this time, I'll bet, the papers are full of it and the sparks are fairly flying from scientific and religious circles."

"She was too funny for words." said Mrs. Hart.

"Perhaps," replied Kerby, "but as soon as I heard of it I knew what had happened. I recognized that particular brand of madness, having suffered from it for years. After that it was easy to find you."

"How fortunate," said the Colonel, with highly polished hypocrisy. "If we had known you were back we would have scoured the countryside. Your return was our constant topic of conversation. Topper and your wife were forever talking about it."

"Were they?" cried Kerby, pitifully pleased. "What a beast I've been."

"They were," continued the Colonel, "but don't worry. It's been a gool summer all around. You've outraged Europe and we've despoiled the New England States. At last we meet. A little misunderstanding, a most natural misunderstanding, is happily if painfully settled. Therefore I propose a final celebration. I feel that my ectoplasm is running low and I fancy we're all about in the same boat. We can't fade away without one last fling, but this time the party will be on us. Mrs. Hart and your servant will give it."

"Where?" asked Mrs. Hart, sleepily opening her eyes. "May I come?"

The Colonel cast her a glance of commiseration.

"The events of the day have been too much for the poor woman," he remarked. "She is sodden with excitement."

"It's not that at all," she protested. "Tell him, Marion. It's just because I'm so frantically sympathetic. No one suffers as I do. No one has such nerves. You wouldn't believe how much . . ."

"The Colonel," George Kerby interrupted impatiently, "has extended to us a very handsome invitation which I, for one, accept on the spot. But where can we stage this celebration? From what I've been able to gather, you people have about exhausted all the hospitality on this side of the Rockies."

"How about right here?" suggested the Colonel. "This is a good, safe place."

"No," put in Topper, "let's go back to the old inn—you know, George, where we pulled our first party. Mrs. Hart and the Colonel would love it there."

Marion Kerby was gazing at Topper with a reminiscent light in her eyes.

"I second the motion," she said. "The old inn would be a lovely place for a farewell party."

At this Mrs. Hart's shoulders began to shake convulsively.

"Don't say farewell," she sobbed. "I can't bear to think of the parting. Quick, Colonel, my glass."

Marion motioned to the Colonel, who immediately lifted the grief-stricken woman to her feet, and, whispering words of comfort in her ear, assisted her from the tent.

Two days later the Colonel and Mrs. Hart left for the inn, there to complete arrangements for the celebration. The others, including Oscar, who had stubbornly refused to dematerialize, were to follow by motor within a few days.

On the morning of departure Topper, still bearing the honorable scar of battle, wandered dejectedly about the place. He was looking forward with but small eagerness to the farewell celebration and would have preferred to linger on forever in this quiet spot where he had spent so many happy and carefree days. Everything spoke to him of Marion, the water, the beach and the trees. Everything breathed farewell, the parting of the ways. If he could only have remained near her, even with her husband present, it would have been better than a final separation. For the first time in many days he thought of Mrs. Topper, thought of her miserably, protestingly and with a little pang of shame. He had treated the poor creature terribly, he realized that, and the realization made it no easier for him to face their inevitable reunion.

To escape his thoughts he put on his bathing suit and went for a parting swim. He swam far out to the mouth of the cove and looked across the water to the distant horizon where tumbled clouds, touched with sunlight, were banked against the sky. He wished that he could swim out there with Marion Kerby and hide with her behind that fleecy curtain, to be protected by it forever from the urgency of life, to prolong there in a curtained land the romance and freedom he had enjoyed for only a few short months. His dream of escape was shattered by a voice floating to him across the water. Looking behind he saw Marion, clad in her bathing suit, gliding towards him in the canoe.

"What are you doing so far from shore?" she demanded. "It's time we were getting started."

"Are you eager to leave?" he asked her.

"My heart is no lighter than yours," she answered, "but I'm not wasting time weighing it. Look out, I'm coming in."

She poised herself and dived lightly overboard, emerging close to Topper. Together they swam back to the canoe, and Topper, with all his strength, pushed it out of the cove.

"Let it drift away," he said, "as a symbol of my departing happiness."

"I'm in on that, old thing," she replied, "but just the same, cheer up. We'd better be getting back to shore or George will be collecting another nice little pile of clam shells."

"But, Marion," Topper protested, "is it really to be the end of things? Can't we go on for a while?"

"I'm afraid not," she replied. "You and George are not proper playmates, and anyway my ectoplasm is growing a trifle frayed. You'll be seeing through me soon."

"You've deprived me of all my old ideas," Mr. Topper answered, "and all I have in their place is an empty, aching feeling, a feeling of loss and discontent, the makings of a rebellion."

"Memories!" she cried. "Memories, Topper. Do they mean nothing to you? Cling to them. The past is made of memories, the future is made of dreams. Hot stuff!"

"Not mine," answered Topper. "Desk tops and legs of lamb."

"Well, then, here's a memory for you," she said, swimming cose to him and giving him a little salt-edged kiss. "Now, quit your mooning and get back to shore."

Topper buried his face in the water and swam to the beach, Marion following easily in his wake. George Kerby was waiting for them with a glass in either hand, and as Topper swiftly studied his face, he fancied he detected in Kerby's eyes a hint of pain, something lonely and hidden, yet reassuringly sympathetic.

"I thought you might like these after your long swim," said Kerby, a shade apologetically.

Something about the situation made it difficult for

Topper to speak for a moment. He accepted the extended glass and pretended to be getting his breath.

"You're thoughtful, George," he said at last. "Here
are my best regards to you."

"Good luck," replied Kerby with a faint smile. "This
place is almost too lovely to leave."

But they left it just the same, left it as it was, the
canoe drifting out with the tide and the tents rippling
in the light breeze beneath a high, glad sun. Topper,
with Oscar on his lap, slouched in the automobile and
refused to look back at the little beach as Kerby drove
across the field and on to the narrow road. No one
spoke, no one seemed inclined to look at the other.
They were occupied with their thoughts, which apparently were not happy. Presently Marion found a
bottle and handed it to Topper.

"What's wrong with this outfit?" she demanded.
"You'd think we were going to a funeral instead of a
celebration. The pair of you depress me."

Topper and Kerby drank, solemnly at first, but
gradually their solemnity faded until at last the three
of them felt moved to lift their voices in writhing
harmony, so painful to the ears that Oscar howled in
protest.

Dusk was drifting over the fields by the time they
reached their destination, and already the old inn
was partly obscured by trees and shadows. They
parked the car behind a clump of bushes and entered
the inn by a rear door, old memories rising up to greet
them as they stood in the dim light of the silent room.
No one was there to receive them, but signs of prepa-
ration were everywhere in evidence. A long table had
been arranged at one end of the room and the great
sideboard was burdened with provisions, glasses and
bottles. In one corner Marion discovered a battered but
businesslike phonograph. Cigars and cigarettes had
been placed by thoughtful hands at all convenient
points. Oscar was behaving strangely. The hair stood
up on his back as he sniffed the air excitedly and gave
utterance to eager whines. Observing the behavior of
the dog, Topper began to feel uncomfortable.

Suddenly three loud raps shattered the silence of the

room and a voice called out, "Attention!" Topper, on his dash to the door, stopped long enough to see the Colonel, in full uniform, emerge from the gloom. The sight reassured him, as did the appearance of Mrs. Hart a moment later. Oscar was barking madly and scrambling at the Colonel's feet. Mrs. Hart was approaching Topper with a tray full of glasses. This decided him to stay. He took a glass and drained its contents.

"Take another," said Mrs. Hart.

"Thanks," replied Topper. "How are your nerves? Mine are terrible."

"Couldn't be worse," she assured him. "The arrangements have been such a strain. I think I'd better join you before I continue with the tray."

"Do," urged Topper. "It would be awful if you fainted."

They drank together quickly and Mrs. Hart hurried away. Topper looked about the room and was appalled by the sight he beheld. Bodies in various stages of formation were appearing in every corner. Heads were floating in the air and bodyless legs were walking across the floor. Strangely detached-looking arms were already snatching food and glasses from the sideboard. And as Topper stood there gazing, the room gradually became peopled with men and women in evening clothes. They stood about in groups and conversed with animation. In the most natural way in the world they consumed sandwiches and cocktails, and lifted their voices in laughter. Marion Kerby came over to Topper and took him by the hand.

"Stop gaping like that," she whispered. "It's only a few of the Colonel's friends he's invited in honor of the celebration, and if you'll take it from me, it's a pretty hard-looking crowd. Don't get giddy with any of the women or I'll have to start something. I want you for myself to-night."

"Never in my life have I witnessed such a wholesale display of horrifying sights," said Mr. Topper. "You are welcome to have me all to yourself to-night. I'm cowed."

"But first we must appear in public," she replied. "Come with me and I'll steer you safely through."

She led him to a table at which George and the Colonel were already seated. Topper was greeted with shouts of joy, and the Colonel thrusting his hand into a bucket, produced a bottle of champagne.

"Topper," he said, "nothing is too good for you. I've been waiting for this moment."

At the sound of the popping cork Mrs. Hart innocently sidled up to the table and sank to a chair with a weary sigh.

"I'm exhausted," she breathed. "Simply exhausted. What's that? Champagne?"

"Yes," said the Colonel. "Do you drink it?"

"I will try to-night," she answered in a resigned voice. "They say it's good for exhaustion."

When the Colonel had filled the glasses he rose and bowed to Topper.

"Topper," he said, "I toast you as a man in a million. On this, our last public appearance, so to speak, I am frank to say that of all the happy things we leave behind you will be the most missed."

Amid enthusiastic shouts of approval the Colonel resumed his chair and Topper in turn got up.

"I toast you all," he said, "as a revelation to me of a larger life and a lighter death. And I thank you all for the changes you have wrought in me. Once I was a law-abiding, home-loving and highly respected member of my community. Within a few short months you have changed all that. Now I am a jailbird, a hard drinker, a wife deserter and an undesirable, dissolute outcast. And I am glad of it. Only a few short miles now separate me from my home, but let me assure you that they will be the hardest miles I have ever traveled in my life."

Topper sat down to be thumped on the back by Kerby and the Colonel. Marion's eyes were like stars and Mrs. Hart's like pale moons, big but dim. More champagne appeared and guests kept visiting the table, gossiping for a moment, then drifting away. Topper was elaborately introduced and frequently reintroduced. This continued for some time. Many flushed faces confronted Topper, many bright eyes challenged his. Thrilling laughter floated through the air, the quick responses to well-turned lines. Arousing perfumes, subtle yet intimate, quickened the expectant blood. A soft light, shed by the lanterns hanging from the rafters, flooded the room, and through this light the dancers revolved to the impersonal music of the phonograph. The Colonel was at his most beaming best, gracious, immaculate and highly charged with champagne. Like a prince he sat at the table and greeted his subjects with jovial words. It was an expansive, heady and fluid evening, a dizzy moment stolen from the lap of time. Mr. Topper, at the urgency of Marion, danced with many fair women, listening to their leading remarks and capping them with his short but pertinent rejoinders. At last he returned to the table and claimed Marion for a dance. They circled the floor once, then ducked through the rear door and wandered off into the woods. Other couples were there before them. Laughter and whispers drifted among the trees.

"Well, Topper," said Marion, "how are you holding your grog?"

"With all my might and main," he answered. "You seem to be quite untouched."

"It's not my fault," she replied, sitting down with her back against a tree. "It just won't work to-night, although I've consumed enough for ten. My heart is not in my glass. Only my reflection, which will soon fade away."

Topper was painfully inarticulate and Marion slipped her hand in his, letting her head rest on his shoulder while she gazed up at the sky through the branches of the trees.

"Did you ever look at the stars so long," she continued, "that you almost became a part of them, so that when a lightning bug flew past your vision it got all mixed up with the Milky Way? Did you ever sit alone for hours chewing the cud of your own futility, hating yourself for being yourself and blaming life for making you so? Well, that's the way I feel to-night. It's time for me to be moving on. I've enjoyed this sort of stuff too long. There are other things to do. I don't mean better things, merely more interesting ones. Our capacity to enjoy life should be measured by our ability to create life, or beauty or some form of happiness. So far I've created nothing, only a constant confusion, a restless, discontented stirring in the ether."

"You've created happiness in me," said Mr. Topper. "You've awakened dreams and left memories. You've made me humble and you've made me human. You've taught me to understand how a man with a hangover feels. You've lifted me forever out of the rut of my smug existence. I'll go back to it I know, but I won't be the same man."

"You never were," she answered logically. "You were never intended to be. Nobody is, but life gets you, life and the economic urge—success, esteem, safety. How many of our triumphs in life spring from negative impulses, the fear of losing rather than the wish to win. It's a lot of talk, Topper, the whole damn show. And no one alive to-day is to blame. We must thank the ages past and bow to their false gods. We dress them up in new garments, but in their essence they're just the same—power, property and pride. You can't get away from them, the subsidized steps to salvation. I talk like this, but I've contributed nothing. We must just keep on and on until the mountains themselves crumble from nausea or we learn to scale them and cool our hands in the sky. Wild talk, Topper. Let's go back and cage a drink."

She would have risen, but he held her back.

"Rest here with me a moment," he said, "and let the world go to hell."

"If you feel like that," she answered, "we'll have to cage a flock of drinks."

They rose and walked back to the inn from which issued the tumult of many voices raised in song and uncontrolled abuse. The room presented a scene of great disorder. Couples not amorously inclined were either gambling or accusing each other of murder, arson and rape. George Kerby was among the gamblers, but the Colonel still sat at his table with a far-away look in his eyes. With the methodical pre-

cision of a wax figure he raised his glass to his lips at
regular intervals. Mrs. Hart was sitting in a corner
devouring a leg of chicken, while Oscar with moist
eyes was trying to hypnotize it out of her hand. The
hour was late, but no one seemed to care about that.
There were still some uncorked bottles. Broken glass
lay on the floor and cigarette ends smoldered beneath
the dancers' feet.

Topper and Marion made their way to the Colonel's
table and sat down. He regarded them with polite inquiry, then automatically passed them a bottle.

"Good evening," he said. "Are you well?"

"We are very well," replied Marion, quite seriously.
"And you?"

"I am well," said the Colonel. "I am well."

He then lapsed into silence as if the last shred of
conversation had been exhausted. Topper and Marion
sat quietly drinking and listening to the din which was
constantly increasing in volume. It had arrived at that
stage of the evening when the women were doing their
specialty dances and the men were imitating animals
or encouraging the dancers to more abandoned efforts.
Suddenly in the midst of this debauch a new and
sinister note was introduced. The doors of the inn flew
open and in each door stood a man with a revolver in
his hand.

"This place is pinched," announced the leader.
"Men and women line up in two separate rows. No
funny stuff now. Get a move on."

As if they had long rehearsed the figure the guests
arranged themselves in two rows and stood swaying
and giggling at one another, all except Mr. Topper.
He neither swayed nor giggled, but trembled in every
limb. The Colonel stood on one side of him and
George Kerby on the other. Marion was directly opposite. The raiding party moved from the doors and
walked between the rows, and as they progressed the
rows gradually faded from view until only Topper remained unhappily present. Each man in turn in-
spected Topper, then turned back to the guests, but
there were no guests to be seen, nothing but Topper
and an empty room filled with chuckling voices and

glasses moving through the air. The raiders huddled together and raised their revolvers, and as they did so the weapons were quietly removed from their hands.

"Out with the lights!" cried the Colonel's voice, and the room was plunged in darkness.

Cries of mortal fear now broke from the raiding party and a scuffling noise was heard. Topper was seized by either arm and carried from the room. He felt himself thrust into the automobile and heard the grating of the gears. There was a furious barking and Oscar sprang into the car just as it wheeled down the path.

"Another pursuit," said Topper. "What a remarkable country this is. Some one is always chasing some one else, and I'm forever it."

"Killjoys," replied Kerby from the wheel. "I was fifty bucks ahead."

"I still have my chicken," Mrs. Hart gloated from the back seat.

"And I have a couple of bottles," announced the Colonel. "Oscar seems to have the seat of someone's trousers."

"And we all still have Topper," said Marion Kerby. "Let's escort him home."

When the party had materialized Topper found himself seated between Marion and George Kerby. George was driving with one hand and reaching for the bottle with the other. Thus they sped along increasingly familiar roads at an increasingly reckless speed. Marion admonished her husband, but he merely took another drink and broke into a ribald song. Marion was clinging to Topper's hand and pressing it from time to time. The Colonel and Mrs. Hart had apparently gone to sleep.

"Here we are," said Marion at last. "We're approaching the old tree. It's our parting point, Topper. Can you take the car from here?"

"It was a fine party," muttered Topper, then the words refused to come. He felt that his world was dropping away from him, and as if to hold it back, he clung with all his might to Marion's hand. The automobile gave a sharp, uneasy bounce, then side-jumped from the road. As the great tree rushed out of the night to meet them, Marion Kerby threw herself on Mr. Topper and held him in her arms. Then Topper's world in reality did drop away. He had a sensation of clinging arms and a warm breath on his cheek. There was a terrifying crash and he caught a strange picture of Oscar describing an arc in the air and vanishing as he turned. The earth sprang up and struck Topper a smashing blow all over. Aching darkness settled down on him.

CHAPTER XXI

Through the Easter Egg

MR. TOPPER WAS ENTERING THE PEEPHOLE OF HIS sugar Easter egg. Once inside he felt that he was in a different world, different yet strangely familiar. A soft, still radiance, more vital and sympathetic than that of the real world, lay over a vast hollow plain which ran in a great green dip to a distant fringe of trees.

What was he looking for? he wondered. Was it for the shepherdess of his youth? He knew that it had something to do with romance. Was he looking for Marion Kerby? That must be it. But where was she? The hollow plain was empty. No living thing moved across it. And Mr. Topper was tired. Never before had he been so tired. He could hardly lift his legs, they dragged so heavily. But he had to find Marion Kerby. She was necessary to him. Already she had been too long away.

With slow, weary steps he set out across the sunken plain to the far-away trees on the other side. Their tops were dipped in a glowing light as the roof of the Easter egg turned on its downward curve, but all was dark at the base of the trees, dark, hushed and mysterious. He wanted to sit down and rest, but his eager-

ness to find Marion urged him onward. Several times
he called her name, but was unable to hear his own
voice. There seemed to be no sound in this Easter egg
world of his. Why was there no sound? Topper became confused. He had a faint suspicion that he was
suffering from an acute hangover.

He leaned against a small tree, and most amazingly
the tree became Marion Kerby. This convinced Topper that he was suffering from a hangover of an exceedingly virulent nature. He took a step back and
eyed her reproachfully.

"Where have you been?" he complained. "I've
been looking all over for you. Looking and calling
and wandering about. I'm going to cut it out, Marion.
Too much grog. What a head I have."

"You do look a bit like the Spirit of '76 after a
hard night," she said. "Sit down before you swoon."

Topper promptly sat down and nursed his head in
his hands.

"Where am I?" he demanded. "How did I find this
place? You're always getting me into scrapes."

"Don't blame me," she replied. "Blame my charming husband. He has a decided flair for trees."

"Oh, yes," said Topper. "There was a tree. I remember now."

"That's why you're here," she explained. "You became altogether too familiar with that tree, but the
effect will soon wear off and then you'll have to go
back."

"But why do I have to go back," he asked. "There
is no other place. And I'm tired, Marion, dog tired."

"You don't belong to our club yet," she told him,
"although you came close to joining. There's still a
spark of life left in you. Furthermore, it would make
things extremely uncomfortable for me with you
hanging around. George, as you know, has some
rather archaic ideas."

"Marion," Topper pleaded, "don't send me away.
You know how I feel. I can't go back to the world
now. There's nothing left for me there."

"How about Scollops?" she suggested. "How about
Mrs. Topper?"

"I'm done for," he admitted, after a heavy pause. "I see I've got to go on. But won't I ever see you again? Won't you ever come back to me?"

Marion shook her head.

"I'm moving on," she told him. "Some day we'll meet again, perhaps, but things will be different then."

"Worse, if possible," grumbled Topper, painfully getting to his feet and gazing ruefully at Marion.

She grinned at his woeful expression and lifted her face to his.

"I do believe you want to kiss me," she remarked.

"Damned if I will," he replied.

"Ah, come on," she urged. "It's the last."

Topper groaned and kissed her.

"You always were a jade," he said.

"How gracious," she retorted. "You're almost like your old self."

"I'll never be that again."

"Don't," she replied. "Don't. Remember this, old thing: Too much virtue will sour the sweetest character. I've taken a sort of pride in you, seeing you change and grow ornery. Don't spoil it all and disappoint me. Life will squeeze you if you let it, squeeze you back into a nice little mold with whipped cream and fixings."

"I know," said Topper drearily. "Squeeze me back into the 7:32."

"But never into white duck trousers," she replied. "Promise me that, Topper."

"I swear it," he answered.

"Good man!" she exclaimed, patting his arm. "It's almost like leaving a son—my own creation."

For a moment she regarded him thoughtfully, then moved away.

"So long," she called over her shoulder. "Good-bye, old dear."

Topper's eyes grew round with desperation.

"But, Marion!" he cried. "Marion! When shall we meet again? Won't you tell me when?"

"When fate sends you up against a larger and tougher tree," she replied. "You're a hard man to kill."

Without looking back again she drifted away among the trees and Topper stood alone on the sunken plain.

"A pretty trick," he muttered. "Leaving me flat like this. Well rid of her, say I. Always getting me into scrapes."

But as he continued across the fields his heart grew heavy for Marion Kerby. Several times he stopped and gazed back, looking for all the world like a small boy reluctant to set out for school.

"The jade," he continued to himself, "the heartless little jade. I don't care a damn. Scollops has better sense. What's happening to the light? I'll never get out of this place. Marion, where are you? You got me into this fix."

Gradually the plain grew dark and faded away as Mr. Topper, panting heavily, struggled through the peephole of his Easter egg world. It was a tight squeeze. He seemed to be hanging in space.

"Still too fat," he growled. "My stomach sticks, damn it!"

When Mr. Topper returned to consciousness he found himself in a small white bed in a small white room. The hospital was close to his home, but Mr. Topper knew nothing of this. During the course of his vacation he had awakened in so many unfamiliar places that he instinctively began to figure out what had happened at last night's party. Where had he been? What had he done? In what place was he lying now?

Then his eyes fell on Mrs. Topper and everything became clear. There were no adventures ahead. He looked at her through half-closed eyes and wondered about the woman. She was crumpled in her chair and her eyes were fixed on some green boughs tapping against the window. Somehow she looked quite pitiful. Strange that was, she had never looked pitiful before. And her face was not so unpleasant, thought Topper, in fact it was almost attractive now that the petulant, self-centered lines had been replaced by those of genuine anxiety. Her hand was resting lightly on the bed and Topper fumbled it into his.

"Hello," he said, "how's the girl?"

With a little gasp she turned in her chair and looked at his sunken face. It was odd to see the tears in her eyes and the uncertain smile on her lips.

"You can kiss me," said Topper magnificently. "I'm too tired to move."

Mrs. Topper was very much afraid. She kissed him, but did not linger over it.

"I might hurt you," she faltered.

"Am I as broken up as all that?"

"You're pretty well cracked," she admitted. "It's lucky you're still alive. The automobile burned up."

Topper heard this with relief. Much damaging evidence had been destroyed.

"It was the same tree," he remarked.

"They're talking of cutting it down," she replied.

A nurse looked in at the door and, seeing the two conversing, hurried for the doctor. Topper was examined and Mrs. Topper dismissed. When she returned to say good-by she found him white from pain.

"Go home," he said, "and take a rest. I've given you a tough time of it. How's the dyspepsia?"

"You know," she replied, "I've been so worried I think I've lost it."

"You'll get it back," he answered consolingly.

"I don't want it," she snapped. "I've got you back and you're trouble enough. No sarcasm, please."

"How's my cat?"

"As useless as ever."

Under her calm exterior Mrs. Topper was radiant. She gathered up her possessions and kissed her husband again.

"Those step-ins," she whispered. "I'm sorry about them. They were lovely. I bought a lot more."

A smile flickered momentarily across Mr. Topper's lips. His eyes moved to the window. The fields and the woodlands stretched out to the dropping sun. Somewhere out there in space was Marion Kerby. But was she there? Had he ever seen her? A remarkable dream? Hardly. Across the fields the old song came back on the wings of memory:

"My husband he did it. The devil would drive,
    The high-flying, low-lying soak.
And that is the reason I'm no more alive,
    For he drove me smack into an oak."

He raised his hand to his forehead. Yes, that was George Kerby's scar. It was still there. And where were the Colonel and the jocund Mrs. Hart and that prince of dogs, Oscar? Gone, all gone. Would he ever see them again? The sun had touched the treetops now, filling their limbs with fire. Topper sat watching the glowing sky until the colors faded. A nurse entered quietly and handed him a glass. Topper obediently drank it.

"Very poor," he remarked. "Very poor. Who bootlegs for this hospital?"

She laughed automatically and departed with the tray. Topper cautiously eased his position in the bed. In a little while he would be leaving the hospital, going home, going back to the distractions and obligations of life, going back to desks, schedules, commutation tickets, legs of lamb and familiar eyes. But things would never be the same. Topper was sure about that. Life would never get him. He would use it differently now. He himself was a different man. Perhaps he would sell his house and go away somewhere. He could get her to agree to that. In a little while he would be going back. Yes, going back home, starting the game all over. It would be good to see Scollops again. And the old girl was not so bad, not so bad, not at all so bad. But somewhere out there between the wind and stars, Marion Kerby was drifting, drifting farther and farther away. Thus meditating, Topper fell into a quiet sleep and dreamed that he was introducing Scollops to Oscar and that Oscar, now thoroughly in control of his members, amused the cat for hours by making his head and tail alternately disappear. Oscar was snappy about it.